METAL GEAR SOLID® 2
SONS OF LIBERTY

Raymond Benson

METAL GEAR SOLID® 2
SONS OF LIBERTY

Original Story by Hideo Kojima

Ballantine Books **DEL REY** New York

A Del Rey Trade Paperback Original

Copyright © 2009 by Konami Digital Entertainment. All rights reserved. Used under authorization.

Published in the United States by Del Rey, an imprint of The Random House Publishing Group, a division of Random House, Inc., New York.

DEL REY is a registered trademark and the Del Rey colophon is a trademark of Random House, Inc.

ISBN 978-0-345-50343-5

Printed in the United States of America

www.delreybooks.com

2 4 6 8 9 7 5 3 1

ACKNOWLEDGMENTS

For their help and support, the author wishes to thank Hideo Kojima, Dallas Middaugh, Peter Miller, and—of course—Randi and Max.

METAL GEAR SOLID® 2
SONS OF LIBERTY

THE BIG SHELL

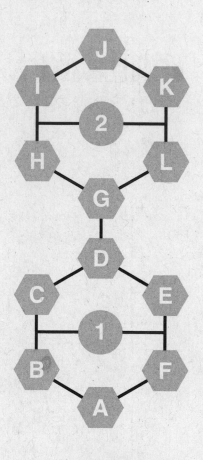

ADDENDUM A: SHADOW MOSES INCIDENT

Pursuant to your clandestine transport of the unit aboard the U.S.S. *Discovery*, it is advised that you study the file regarding the so-called "Shadow Moses Incident," which occurred two years ago in the Alaskan Aleutian Islands. Briefly, Shadow Moses was a nuclear waste disposal facility run by DARPA and ArmsTech. It was also the undercover testing ground for an earlier prototype of Metal Gear. The facility was taken over by renegade FOX-HOUND operatives led by LIQUID SNAKE and his compatriots, namely a Russian named REVOLVER OCELOT. The terrorists held the U.S. government for ransom, threatening to use Metal Gear if, among other demands, the remains of the former FOX-HOUND operative BIG BOSS were not turned over to them for DNA cloning purposes. FOXHOUND, under the command of COLONEL ROY CAMPBELL, sent in lone operative SOLID SNAKE to neutralize the situation. During a twenty-four-hour period, SOLID SNAKE was able to rescue Shadow Moses hostages, among them DR. HAL "OTACON" EMMERICH, and Campbell's daughter, MERYL SILVERBURGH. The Metal Gear was destroyed and all but one of the terrorists—REVOLVER

OCELOT—were killed. As you know there were a number of governmental shake-ups after the incident, including the resignation of President GEORGE SEARS and the disbanding of FOX-HOUND.

To date, the whereabouts of OCELOT are unknown.

SOLID SNAKE and DR. EMMERICH formed an anti–Metal Gear organization called PHILANTHROPY, which is recognized by the United Nations but not by the U.S. government. It is imperative that the details of your transport along the Hudson River do not fall into the hands of PHILANTHROPY.

1

"THE HUDSON RIVER . . . *We had classified intelligence that a new type of Metal Gear was scheduled for transport. The whole thing stank, but our noses have been out in the cold too long . . .*"

Solid Snake stood on the middle of the George Washington Bridge in the torrential downpour, overlooking the water below. The tanker U.S.S. *Discovery* was approaching and nearly at Snake's "Point of No Return." Snake looked out from under the hooded rain poncho and eyed the traffic on the bridge moving in both directions. Just headlights. No other figures on the walkway. If any people in vehicles saw him, they'd think he was just another suicide statistic. No cause for alarm.

That thought made Snake smile wryly.

Visibility was close to zero due to the heavy rain and high winds. The tanker was just a big, black shape moving along the river.

Time to go.

Snake unzipped the poncho and shrugged it off of his body, revealing the dark sneaking suit that was his trademark uniform, the same old gear he had used during the Shadow Moses affair two years earlier. The uniform showed signs of repair in several places, and there were no protectors in place. Snake was armed only with a Beretta, worn on a hip holster.

He adjusted the goggles over his face, careful not to disturb the signature blue bandana that was also as much a part of his body as the black hair on his head and stubble on his face. Snake checked the small parachute's harness and confirmed that it was snug. He then shimmied up the slippery supports using gloves that were made of special fabric that induced friction even when wet. He climbed onto the rail, stood upright, found his balance, and stretched out his arms to prepare for the dive.

The *Discovery*'s deck moved into position directly below the bridge.

Snake leaped off and the AOD—Automatic Opening Device—caused the stealth parachute to blossom across his back. From that point on he was invisible to radar, sonar, and the naked eye, although the sheets of rain streamed off the parachute wings and drew its outline in the night sky. But no one would notice.

As graceful as a seagull, the former FOXHOUND operative managed to avoid the gusty effects of the wind and glided safely to the ship's deck. He landed lightly in a crouching position, facing the ship's stern. The impact of the landing rendered the stealth camo ineffective, so Snake was forced to deactivate the stealth function and become visible. He cut himself loose from the parachute and attached the wings to the filament on his back. The parachute, fragile as an angel's wings, sat on the filament and tightened with the ship's movement—its other end was tethered to the bridge railing high above. When the wire was fully taut, Snake released the gear; it disappeared into the murky black sky, carried off by the filament. The retractor reeled in the parcel and the pack came to rest unseen in the safety of the bridge.

THE HELICOPTER PILOT struggled with the controls but kept the aircraft steady as it hovered over the bridge and the tanker below.

The storm made it extremely difficult, but the pilot was a good one. He had to be, considering who his passenger was.

The man in the seat behind him had night-vision binoculars to his eyes and was focused on the tanker's deck.

"Our boy is right on schedule," he said. Involuntarily, he drew the six-shooter from the holster on his belt and twirled it in his left hand, gunslinger-style. Just as quickly, he shoved the revolver back into the holster and then reached up to twist his long mustache. His long yellow-white hair came down to his shoulders. He had often been told he resembled the legendary General George Custer, something he considered a compliment. After all, Custer had been a valiant, brave soldier of the U.S. Cavalry.

Revolver Ocelot watched Snake stand on the tanker deck. He lowered the binoculars and then spoke into his cellphone, "He'll know soon enough."

SNAKE MOVED BEHIND the windlass and activated his Codec. He punched in the memorized frequency on the device around his wrist and waited for the face of his partner to appear on the Codec's screen.

"This is Snake. Do you read me, Otacon?"

The Codifying Satellite Communication System incorporated anti-wiring coding, digital real-time burst communication, sonar utilization, and radar. Normal communication was instantly codified, compressed, and transmitted in a burst of one microsecond in length. However, Snake could receive it in real time, unscrambled and decoded. The nanomachines in his body received the transmission and stimulated the small bones of his ear so that no one would hear the sound but Snake. And he could contact his partner with a speed-dial button corresponding to a code frequency. If necessary, he didn't need the actual Codec on his wrist. The nanomachines could provide a conduit for conversation in his head, hands free.

"Loud and clear, Snake." Otacon, aka Dr. Hal Emmerich, was probably the closest thing to a "best friend" that Snake had. They had met during the Shadow Moses ordeal and since then had been working together. Although he was younger than Snake, Emmerich's brains and science background were the perfect pairing to the operative's more *physical* approach to things.

"Kept you waiting, huh? I'm at the sneak point," Snake said.

"Everything going okay?"

"The stealth camo's busted. Landing impact."

"We must have overused it. Sorry, but you're going to have to deal with it. You're not in the military anymore."

"Right. I didn't plan on relying on this gadget anyway," Snake said with not a little sarcasm in his voice.

"Hey, the private sector's not so bad, is it? Privacy guaranteed!"

"I'm happy as long as no one gives me any more unwanted *gifts*."

"You mean that thing with Naomi?" Otacon didn't have to bring up the fact that Snake was still carrying the FOXDIE virus that he had acquired during the Shadow Moses incident. Thanks to Naomi Hunter, FOXHOUND's chief medic at the time. Whether it had been for Snake's own good or not was still a question.

"And I can't say I miss the chattering nanny," Snake added.

"Oh, Mei Ling's not so bad."

Actually, Snake had found FOXHOUND's communications officer rather cute, a *manga* character come to life. She did talk a lot, though.

"That reminds me," Otacon continued. "I have to get in touch with her again about that new Natik flashware."

"Diverting toys from the SSCEN again? Give her a message from me. Someone will find out, sooner or later. She's better off assuming it's sooner and quit while she's safe."

"Too true. Okay, Snake, let's get to work."

Snake heard the faint sound of a helicopter. He looked up but couldn't see anything through the rain and darkness.

"You know how the technical specs of Metal Gear were sold on the black market after Shadow Moses?"

"All Ocelot's doing," Snake answered.

"Exactly. And now, every state, group, and dotcom has its own version of Metal Gear."

"Not exactly a classified weapon for today's nuclear powers." Snake still had dreams—and sometimes nightmares—about his encounter with the gigantic, mobile nuclear weapon–launching system that walked like a Transformer come to life.

"This new one seems to have been designed to wipe the floor with all the other models. The only consistent description is that it's an amphibious, anti–Metal Gear vehicle."

"And that explains why this one is under Marine Corps jurisdiction?"

"Right. The mission objective is to make visual confirmation of the new Metal Gear being transported by that tanker and bring back photographic evidence. But I want you first to go up to the top level of the infrastructure, to the bridge. That's Deck-E. We need to find out where the tanker is headed."

"A little reconnaissance, huh?"

"There's too much we don't know about this new prototype. Capabilities, deployment method—we don't even know how close it is to completion. If we know where the testing arena is, I can start to draw some reasonable conclusions."

"All right, I'll head to the bridge ASAP."

"Try to avoid confrontations! Our goal is to collect evidence on Metal Gear development and expose it to the world. It would be best if you could get out of there without alerting anyone."

"Don't worry. I know the drill. We're not terrorists."

"Very good. Don't you forget that you're part of Philanthropy now!" Snake could hear the pride in Otacon's voice. He mouthed the exact words as Otacon repeated them for the thousandth time. "We're an anti–Metal Gear organization and—"

"—and officially recognized by the U.N. I know! Recognized, but still *fringe*, Otacon."

"All right, all right. So, how's your gear?"

"Seems to have survived the jump."

"Your weapon is a tranquilizer gun converted from a Beretta M92F. It's a little hard to work with, because you'll have to reload after each shot since the slide locks."

"It's better than scavenging at the site. It's got a good suppressor, too."

"The chemical stun will take effect in a few seconds and last for hours. You can take down an elephant with that thing. The effects of the anesthetic round will vary depending on what part of the body is hit. We're talking about a difference of tens of seconds between hitting the limbs, chest, or head. Check out the laser sighting, too!"

Snake grunted his approval.

"As for the equipment . . ." Otacon did a quick scan of Snake's suit using the Codec sensors that were built into it. "Cigarettes? Snake! What's wrong with you?"

Snake shrugged. "It's kind of a lucky charm." With that, he immediately drew one out of the pack, lit it, and inhaled the smoke deeply. It relaxed him.

"You haven't read the Surgeon General's Warning, have you?"

"Drop it, Otacon."

Otacon shook his head and went on. "Okay, your digital camera works almost the same way as your old one. It's just a matter of a few images we need, so just use it to get us the evidence of the new Metal Gear."

Snake held the camera to his face and surveyed the tanker's superstructure and guard stations. A few maintenance workers dressed in rain gear were patrolling the second, fourth, and fifth decks of the crew's quarters. The camera's viewfinder zoomed in on the sentries.

"They don't look armed," Snake commented.

"Hey, Earth to Snake. These are nice, upstanding Marines, not terrorists. Don't get caught; you're in stealth mode from now on."

"Sure. But if it comes to that, a little beauty sleep never hurt anyone."

Snake moved the viewfinder to another sentry. The men did indeed appear to be wet, bored Marines that were unlucky to pull deck duty during the storm, although they were not dressed in uniform.

"By the way, Otacon, are you sure of this intelligence?"

"Absolutely. Hacked it out of the Pentagon's classified files myself."

"No traces?"

"Oh, please. I'm too good for that."

"We can't rule out the possibility that this is a trap. Remember, there's a price on our heads."

"You're just being paranoid."

"I hope so."

Snake continued to study the sentries. "Those men—you wouldn't think they were anything but civilians from here."

"With all the ships passing on the river and in the harbor, putting uniformed Marines on the deck would be a bad idea. People can get a clear view of the water from riverside, too. It's a classified operation, Snake. No one's supposed to know the Marines are on the tanker."

A flash of lightning illuminated the sky enough to give Snake a view of the *Discovery*'s port side. "The waterline is too high," he said. "According to the navigational plans, this ship should have discharged its cargo upriver."

"That's because the new Metal Gear is in there," Otacon answered. "No doubt about it."

Snake didn't like it. As he looked around the deck, he felt as if something wasn't right. "The military trains you to watch for threats from the stern of a boat. That's SOP for counter-terror ops, too. Security should be tighter!"

"You worry too much."

"So where's the target?"

"Satellite surveillance is a major international pastime these days. I'd say it's in the cargo holds, safely below deck. Do you see the entrance to the holds?"

Snake swung the camera back to the superstructure. There were several doors on different levels above deck connected by staircases. "Looks like there are a few entryways into the crew quarters."

Then he heard it again—the distinct sound of a helicopter. Snake looked up, and this time he saw it, but it was too rainy and dark to be able to identify what kind of aircraft it was.

"A chopper!"

At that moment, a sudden movement to his right attracted his attention. He focused the camera in that direction and witnessed a sentry being attacked from behind. A hand clamped over the man's mouth and a knife smoothly slit the guard's throat. Snake watched in horror as the sentry slid to the deck amidst a spreading pool of blood. The killer was dressed in brown camouflage and headgear equipped with night-vision goggles. On his back was a boxy rucksack.

More movement to the upper left. Snake aimed the camera to Deck-B in time to see another camouflaged newcomer slice a crewman's throat.

"Uh . . . looks like we're not the only ones after Metal Gear tonight," Snake whispered.

"Is that a chopper I heard?"

"Affirmative. Probably another cavalry."

Snake searched for the other sentry he had seen earlier but saw yet a third camouflaged figure dragging the guard's body over the low deck railings. The killer rolled the corpse overboard. No one could hear the splash for the sound of the heavy rain.

"What's their game? Hijack?"

Otacon didn't know, but he ventured, "They're probably targeting the ship's controls."

"Otacon, how many men do you need to take over a tanker of this size?"

"The ship is run by a computer so . . . I'd say about eighteen people."

By now, several other camouflaged men had assembled on the superstructure area. Each one sported a machine gun, the stock extended and a silencer affixed to the muzzle.

"AKS-74u's," Snake said.

His eyes drew toward a mustached older man wearing a fur coat and fur hat giving orders to the soldiers. Snake didn't recognize him, but he thought the man to be in his late sixties. Even from Snake's position, the leader exuded a powerful, charismatic presence. The man seemed to be oblivious to the wind and rain and had a somewhat imperious attitude toward the rest of the men. Snake figured the guy had spent a lifetime in the military.

"Russians?" he whispered.

The leader barked a command into a radio. Snake was almost positive that was the language he heard.

"Are you sure?" Otacon asked.

"No Marine barber touched that head of hair."

Snake snapped a picture of the man. "I'm transmitting a photo. Let's get an ID on him ASAP."

"I'm on it."

Snake watched the men spread out over the superstructure. "Looks like the tanker's theirs now."

The sound of the helicopter grew louder. Snake looked up and saw the vehicle soar above him. The noise of its Fenestron-type tail rotor, which made a distinctly different sound in flight from other types of choppers, was familiar to Snake.

"KA-60. Kasatka," he said.

"Kasatka? Kamov chopper, right? A 'Killer Whale.' "

This was more serious than Snake had planned on. He put the camera away and crouched low.

"Otacon, we need to get a fix on who they are."

"Judging by their transport, aren't they some kind of military commandos?"

"Not necessarily. That chopper could've been the KA-62, the civil model. I wasn't too sure."

Snake heard the uneasiness in Otacon's voice. "Look, Snake, all we need is the photographic evidence of Metal Gear. As long as we have it we can put it online and blow the whole thing wide open. So no pyrotechnics, okay? Leave 'em alone!"

"All right. I'll do my best."

"This isn't Shadow Moses. Reach me if anything happens. I'll be waiting just past the Verrazano Bridge. You need to be off that ship by then. Okay?"

"I'll be in touch."

Snake signed off and rubbed his chin.

Great, he thought. *Sneak into a Marine tanker while it's being hijacked by Russian commandos, take a few pictures, and get out without being seen. No problem.*

Best to get moving, do the job, and evacuate fast.

Snake moved out of his hiding place, trotted around to the port side of the superstructure, and encountered the back of a commando. He drew the Beretta, held it in both hands, and aimed. "Freeze," Snake ordered as quietly as he could. But the Russian turned. Snake squeezed the trigger. A tranquilizer hit the man in the neck, the only part of his body that was exposed. The Russian dropped to the deck. Snake quickly reloaded the gun and then grabbed the sleeping commando by the arms. He dragged the man to the side of the railing and hid the body behind a lifeboat. Snake then moved to the first door he saw, which led to Deck-A.

It was obviously the crew's quarters. Snake hugged the wall as he trod quietly down a corridor. It took a sharp left. As he moved along, Snake heard footsteps behind a door marked LOCKERS. He readied the Beretta and cracked open the door. Sure enough, one of the Russian commandos was searching the locker room. Snake aimed through the space in the open door and shot the man in the back. He waited until the interloper was down, and then he silently entered the locker room. No one else was inside. Snake opened one of the vertical metal lockers, hoisted the heavy man up by the shoulders, and stuffed him into it. A pinup of a gorgeous bikini model was taped to the inside of the locker door. Snake pulled out the digital camera and decided to play a joke on Otacon. He snapped a picture of the pinup, muttered, "Good," and closed the door.

After reloading, Snake carefully looked out of the locker room, scanned the empty hallway, and moved on. Eventually he came to another door, opened it, and scampered up the stairs to Deck-B. He entered the hallway and immediately saw a shadow moving along the wall. Snake ducked back into the stairwell and waited with his Beretta ready. The sound of footsteps came closer. Snake could hear the man breathing just a few feet away. He stepped out, pointed the gun, and commanded, "Freeze!"

The commando raised his hands.

Snake figured it wouldn't hurt to have an AKS-74u. He took the man's weapon and slung it over his own shoulder. Then he shot the Russian with a tranquilizer. He caught the soldier mid-fall so that the body wouldn't make a lot of noise on the metal floor. Snake dragged the guy into an empty locker room, opened a toilet stall, and sat him on the commode. He closed the stall, reloaded the Beretta, and went back to the hall.

Another door led to Deck-C, which contained more crew's quarters.

Where is everyone? Snake wondered. *There's not a Marine in sight.* He tapped the Codec and called Otacon.

"What is it, Snake? Why aren't you on the bridge yet?"

"I'm making my way up. I'm on Deck-C."

"I know. I'm tracking you."

"Listen, there's no one around. Where are all the Marines?"

"I'll bet they're in the holds. They probably left a skeleton crew on deck and in the crew's quarters. That's why those Russians got control of the ship so easily."

"I don't think the rest of the Marines even know they're here!"

"Never mind, Snake! Get up to the bridge. Hurry!"

He signed off and sprinted through the empty deck to the door at the end of the corridor. Snake ascended to Deck-D, which apparently contained more rooms than the lower levels. Upon entering the mess hall, he heard movement on the other side of the wall. Someone was heading his way, so Snake flattened himself next to the door. It opened and a Russian commando stepped inside. Snake took the opportunity to approach the guy from behind and execute his trademark stranglehold. The soldier struggled fiercely but Snake maintained the pressure on the man's neck with his forearm until the guy lost consciousness. Snake then pulled the limp body to a cabinet, opened it, and hid him inside.

The former FOXHOUND operative crossed the mess hall and left through the door on the starboard side. He was moving along the corridor when the Codec burst with a transmission from Otacon.

"Snake! Don't move!"

He froze. "What?"

"Look at the walls on both sides of the hall."

Snake thought he saw pinpoints of red lights on two bulky packs attached to the walls.

"I see some kind of device on both sides of the hall. Infrared sensors?"

"Right. And they're probably linked to—"

"Let me guess. Semtex."

"Exactly. Plastic-explosives-R-Us!"

"Otacon, I think the Russians put that stuff there. They're going through the crew's quarters installing it!"

"Snake, you know you can't go through the infrared beams. If you touch them, the explosives will detonate and the ship will be pulverized."

Snake sighed. "I'm not in the mood to go sleep with the fishes. There are too many sensors. Looks like I'll have to find another way up."

"No need to worry. You can get through if you know where the beams are. Use the usual method!"

Snake understood and looked up and down the hallway for a fire extinguisher. There was one fastened to the wall on the *other* side of the Semtex.

Piece of cake.

He aimed the Beretta and fired it at the canister. The hose burst, spraying a cloud of extinguishing chemicals all over the corridor. The infrared beams were then clearly visible, crossing the corridor. The lowest one was two feet off the floor. Snake could easily crawl beneath it.

Once he was on the other side of the Semtex, Snake stood and reloaded the gun. He rounded the corner and came face-to-face with a Russian commando. The element of surprise was on Snake's side and the Beretta was already in his hand. Before the soldier could react with more than a deer-in-the-headlights expression, Snake shot him with a tranquilizer.

No time to hide the body. He had to get to the Bridge, find out where the *Discovery* was headed, and hurry down to the Holds to take the damned pictures of Metal Gear, if he could find it. The fact that the Russians had set Semtex on the ship added yet another complication to the increasingly difficult "little" mission.

Snake made his way to the stairwell and ascended to Deck-E. Once again, he carefully opened the door to the level and peered into the Bridge. There were no Russians in sight—only a few unfortunate Marines. They lay sprawled on the floor and slumped over desks, soaking in their own blood. Snake winced and then stepped out of the stairwell. He entered the Bridge and made a quick sweep of the place to make sure someone wasn't still alive. He didn't know what he would have done if there had been. He had no time to play doctor.

The sound of the chopper was very close. Snake stepped to the large window in front of him and got a clear view of two transport helicopters hovering over the deck.

"So they are Kasatkas," he murmured. "Russian choppers . . ."

The high winds made it difficult for the helicopters to maintain their balance, so the two crafts gave each other a wide berth, one below the other, to prevent collision. Then, cables were thrown from the choppers. Soldiers, armed to the teeth, descended with fluid rapidity through the drenching waves and near gale-force wind. Snake noticed snipers inside both helicopters, keeping watch over the safe descent of the men. Once on deck, the soldiers quickly infiltrated the tanker's interior through various entryways. The precision of the process informed Snake that this was a thoroughly trained operation.

Once the last man was on the ship, the two Kasatkas veered up and away.

Snake shook off what he had seen and went straight to the helm. As he studied the computer monitors, the Codec burst on.

"Snake, did you find out where that ship is headed?" Otacon asked impatiently.

"I'm looking at it. Thirty-five degrees longitude, latitude around fifty-eight."

Snake saw Otacon remove his nerdy glasses and rub his eyes. The scientist replaced them and said, "That's more than eight hundred kilometers off the coast of Bermuda, out in the middle of the Atlantic. So . . . the prototype is ready for solo testing. It's basically combat-worthy. That area is out of the Navy's operational range, too. It must be a stand-alone Marine Corps project—

which means this prototype Metal Gear must be designed for independent deployment, without any naval assistance. But analysis can wait till later. Snake, you need to go down to the holds and locate the actual Met—"

A loud *clang* outside the window startled Snake and interrupted Otacon. Snake ducked and then slowly peaked over the counter to see what was out there.

A woman? Hmm.

She was dressed in camouflage pants, combat boots, and military-issue tank top with the distinct horizontal striping of the Russian army. However, Snake noted that the rain gave the clothing a flattering effect that the army most likely never intended. She was armed with a PSS pistol. An army cap was pulled down over her forehead, shading her face, but she had closely cropped hair like a boy. In fact, she was very wiry, but obviously muscular.

She held a radio to her face and was talking.

Snake crept out the door and onto the deck, slithered along the wall, and crouched out of sight so that he could listen in on the conversation. A man's voice sputtered through her radio. Snake assumed it was the leader, the older man he had seen earlier. They spoke Russian—the courses Snake had taken at FOX-HOUND came in handy.

"—and Shalashaska has landed. I'm on my way to the tanker holds. Report your status."

The woman answered, "Control room, communications, and engine room are under control. All entry and exit points to the tanker holds secured. Infrared sensors placed and operational."

"Good work. Are the explosives in place?"

"Yes, they are all planted."

"Listen. Once we have what we came for, the tanker will be scuttled."

There was a burst of static but it quickly cleared.

"Did you read that?" the man asked.

"Affirmative. And the vehicle's pilot?"

"He's the only one who underwent the VR training. No one else can do it."

"Are you sure you can trust him?"

The older man didn't answer. "Your part in the mission is complete. You are to leave at once."

"No! It's not over yet!" She shook her head in dogged defiance.

"I can see the moon, even in this storm. Pale as death. I have a bad feeling about this mission. You swore this to me. That you would leave the unit, once the mission was complete! Do not worry. This is a country of 'liberty.' "

"No! This is where I belong, with the unit. I have nowhere else to go!"

The woman pulled her PSS pistol from the holster and cradled it against her chest, as though it reassured her.

"Father, I want to stay and fight," she said.

"There is no choice to make here, Olga! Need I remind you that you are carrying my grandchild?"

The woman stared down at her stomach and gently placed a hand on it.

The man ordered, "You will be on the helicopter out of here! Now!"

And the radio abruptly cut off.

"Damn it," she muttered.

One of the Kasatka choppers hovered above her. She waved it away, but the pilot gestured for her. Again she indicated a refusal, and finally the chopper turned and sped away. The woman called Olga stared at the departing craft and lowered her radio to waist level.

"Freeze!"

Snake was behind her, the Beretta aimed at her back.

The woman stood completely still but didn't appear fazed by Snake's presence.

"Hands over your head! Now!"

She slowly complied.

"Toss your gun overboard. Slowly!"

Obeying the command, Olga took the PSS by the barrel and threw it in a wide arc into the sea.

"Show your face."

She carefully removed the cap and let the wind snatch it from her hand. She turned and faced Snake.

Olga was beautiful—in a boyish way. There was no trace of fear on her face.

"Who are you?" he asked.

"We are nomads," she answered in heavily accented English.

She started to inch sideways. Snake sensed she might be preparing a sudden move. "Stay still!"

"Americans . . . so you shoot women, too?"

"I'm a nomad, too."

Then Snake spotted an NR-2 Special Scout Knife strapped to her waist. "Take that knife and toss it!"

Olga slowly pulled the weapon out of its sheath, pointing the tip toward herself. She started to lean over to place it on the deck.

"Not there. Toss it overboard!"

The woman straightened and glared at him defiantly. "You know what you're doing."

A tremendous wave rocked the ship and suddenly, as if a huge spigot in the sky had been shut off, the rain ceased. Olga looked up and over at the Manhattan skyline. A full moon hung over a cluster of skyscrapers.

"Not too shabby, is it?" she asked with a flourish. "New York, I mean."

Her words threw Snake. Olga detected that she had slightly diverted his attention. With the grip of the knife pointed toward Snake, she pressed an inset trigger. A chamber concealed inside the grip explosively propelled a single round at the operative. But

Snake, whose reflexes were razor sharp, noticed the sudden jerk of the woman's triceps and bent backward during the second that the bullet zipped past him.

The woman used the surprise attack to conceal herself behind a stack of crates. She then drew a USP handgun that was concealed behind her back. Sensing what was coming, Snake dived behind the corner of the bridge.

"And that brings our tour to its conclusion!" she shouted.

"Scout knife with a surprise, huh?" Snake hollered at her. "You a Spetsnaz?"

"I think you deserve a little credit. No one's ever dodged that shot of mine. But no one gets lucky twice!"

She aimed the USP around the crates and fired several rounds in Snake's direction. He was pinned—unless he went around the Bridge to the other side.

"I've been with the unit since I was born!" she shouted. "I grew up on the battlefield. Conflict and victory were my parents!"

Snake rushed to the port side and headed toward the stern. But by the time he had made it around the deck, Olga had figured out what he was up to. He was met by a volley of USP 9-mm rounds. Snake leaped behind a bundle of cargo that was secured to the deck, barely escaping injury.

"The unit is my life! My family!"

Was this woman nuts? Snake asked himself.

"I have no one—nothing except the unit! Nothing else matters to me! Whoever you are, you're not stopping us!"

Then there was a clatter on the deck next to him. A small metallic object had landed next to him and rolled across the metal floor.

A grenade!

The only thing Snake could do was bolt across her gauntlet of fire toward the Bridge, hit the deck rolling, flatten himself, and hope that he was far enough away when the grenade went off.

The blast shook the deck, and Snake felt pieces of debris shower him, but he had apparently avoided the shrapnel.

One thing was for sure. The woman wasn't lying. She was as professional a soldier as he had ever seen. And if the boss was her *father*, what kind of foe would *he* be?

He heard her running toward him. Snake jumped to his feet and hustled behind another stack of crates. She came around the corner firing, forcing Snake to crouch behind the cover with no clear shot at her. He only wanted to put her to sleep. Why wouldn't she cooperate?

Finally, she was out of ammunition. He heard her run back to cover, so Snake used the opportunity to advance. He skirted around the crates and rushed in her direction, took a position at the side of the cargo that had been damaged by the grenade. It was a risky move, for he was in clear sight—the advantage was that she wouldn't expect him to be so close when she appeared again.

He sensed that she was behind a different stack of crates, reloading her weapon. The only way she'd be able to fire at him was from her left side—not easy for a right-handed shooter. Snake pointed the Beretta at that space and waited.

Sure enough, Olga's left shoulder and arm jutted out so that she could shoot at him with the gun in her right hand. That was all Snake needed. He squeezed the trigger and the Beretta jerked once. The woman gasped, dropped the USP, and wavered for a moment before falling to the deck. Out cold.

Snake reloaded, stood, and approached her. He took the USP and tucked it into his belt for safekeeping, and then searched the zipped pockets in her pants. He found a box of 9-mm ammunition and an extra fragmentation grenade and stuck them in his own backpack. The woman yielded no other form of identification or clues as to who she really was or what her unit was up to. He decided to snap a picture of her with the digital camera. He did so, but then a soft, whirring sound above him diverted his attention. A small, strange device that resembled a life buoy was *flying* not five meters away from him. When Snake saw the camera pointed at him, he knew exactly what it was.

"Cypher!"

On instinct, he raised the Beretta and started to shoot at it, but the thing jerked and zipped away as if it were a hummingbird. Snake cursed to himself and holstered his gun. There wasn't much good a tranquilizer round would do to a Cypher anyway.

He punched the Codec and waited for Otacon's face to appear on the screen.

"The ship appears to be under their control. The men have Russian gear, but I haven't been able to find out anything else about their motive or origin."

"I know who they are," Otacon said somberly.

"You do?"

"We've ID'd the old man."

"Who is he?"

"Sergei Gurlukovich."

Snake blinked. "Gurlukovich! He's . . . he's one of *Ocelot's* allies!"

"Yeah. The GRU colonel. He's the one Ocelot was supposed to meet up with after Shadow Moses."

"Then they're after Metal Gear."

"Everything's changed. This is not going to be as simple as we thought."

"You could say that. And I saw a surveillance remote just now. It looked like a Cypher."

"A Marine Cypher-T?"

"No. Army."

Otacon wiped his brow. "First the Marines, then the Russians . . . and now the *Army*?"

"You're right, this isn't going to be simple."

"Snake . . . there's something I have to tell you."

"What?"

"We didn't dig up this info—about the new Metal Gear—on our own. Not like usual."

"How did you find out, then?"

"It was a tip. An anonymous tip."

"Anonymous? You've never trusted those! Why would you now?"

"I, uhm, I have a younger sister. A stepsister. We have different parents." Snake wondered what that had to do with it, but Otacon continued. "I only knew her for two years."

"You never mentioned her before. So?"

"The sender of the tip was 'E.E.' "

"E.E.?"

"Her name is Emma, but I always called her E.E."

"Emma Emmerich?"

Otacon sighed. "Yeah. It just caught my eye, you know? I figured it was a coincidence, but I couldn't get it out of my mind. There's really no one out there who knows about her."

"When was the last time you saw her?"

"Over ten years ago."

"You think it's a trap? To lure us out here?"

"I don't know. After I got the tip, I did break into the Pentagon system to get confirmation."

"Okay."

"Watch your back, Snake. Maybe I screwed up."

2

SNAKE LEFT THE BRIDGE and stealthily made his way down the stairways, past the lower crew's quarters, and, finally, below deck. He found himself in the massive, three-level Engine Room on the starboard side. The place was extremely noisy with rumbling machinery, so it was difficult to detect if any of the Russians were nearby. Snake moved slowly through the upper level, past the large freight lift that traversed the entire depth of the ship, and eventually came to an alcove containing more vertical metal lockers. Something caught his eye on the floor, so he cautiously approached the lockers to get a better look.

Blood. Seeping from one of the lockers.

Snake readied the Beretta, grasped the locker handle, and opened the door.

The recently murdered body of a Marine tumbled out and collapsed onto the floor like a rag doll.

Snake cursed under his breath. He started to move the corpse into a more dignified resting position when he heard the sound of the lift stop on his level. There was no time to do anything but hide—so he stepped into the empty locker and shut the door. He grimaced as he stood in the dead Marine's pool of blood, but there was no other alternative. As with all lockers of that type, there were three horizontal ventilation slits in the door through which Snake could peer out into the room. Sure enough, a Russian commando came around the corner from the lift to investigate. The soldier saw the dead Marine on the floor, aimed his assault rifle at the body, and then slowly stepped toward it. The commando nudged the Marine with his boot to make sure the man was dead. Snake held his breath. The Russian was just on the other side of the locker door. Snake watched as the soldier scanned the room and then finally moved on. Snake breathed but waited a minute for the Russian to gain some distance. Snake quietly opened the locker and stepped out and over the dead Marine.

He worked his way down to the middle level, made a quick reconnaissance to ensure there were no more guards, and then descended to the lower level, near the gargantuan turbine. The way out and down to the bowels of the ship was through a sealed watertight hatch at the end of a corridor.

The Codec spurted on. "Snake?"

"Yeah?"

"There's more Semtex in front of you. Do you see it?"

Sure enough, there were two bundles of explosives attached to the opposite sides of the corridor.

"Yeah. I don't see a fire extinguisher anywhere, though. Think I can crawl under the beams?"

"Do you see the thing with blinking green lights right next to the explosives?"

Snake squinted and pinpointed the small control box attached to one of the bundles. "Yeah."

"Destroy that and the sensors stop functioning. But you can't get in close enough to touch it, so you'll have to shoot it out. The Beretta's knockout rounds won't work. Did you find another weapon?"

"I picked up that woman's USP. I'll use that."

Otacon signed off as Snake checked Olga's handgun and re-loaded it with the stolen ammunition. He then stood in a Weaver stance and aimed at the Semtex control box. If he missed and hit the explosives instead of the target, it would be *adios, amigo*. He wished he had some Pentazemin, a mild antidepressant that also had a calming effect and improved one's nerves. Snake found that the stuff improved his aim. But in this case, he had to make do without.

He lined up the shot and squeezed the trigger. The USP nois-ily recoiled, but the control box was history. No more blinking light or infrared pinpoint dots on the explosive packs. The prob-lem now, though, was that the loud gunshot may have attracted more commandos. Snake rushed down the corridor, turned the wheel on the sealed hatch, opened it, and stepped through.

Snake descended to Deck-2 and silently entered a corridor just as a booming voice on the ship's PA system announced, "Ver-razano Bridge checkpoint passed. All non-essential personnel re-port to the holds in ten minutes' time for the scheduled briefing session with the Commandant. You are ordered to continue man-ning your posts until that time."

Damn! he thought. *We're running out of time.*

He was on the port side of the deck. According to the ship's blueprints that Otacon had provided—readily available on the Codec screen—Snake needed to get to the starboard side in order to access the cargo holds. The corridor was U-shaped and was ap-proximately sixty meters long. Normally that wouldn't be much of a problem, but he had no idea how many of the enemy he might encounter. The bright illumination was also a detriment to successful stealth maneuvering. Snake considered shooting out the lightbulbs along the corridor, but he didn't want to waste the knockout rounds in the Beretta, and the USP was too noisy.

Nevertheless, he hugged the wall and slid along it quickly, his eyes and ears open for any untoward movement or sounds. As luck would have it, he came to a door marked ELECTRICAL ROOM.

He shrugged, tried the door, and found it unlocked. Snake stepped inside and studied the banks of circuit breakers. If he wanted, he could douse the lights throughout the entire tanker, but that would arouse too much suspicion. The commandos might think they'd been discovered and would begin slaughtering the Marines. Best to simply shut off the electricity on Deck-2. He found the appropriate circuit breaker box, flipped the switches, and the room was plunged into darkness. Snake slipped on his night-vision goggles, turned, and stepped out of the room.

He heard voices in the distance. The Russians on the level were obviously concerned about the sudden blackout. Footsteps were headed his way. Before he had time to hide, two men rounded the far corner and faced him. Snake was ready—he fired two shots from the Beretta at a distance of ten meters—and hit both targets in the shoulders. The men went down, and Snake rushed forward to head off any reinforcements that might be behind them, but the corridor leading to the starboard side was empty.

Snake continued along the level until he finally came to the hatch he needed. But as he approached it, the wheel began to turn by itself. Someone on the other side was coming through! Snake slipped behind a wall in an alcove near the hatch, readied his weapon, and crouched. He heard the hatch open; three commandos entered and shut it behind them. One soldier was talking on his radio. Snake's Russian was adequate enough to understand the conversation.

"Colonel, we have sealed the stern hatch."

"All right." Old Man Gurlukovich's voice.

"The lift is also under our control."

"Good. We're on the foredeck. About to descend into the holds."

"Sir, the Marine commander has started his speech."

"We will complete the preparations before the end of the speech."

"All communications to the holds have been severed. No one

is aware of our presence. Except for the men we have already taken care of."

One of the other guards chuckled.

"Let no one down into the holds until we are out," Gurlukovich ordered.

"Yes, sir! We will secure your exit with our lives if necessary."

"There is one more thing . . ."

"Yes, sir?"

Gurlukovich paused a moment. "My daughter. Keep her safe."

"Yes, sir!"

Snaked frowned. The Marines were being sealed inside the holds. Something bad was definitely going down.

"What happened to the lights?" one Russian asked.

"I don't know. Use your night vision."

The men began to move along the corridor toward the alcove where Snake was hidden. He kept perfectly still as they walked past him, but one of the three men turned his head and looked into the space.

"Hey!" the man shouted, swinging his assault rifle around in Snake's direction. But Snake had equipped himself with the USP. No more Mr. Sandman—he had to play for keeps now. The handgun erupted and the soldier fell back against the corridor wall, his chest now a blooming spread of redness.

The second of the three men turned to fire at Snake while the first one had the sense to dash forward, out of the alcove's line of sight. Snake took down the second man with another round from the USP—this time to the commando's forehead.

Now, however, the remaining lone soldier had taken a position somewhere down the corridor. Spray fire from the Russian's AKS-74u pinned Snake in the alcove. He waited until the commando ceased firing and then reached into his pack for the frag grenade he had pinched from Olga. Snake pulled the pin with his teeth and then tossed the grenade around the alcove corner. He heard the thing hit the floor and rattle as it rolled toward the enemy soldier. The commando actually cried out in alarm, but it was too late for him to escape. The blast shook the deck. There was no more machine-gun fire after that.

Snake emerged from the alcove and approached the sealed hatch.

The Codec snapped on. "Snake, are you in yet?"

"It's taking longer than I expected. We've already passed the Verrazano Bridge."

"All right. We'll use another recovery point."

"They may be planning to change course."

"What?"

"The exits to the deck are all sealed."

"What are they planning?"

"If they get Metal Gear, we're going right off the fringe!"

Snake turned the wheel, opened the door, looked inside to make sure it was clear, went through, and shut the door behind him.

A LONE RUSSIAN COMMANDO had been watching the whole thing. He had avoided the grenade blast and witnessed the infiltrator go through the hatch to the holds. The orders were to either keep anyone else from going in—or keep them from coming out. The commando went to the hatch and turned the wheel to the locked position. But then the sound of clinking footsteps caused him to turn, his weapon ready.

The man behind him was tall. He had long golden hair, a mustache, and was wearing a gray duster coat and cowboy boots—with spurs, the source of the *clinks*.

The commando sighed with relief and lowered his weapon. "Oh! Shalashaska."

Revolver Ocelot nodded.

"Why are you here? We thought you were with the Colonel," the commando said.

Ocelot didn't answer. He merely raised his six-shooter and shot the Russian with two rounds in the head and chest. The gunslinger then stepped over the body and confirmed that the hatch was sealed tightly. "Yes," he said to the corpse. "The colonel will be joining you soon. Comrade."

THE CAVERNOUS THREE-LEVEL cargo holds in the lower part of the ship were giant tanks that would normally store crude oil. But because of the *Discovery's* true purpose—the transport of Metal Gear—the tanks were empty. The landing outside of the hatch was approximately seventy feet above the floor, where approximately fifty Marines stood at attention in orderly rows, facing their commandant, General Scott Dolph, a by-the-book African American career soldier in his fifties. From Snake's vantage point, he could see the portion of the hold behind the general, which was obviously where Metal Gear was stored.

General Dolph had just begun addressing the troops, and his voice echoed loudly throughout the vast space. *"At the moment, every industrialized nation in the world knows the specifications for Metal Gear. Even worse, so do a number of rogue states. They are all working on deploying their own Metal Gear force to compete with U.S. nuclear strike capabilities. The world is about to see a swarm of these Metal Gear derivatives. We initiated the development of Metal Gear RAY as a countermeasure to these pirated weapons forces."*

Snake spoke through the Codec. "The men down here are definitely Marines."

Otacon stated the obvious. "If the deck is sealed off, they have no way of knowing that the ship's been taken over."

"I'm not interested in fighting these guys. The weapons won't do me much good here."

"Can you see Metal Gear?"

"No. I'll have to go around the bow. They have some serious

defenses here. I doubt the recent arrivals want to blast their way through the Marines, either."

"Wonder where they're headed . . ."

"I don't know. Not the beach, that's for sure."

"Okay, Snake, let's go over this one more time. We need four photographs. Metal Gear from the front, front-right, and front-left. And then we need a close-up of the Marine Corps marking."

"Marking?"

"There should be a Marine Corps insignia on the body of Metal Gear. Just let someone try explaining away a clear shot of that."

"All right."

"But there's actually one little thing . . ."

"Just spit it out. I'm used to things going wrong."

"It looks like someone's monitoring our transmission."

"Who?"

"I don't have a clue. All they're doing is listening and watching—it would creep me out less if they tried to interfere with our communications."

"Could it have something to do with the Cypher I saw?"

"Maybe. I've switched the encryption protocol for our burst transmission for now. What I want to do now is use a different method for sending your camera's photos. Just in case."

"Instead of using the Codec?"

"Exactly. There's a workstation in the southeast corner of the block where Metal Gear is housed. I've made arrangements so that you can send the pictures from that machine."

"Arrangements?"

"I hitched a ride on Link-16 into the U.S. military's proprietary network. Managed to get into that workstation and over-wrote a part of the system software so I could remote-install a little app I wrote."

Snake shook his head in frustration. "Why bother with anything complicated—?"

"No, it's pretty simple, really. Look, all you have to do is stand in front of the machine and log onto the main screen. Place the camera on the port. The app will automatically launch and download the image data from the camera, split the files, and encrypt them individually. The data packets can then masquerade as—"

"Okay, okay! I get it!"

Otacon rolled his eyes. "Fine. One more thing. You need to get the pictures before the Commandant's done talking. Otherwise, they'll disperse and spot you!"

"How much time do I have?"

"I hacked into the general's personal files and took a look at the text of that speech. I'd say you have seven more minutes—longer if he throws in a joke or two."

"With these kinds of odds, I won't be making any sudden moves. But that doesn't mean we can just let Metal Gear be hijacked."

"Okay, okay. But first the photos!"

"All right. We'll cross that other bridge when we come to it."

"Stay low."

Snake signed off and began the trek around the landing of the first hold, which was much like a metal grid catwalk in the fly space of a theater. Luckily, the shadows up there were his friends.

"The only thing that can stand up to a Metal Gear is, of course, another Metal Gear. With RAY, the hundreds, if not thousands, of Metal Gears that exist all over the world are no longer a threat. The blind rush to nuclear proliferation will be contained. And it will be the Marine Corps—and our RAY—that will accomplish this!"

Snake found a rung ladder that descended to the second landing, and it was far enough to the side of the Marines that they wouldn't notice him—as long as they each remained at attention. Should one of them happen to turn his head . . .

Snake quickly scaled down and crouched on the middle catwalk. And then he saw it.

The gigantic shape of Metal Gear RAY loomed ahead. It had a presence and heavy, brooding feel that bore no resemblance to its predecessor. It appeared almost organic, with a parched look of a beached marine creature. Its surface design owed more to biology than metallurgy and was almost opalescent with the soft gloss of seashells. Snake thought it looked like a mutant merging of a bird and a sea mammal. Except for the fact that it stood thirty-five meters high.

General Dolph stood on a small podium in front of the mechanical beast, but his image was projected on a giant screen above Metal Gear so that all of the Marines could see him as he spoke. *"Ours is not the only military project devoted to Metal Gear development, but it cannot be more different in nature from the Navy's. Theirs is a program that will add fuel to the uncontrolled fire of nuclear proliferation. It is a fact that players in favor of such a policy are attempting to derail our own RAY project. But I promise you that they will not succeed! Some say that the strategic importance of aircraft carriers will be reduced by the completion of RAY."*

Snake was forced to sneak backward, the opposite way around the room, because of a large spill of bright illumination from the overhead work lights. That was going to take at least another minute of travel time. But he hurried along, willing the soldiers to keep focused on their commander, even though the speech was deadly dull. Snake figured he would have dozed off by now had he been down there on the floor.

After what seemed like an eternity—but was really only fifty-five seconds—Snake found another rung ladder that led down to the floor of the hold. He scaled it like a spider, crouched low on the ground and scooted behind a cargo crate that was directly behind the Marines. Snake glanced to his right—at the southeast corner—and saw the workstation Otacon had mentioned. Now he had to get around the side and up to the front of the space so he could snap the pics. But that was easier said than done.

"This project is vital to the Marine Corps. The enemy is some-

times closer to home than you think, gentlemen. Always bear that in mind. This weapon will render all other Metal Gears obsolete. We, the Marine Corps, will play a central role in the shift of the balance of power in the world."

Snake crept between blind spots as quietly and quickly as he could. But when he got halfway toward the bow, the general announced, *"You look a little tense, men. Let's do a little stretching, shall we?"* And for the next minute, he drilled the troops in head and shoulder exercises. He ordered them to look up, down, left, and right. At first Snake thought this was a disaster, but then he realized that the three counts in which the men were looking up, down, and to the left were to his advantage—it gave him that much more time to move forward without being seen.

When he reached the front of the room, where the general and Metal Gear RAY were located, the Marine stopped the exercises. *"Very good, men. Now, where was I? Oh, yes. Men, I have a daughter. I hope she never has to experience the horror of nuclear war. As a father, I want to leave a better world for the future generation."*

Snake pulled the camera from his pack and shot the front-right picture. He then ducked beneath a tarp and crawled, belly to the floor, around Metal Gear to the other side, and then snapped the left-front picture. Luckily, the Marine Corps insignia Otacon had mentioned was there as well, on the beast's underside. Snake lay on his back and zoomed the lens to get a close-up.

"The National Missile Defense program was initiated at the end of the twentieth century. However, the NMD trial conducted in the year 2000 was a complete failure. There was no technological solution in sight, and the program was already attracting strong criticism from Russia and China for its potential violation of the Anti–Ballistic Missile Agreement. The fact that any development in missile defense would trigger accelerated weapons development has been pointed out from the very beginning."

The last shot—front-center—was going to be risky. The only thing Snake could do was worm along the floor on his back beneath the mecha weapon until he reached the back of the podium upon which the general was standing. Would the Marines see him? The lighting was in his favor—a lone spot shone on the general, but the space directly behind him was in shadow. If he moved slowly . . .

"RAY is deployed from under water. It can move in undetected and make its landing on any shoreline. Its onboard Joint Tactical Information Distribution System identifies targets with unerring accuracy and takes them out with massive firepower. It is the ultimate weapon, and it is yours to guard."

He was in position. Snake held the camera close to his chest, for to raise it to his eyes would certainly be noticed. He had to hope that the shot he wanted was correctly in the frame. He snapped the picture and then slowly reversed his snail-like crawl back to the belly of Metal Gear RAY. From there it was relatively simple to slip out from under and make his way back along the side of the hold to the southeast corner where the workstation sat.

"We have intelligence that anti–Metal Gear terrorists are planning to target this ship. Should that actually happen, I expect you to be prepared. We cannot and will not give up RAY. Stay on your guard at all times!"

Even though the general droned on, Snake knew he had less than a couple of minutes to get the photos uploaded. He made it to the workstation, used a mouse to access the main screen, placed the camera on the port, and—voila!—Otacon's app suddenly activated. Snake had to hand it to the guy. Hal Emmerich was one smart dude.

"Okay, Snake, I'm receiving your photos," the scientist said through Codec. "The first one's coming in and . . . hey!"

Snake smiled. The first shot he had snapped on the camera was the one of the pinup babe in the locker room.

"Snake! What is this? I'm not even going to ask you about it— I'll just, uhm, make a backup copy of it and move on." The next four shots uploaded and Otacon breathed a sigh of relief. "Okay.

Very good. You got exactly the four shots we need. You're a pretty good photographer, Snake. Say, if this stealth thing doesn't work out for you . . . oh, never mind. We got what we need. Get out of there now!"

"To move on . . . the brain drain of nuclear specialists and the black market trade in weapons-grade plutonium have been fueling a cottage industry in nuclear weapons since late last century. Add Metal Gear to the mix, and the result is the renewed proliferation you see the world over. We, the Marines, will lead the charge into a new world order with Metal Gear RAY! That is all. Dismissed!"

As Snake moved toward the hatch, the general saluted the Marines. The men immediately snapped to attention and returned the salute.

A dull *crash* suddenly reverberated through the hold. Snake flattened himself behind a pillar as the men looked around for the cause of the noise. Then there was the echoing sound of hand claps—a lone person applauding the general. Dolph scanned the room and murmured, "What the . . . ?"

Snake peered around the pillar—and couldn't believe what he saw. Stepping out from behind Metal Gear RAY was none other than Revolver Ocelot, dressed in his full trademark gear of duster, boots and spurs, and six-shooter at his waist.

"Excellent speech, my friend," the gunslinger said as he approached the general. "Gift of the silver tongue. They say it's a mark of a good officer."

Snake noticed that Ocelot's right hand was blanched from the elbow down, the fingers twisted into a deformed fist.

"And of a liar," Ocelot continued. "Americans arc too in love with the sound of their own voices to speak the truth."

"Identify yourself!" Dolph shouted.

The Marines raised their weapons and assumed ready-to-fight positions. All they needed was a command to fire.

"I am Shalashaska!" the golden-haired man announced proudly. "Also called Revolver Ocelot."

The men moved closer, but the general raised his hand to halt them. "What do you want?" he asked.

Ocelot gestured to RAY. "This machine will be quite useful."

The general almost laughed. "What are you planning to do, steal it?"

"Steal? No, no, I'm taking it *back.*"

General Dolph smiled in derision at Ocelot's reply, but suddenly a Makarov pistol was jabbed against his throat. The Russian, Colonel Gurlukovich, had noiselessly appeared behind the podium, climbed atop, and stepped behind the Marine commander. The rest of the soldiers on the floor were startled, unsure of what to do. Then they turned and aimed their weapons at both Gurlukovich and Ocelot. But it was a stalemate. The Russian indicated he would blow a hole in the general if anyone moved.

Ocelot raised his left hand in the air. He was holding some kind of remote control. "Nobody move! Understood?" The men continued to murmur to themselves, bewildered by the sudden appearance of the two interlopers.

"This ship now carries enough Semtex on its key structural points to blow it out of the water—at the touch of this button," Ocelot proclaimed.

Snake moved closer to the melee but stayed behind cover. He, like the Marines, could not believe what was happening.

The soldiers kept their guns aimed at the two infiltrators, but Ocelot sensed the men's hesitation. "That's right. No one has to die needlessly," he said.

And then several coils of rope dropped from above and several Russian commandos descended rapidly to the floor. Once there, they surrounded the Marines and raised their weapons against the American soldiers. Several of the Russians positioned themselves near Metal Gear RAY's legs.

Tense silence.

Great, Snake thought. *Now what?*

3

OCELOT ADDRESSED the Russian commandos. "We're almost at the target. Get a move on!" The men immediately rushed to the cables that fastened Metal Gear RAY to the floor and began to unlock them.

General Dolph recovered some of his composure and asked through gritted teeth, "What do you intend to do with RAY—sell it on the streets?"

Gurlukovich moved the pistol barrel from the general's neck to the Marine's temple. "I was raised in Snezhinsk, also known as Chelyabinsk-70, the nuclear research outpost," he said in heavily accented English.

"What are you talking about?" Dolph asked.

"After the Cold War ended, my home was bought out by the Americans."

"Is there a point to this sad story?"

"None that you would understand. Land, friends, dignity . . . all sold to the highest bidder. The *only* bidder—the United States of America. Even the technology that gave birth to the weapon we see here is Russian, developed by us!"

Dolph narrowed his eyes and asked again, "What do you intend to do?"

"Russia will rise again—and RAY is the key!" Gurlukovich glanced at Ocelot, seeking a show of solidarity. But Ocelot began to chuckle while caressing the transmitter in his right hand.

The gunslinger said softly, "I regret to inform you, Sergei, that I have no intention of selling Metal Gear. As I said, I came to take it back."

Gurlukovich seemed bewildered by Ocelot's words.

"Yes, returned," Ocelot continued. "To the Patriots!"

General Dolph jerked violently at Ocelot's words. "The *La-le-lu-le-lo*? How is that possible?"

Snake blinked. *What did the general just say?*

Gurlukovich glared at the gunslinger. "Ocelot, you—have you sold us out?"

"I was never in your employ, Gurlukovich."

"Are you . . . are you still in league with Solidus?"

"No hard feelings, Colonel. Mother Russia can rot, for all I care."

"Since when, Ocelot? When did you turn?"

"I'm glad you noticed, *comrade*. I abandoned 'her' during the Cold War."

"You traitorous—" Gurlukovich trembled with rage.

Ocelot called out to the Russian commandos, "Metal Gear only has room for one!"

The commandos, waiting for a cue from their colonel, showed signs of confusion. Who were they supposed to listen to? Ocelot had been sharing the command with Gurlukovich. Who was really in charge?

Despite the puzzlement, six of the commandos stepped to the podium and aimed their assault rifles at Ocelot.

"Gurlukovich, you and your daughter will die here," Ocelot said calmly.

"Damn you!" the colonel spat. He suddenly released General Dolph and shoved him forward.

It all happened so quickly that it might as well have been in slow motion, and it wouldn't have made a difference. Gurlukovich swerved his Makarov toward Ocelot. At the same time, Ocelot removed his duster with a flourish and threw it in the air as a matador might do with a cape. The coat sailed toward Gurlukovich, twisting and rippling, blocking the Russian colonel's view.

"Die, you dog!" Gurlukovich shouted. He fired, blowing a hole in the duster in midair. Ocelot, however, was no longer in the bullet's trajectory. He moved in rhythm with the duster's progress, shielding himself from view as he drew his revolver with his left hand and fired six shots in rapid succession. The slugs all punched through the coat, which was still falling toward the ground. All six bullets found targets—in both Gurlukovich and General Dolph. As if it had been planned for a circus act, all three hit the floor at the same time—the duster, Gurlukovich, and Dolph.

Then, before the six Russian guards could react, Ocelot dropped the six-shooter, drew another single-action army pistol from a back holster, and pulled the trigger with lightning speed.

All six commandos were hit; they twirled on their feet and dropped to the floor like bowling pins.

Revolver Ocelot spun his pistol like a Western gunfighter and returned it to the holster.

The Marines were outraged at the loss of their commander, but still they hesitated to act. The remaining Russian commandos kept their weapons on the Americans.

Ocelot held up the transmitter and shouted for all to hear, "Show's over! If you wish to live, I suggest you run now! This ship is still in the Lower New York Harbor. You may yet make it to shore if you swim for your life!"

With that, he pressed the button. The tanker rocked violently as an ear-shattering blast filled the holds. A succession of equally powerful explosions went off like dominos throughout the *Discovery*'s several decks. It was as if the gods had picked the huge boat out of the water and shaken it with aggression.

Chaos ensued.

The Marines and Russians all shouted in alarm. Some of them fired weapons at the enemy. Bullets ripped through men with bloody precision. Others ran for it as Ocelot suggested. The holds quickly filled with smoke and fire—and then the sea came gushing in. In less than thirty seconds, the water was up to everyone's waist. The *Discovery* would be at the bottom of the harbor in minutes.

Throughout it all, Revolver Ocelot calmly climbed a ladder that was attached to a platform built next to Metal Gear RAY's cockpit.

Snake trudged through the climbing waterline toward RAY as fast as he could. He aimed the USP at his former enemy and shouted, "*Ocelot!*"

The gunslinger heard Snake's voice and turned. And then something extraordinary occurred. Ocelot's right arm—which Snake could now see was a prosthetic made of uncannily realistic material—began vibrating uncontrollably. The gunslinger grabbed it with his left hand and attempted to stop the tremors. Whatever was instigating them was also causing Ocelot a great deal of pain. The man cried out in anguish.

And then he pointed at Snake with his right hand. "It's been a while, brother!" the gunslinger shouted, but it was not Ocelot's voice.

Snake's eyes narrowed. He knew that voice!

What the hell . . . ?

Ocelot straightened and held himself in a completely different posture. It was as if he had been infused with someone else's body language.

"Who are you?" Snake called. He didn't know whether to fire at the guy or not.

"You know who I am."

Ocelot clenched his right hand, which was a habit of someone else Snake had known. Something *in* the gunslinger's prosthetic arm was controlling Ocelot's mind and body and somehow speaking through him.

Snake couldn't believe his eyes and ears. It was too unreal. *"Liquid?"*

Liquid Snake. His brother, cloned from the DNA of their father, Big Boss. The FOXHOUND traitor who had masterminded the Shadow Moses incident.

But Liquid Snake was killed at the end of that gory affair!

"Not so young anymore, eh, Snake?" Liquid/Ocelot taunted. "You're drowning in time. I know what it's like, brother." The man laughed at the look of confusion on Snake's face. "No wonder Naomi passed you over for the FOXDIE program!"

Suddenly Ocelot grabbed his right arm and screamed at it, as if he were wrestling a demon out of the appendage. "Get out! Get out of my mind, Liquid!" he shouted in his own voice. He then did something equally bizarre—Ocelot bit into his arm, drawing blood. But it was to no avail. The right arm once again suppressed its host personality. Ocelot straightened and addressed Snake again in Liquid's voice.

"The price of physical prodigy. A few more years and you'll be another dead clone of the old man! Our raw materials are vintage, brother. Big Boss was in his late fifties when they created his copies. But I . . . I live on, through this arm!"

"Liquid's *arm?*" Snake asked, totally freaked out.

The water was rising rapidly. The Marines and Russians were still attempting to fight their way out of the holds through whatever passageways were accessible. Many were sealed tightly and locked. Trying to swim out of the flooding holes proved impossible. The rushing torrent swept Colonel Gurlukovich away—but the man had enough life still left in him to think of the one person who meant anything to him . . . *Olga* . . . the last thought in his mind as his lungs filled with water.

Another explosion jolted the tanker, knocking Snake off balance. He began to climb the ladder to RAY's cockpit platform.

Seeing Snake coming for him, Ocelot/Liquid uttered a sharp grunt, leaped into the cockpit, pulled down the hatch, and donned a pilot's headset. He moved an eye module used in attack helicopters over his right eye and rapidly locked his seat belt in place. He punched a few buttons and maneuvered some levers.

Metal Gear RAY came to life.

"You don't have what it takes after all!" Liquid's voice jeered through RAY's PA system. "You're going down, Snake—with this tanker!"

Snake climbed onto the platform, too late to stop Ocelot.

"Otacon, we have a problem!" he shouted through his Codec.

He watched in shock and awe as RAY moved like a bird stepping out of its nest. The machine was truly a monster of frightening design. It had legs for walking, wings for flying, and a tail and fins for swimming. It moved like a prehistoric reptile made of metal.

A heavy wave hit Snake and knocked him off the platform and into the water.

Marines that happened to be on the upper levels of the hold fired their weapons at RAY. The bullets merely bounced off of the shell. As if it had been angered by the annoying rounds, RAY lashed out with its "beak" and destroyed the platform on which the Marines were perched. The men dropped, screaming, into the gushing torrent.

RAY actually *howled* like a beast that had found itself back in its element.

It then dunked its head into the water and aimed at a portion of the tanker's hull. A built-in V17 Vulcan Cannon Searing

LaserStorm High-Energy Cutter, which was the state of the art in laser weaponry, could slice and dice anything in RAY's path. Ocelot proceeded to test its functionality by cutting a hole in the tanker large enough for RAY to swim through. Doing so, of course, ultimately hastened the *Discovery*'s sinking. The holds completely filled with water, drowning anyone who was left inside.

Unconscious, Snake was swept away with dozens of soldiers. He didn't hear Otacon on the Codec, frantically shouting, *"Snake! Snake? Snake!"*

Metal Gear RAY emerged from the tanker and swam to the surface of the Hudson. It then sprang into the air and hovered over the sinking ship.

After losing sight of Snake, Ocelot regained control of his right arm—and personality. He pulled a radio from his pocket and made contact.

"No problems. Proceeding as planned, sir," he announced. He listened to the man on the other end and nodded. "Yes. At the location we discussed." Another question. "Yes. I have photographic evidence of Snake on the scene. The Cypher was most useful. I look forward to tomorrow morning's news flash. I would say the Marine Corps' plans are on indefinite hold." Ocelot listened to a final instruction and answered, "Yes, of course, Mister President!"

RAY proceeded to glide through the air, and then it abruptly dived into the water, as efficient and graceful as its namesake, the manta ray. It accelerated in a single thrust of power and darted away from the New York Harbor.

4

THE SKY WAS A DEEP, cloudless blue, but it was also dotted with several military and police helicopters making passes over the Big Shell facility in the Hudson River. The Verrazano Bridge was sealed off as soldiers and policemen stood in alert position. Global positioning satellites relayed data in real time to various monitors. The scattering of bright lights over the harbor area indicated the scope of the security forces at work guarding the plant. Something big was up, and it would be a challenge to keep the media from finding out about it before it was too late.

The Big Shell. A massive environmental containment unit built to prevent ecological contamination due to the massive spread of crude oil spilled during the sinking of the U.S.S. *Discovery* two years earlier. An impressive structure, the plant was made up of Shells 1 and 2 that appeared, when looking down at them from the sky, to be two hexagons connected end to end. Both hexagons were actually composed of a Central Core surrounded by six likewise hexagon-shaped "Struts" that served different purposes in the facility's functions. The Struts, named A through F in Shell 1, and G through L in Shell 2, and the Central Cores, labeled 1 and 2, stood on the ocean floor and jutted straight up above the surface. The Struts were connected to their respective adjacent structures by a series of open-air bridge walkways. Shells 1 and 2 were connected by a bridge between Struts D and G. The Central Cores were connected to the Struts by only two bridges each—the B–C, E–F, H–I, and K–L bridges were T-sections— the connecting conduits led to the respective Central Cores. The roofs of each Strut and Central Core were plainly visible to the military personnel and the helicopter pilots.

"Snake, do you remember the sinking of that tanker two years ago?"

The Colonel's voice came through loud and clear over the Codec.

The young operative now known as "Snake" swam unseen by the prying eyes above the surface. He had pushed off from a fishing boat in lower Manhattan and, with the aid of elaborate SCUBA gear provided by FOXHOUND, was able to swim out into the bay toward the Big Shell. He held a cylindrical oxygen module in his mouth that still enabled him to speak, and he wore a scroll-like pair of goggles that allowed him to see clearly in the murky darkness.

"Of course," Snake replied.

"Terrorists blew a hole in an oil tanker full of crude, barely twenty miles off the shore of Manhattan—your classic nightmare. It didn't take long for the government to put an oil fence around the whole mess. And then that massive offshore cleanup facility went up inside."

"I hear the Big Shell's cleanup isn't quite over yet."

"It takes time. But in the meantime, the Shell's become a landmark, a symbol of environmental protection."

Above the surface, the choppers flew low, dodging dozens of squawking seagulls that flew around the Shell. Military and police craft bobbed on the water near the bridge trestles, blocking sea traffic into the harbor. Had Snake been tuned in to the same frequency, he would have heard a SEAL team leader's radio call ordering Teams Alpha and Bravo to deploy onto the Big Shell as scheduled.

"Now are you going to tell me what I'm doing here, Colonel?" Snake asked. As far as he knew, the "Colonel" he was talking to was the legendary Colonel Roy Campbell, veteran FOXHOUND leader. At least Snake *assumed* it was he. Snake had never met the man in person but had received periodic communications from him during the training.

"Approximately six hours ago, the Big Shell was seized by an armed group."

"Do we have an ID?"

"There's evidence that they are former members of the Navy SEALs' special anti-terrorist training squad, Dead Cell. Russian private army members may also be involved. It's a highly trained group, and they have the Big Shell under complete control."

"Who's the leader?"

"At one time, Dead Cell's leader was Colonel Reginald Jackson, but he was arrested recently and thrown into the brig. As for Dead Cell's boss now, we'll discuss that later."

The choppers moved in closer to the structure. A SEAL leader called out to his men to get ready to fast-rope down to Shell 1.

Snake continued to swim below the surface with his infrared goggles activated. He approached the oil fence that was emblazoned with military warning signs—NO ENTRY, DANGER—HIGH VOLTAGE, AUTHORIZED PERSONNEL ONLY, DECONTAMINATION FACILITY—but he ignored them. Dead fish floated in front of the barrier. As Snake came closer, he saw that a hole had been cut in the fence, large enough for a single person. He examined the hole and could see the jagged edges in the metal—there was no doubt in his mind that someone had caused the damage for infiltration purposes. And it was recent. Not that it mattered . . . he had a job to do. The hole just made it easier. He swam through the opening, taking care not to come in contact with the fence.

"What are their demands?" he asked.

"Thirty billion dollars," the Colonel replied.

"Thirty *billion* dollars! What makes them think they can get that much?"

"There was a government-sponsored tour going on at the Big Shell."

Snake understood. "Hostages, huh?"

"A VIP from one of the major conservation groups, and one from our own government—the *Most* Important Person in a sense."

"The most important person?"

"James Johnson."

"The President!" Snake was so stunned by the news that he stopped swimming. Johnson had been in office only a short time.

"Unless the demands are met, the terrorists intend to blow the Big Shell out of the water."

"And the crude will ignite, turning the Manhattan Harbor into an inferno."

"That's not the worst-case scenario. If the chlorides being used to decontaminate the seawater go up with the oil, toxins containing catastrophic levels of dioxins will be released. In other words, the bay's ecosystem will be wiped out and the sea will turn into a toxic soup for centuries—becoming the worst environmental disaster in history."

Snake resumed his journey toward the structure. Dead fish also dotted the inside of the fence. Snake looked up at the surface and saw that the thick film of crude blocked out the sun entirely. Directly ahead of him lights affixed to a Strut pointed the way. He switched off the infrared, moved along the ocean floor, and located the plant's barnacle-encrusted maintenance outlet for Strut A. He climbed the ladder into the hatch.

"You have two mission objectives," the Colonel continued. "Number one—infiltrate Big Shell and safeguard the President and other hostages. Two—disarm the terrorists by any means necessary. You should know that SEAL Team Ten is also conducting a rescue operation at this moment."

"Is this a joint effort?"

"No. FOXHOUND remains a covert body. Don't alert them to your presence—that is an order."

Snake broke the surface of the infiltration pool and quickly climbed the ladder into the Deep Sea Dock. Several groupings of sea lice scattered out of his way. Snake looked at them with disgust and made sure none had attached themselves to him. A small, two-man deep-sea submarine was docked in the pool.

"I'm now inside Strut A of Shell One," he announced.

"How are things?"

Snake looked around. The place was dimly lit and empty. Just in case, though, he reached for the M92F holstered at his waist. The lightweight handgun was perfect for infiltration ops, equipped with laser sighting and an optional suppressor.

"We're in luck," he answered. "Looks like there are no sentries posted here."

"What's the visibility?"

"The lights on the plant's Struts are functioning. I won't have to use the IR goggles."

"Any problems?"

"There was a brand-new hole cut through the oil fence. There's someone else besides me that wanted to get in badly."

"That's not possible."

"What about SEAL Team Ten?"

"They landed on the roof of the Big Shell as planned. And by the way, Snake, we're changing your code name for all following communication."

"What's wrong with 'Snake'?"

"Just a precaution. You are now designated 'Raiden.'" The Colonel pronounced the name as *Riden* with a long *I*.

The young operative blinked. He didn't particularly like the new name, but it wasn't his job to question authority.

"All right, Raiden, you've already covered infiltration in VR training."

"I've completed over three hundred missions in VR! I feel like some kind of legendary mercenary . . ."

"But this will be your first sneaking mission. The M9 you already have, but other weapons and ammunition will have to be procured on-site. Make sure nobody sees you. If you need to, contact me by Codec. You know the frequency."

"Right."

"First, make your way to the upper section of the Big Shell."

"How do I get to the next level?"

"There's an elevator at the far end of that area. Use that."

Raiden peered across the pool and saw the doors. "Sounds good."

"Your new Sneaking suit uses electrofiber technology, a by-product of fiber-optics research. The texture isn't far removed from rubber but the material protects against a wide range of toxic substances. The suit itself has built-in sensors. It is referred to as 'Smart Skin' in military R and D. Data about damage to different regions of the body, including blood loss, is exchanged between the suit and the intravenous nanomachines to create a feedback system."

"There's a lot of pressure on my torso."

"Relax. The suit applies varying pressure to major internal organs to maximize performance and safeguard their functions. They call this the 'Skull Suit' in FOXHOUND."

"Skull suit—seems appropriate somehow."

Indeed, the suit fitted Raiden's body so tightly that it was as if it were another layer of skin. The hood made Raiden's head appear like that of an ant—two egg-shaped eyepieces were the only facial features visible.

"The elevator is on the other side of the hatch with a circular handle, beyond the infiltration pool. Locate the hatch first."

"Copy that. Moving onto main mission objectives."

5

RAIDEN MOVED QUICKLY to the hatch, turned the wheel, and opened it. There was a sentry on his hands and knees in the hallway, maybe thirty feet ahead of him. Raiden quickly ducked back into the Dock area.

Wait . . . on his hands and knees . . . ?

Raiden risked a peek around the hatch opening. The guard was slowly getting to his feet. He wore tiger-stripe camos, a skullcap, and an Abakan assault rifle over his shoulder. Grenades on his belt. The man shook his head, as if he were sweeping away cobwebs. Something had happened to him. He had been knocked out by someone.

Raiden watched the sentry get his bearings, pull a radio off his hip, and try to reach others. The radio produced nothing but static. The guard pulled a handgun from a holster, and then slowly moved down the other leg of the L-shaped corridor, out of sight.

"Colonel, I've sighted an enemy sentry. AN-94 and a Makarov. The grenades . . . all his equipment is Russian-made."

The Colonel replied, "Must be a Gurlukovich man."

"Gurlukovich?"

"A Russian private army that was in line to work the Shadow Moses takeover group, four years ago."

"What's their stake in this one?"

"They must have a deal—an arrangement with the terrorists. They've become a band of mercenaries, an army without a country. A sentry would normally call in reinforcements at the sight of you, but he can't do that in the area you're in now. The supplementary radio antennae in the walls are completely corroded. Radio communication is effectively impossible inside that area."

"What about our communication system?"

"No effect on nanomachine-supported networks, only on ordinary radio transmissions. But even if they're cut off from each other, the enemy is armed. Exercise extreme caution, Raiden."

Raiden signed off and entered the hallway. Unlike the Deep Sea Dock, the area was well lit. The elevator cage up ahead had just begun an ascent—and then the Russian sentry Raiden had just seen catapulted out of it! The soldier landed on the floor in front of the lift, unconscious. Next to him were two more men wearing the same style camo, also out cold. Raiden stared at the ascending elevator and caught sight of a figure wearing what appeared to be an old, outdated sneaking suit. The man's back was to Raiden, so he couldn't be identified.

As soon as the lift cage was out of sight, Raiden stooped to one knee and made another call on the Codec.

"Colonel, there's definitely another intruder in here besides me."

"That's not a possibility."

"I just saw him, Colonel! Not a team—looks like a solo job."

"One man . . . ?"

"He managed to take care of every sentry in the area. They're all out cold. Whoever he is, he's got some skills."

"Hmm. We need to get an ID. But for now, you can take advantage of the situation and get to work. There's a terminal in front of the elevator. A *node*."

Raiden put a hand to his ear. "Did you say 'nerd'?"

"Not 'nerd'—*node*."

"Oh."

"Use the node to gain access to the Big Shell's facilities network."

"Then what?"

"Pull up the map of the structure; that'll let you activate the Soliton Radar. It uses biological magnetic fields as input. These estimated enemy positions are projected onto a map according to reference points collected via GPS signals and field personnel reports. We need to get to the map through the Big Shell's node to put this data processing to practical use. The node unit is about three feet high—should be colored blue. Each area has at least one, usually built right into the wall."

"I know about Soliton Radar. It came in handy during VR training." Raiden scanned the space around the elevator and saw the small blue box. It looked like a computer workstation made for a dwarf. "How do I gain access?"

"There should be an activation control on the front of the node. The nanomachines in your body will take care of the security clearance and allow you access to the node. Complete the procedure before those sentries gain consciousness. If they spot you, you won't be able to gain access for a while. You'll need to access the node in every Strut as you go through the Big Shell. Stay on guard."

"Got it."

Raiden gingerly stepped around the fallen sentries and stooped in front of the node. He found the appropriate controls, manipulated them, and then held out his palm. The nanomachines inside his body responded—ribbons of plasma quietly spewed out, and for a second Raiden's hair stood on end. It wasn't an unpleasant feeling, but it surprised him. Then the access message appeared on the terminal screen. Good enough.

Raiden stood and glanced at the unconscious sentries. One of them had three chaff grenades clipped to his belt. Could be useful. Chaff grenades were silent, non-fragmenting explosives that spread a cloud of tiny metallic pieces, disrupting any electronic equipment in their range. Raiden bent down, took them, and shoved them into his backpack.

The Colonel buzzed. "Good work, Raiden. We're reading the node here."

"The radar is functioning now?"

"Remember your VR training sessions. The tool is exactly the same one—it maps the terrain as well as the position of enemy personnel."

Raiden was about to sign off when a woman interrupted the Colonel's Codec transmission. "Jack—are you all right?"

Raiden gasped when he saw her face on the Codec monitor. "Wha—what are *you* doing here?"

"Jack, can you hear me?"

"Rose! You're not supposed to be involved!"

He couldn't believe it. His girlfriend was talking to him on the Codec!

A pretty brunette, Rose was dressed in a beige suit with a blue blouse, revealingly unbuttoned. A pair of earrings and traces of makeup completed the somewhat unreal effect.

"What's going on?" Raiden demanded, a bit angry but more confused.

"Jack, I'm part of the mission."

"Colonel, what the hell is going on?"

The Colonel's image reappeared on the Codec. "Raiden, meet the mission analyst. She'll be overseeing the data saving and support."

"Why her?"

"The FOXHOUND analyst that was supposed to take part in this mission was in an accident. Rosemary was brought in as a replacement."

"An accident?"

"And according to the files, she knows you better than anybody else."

"Rose may be in the service, but an intelligence analyst is no field officer!"

"Not to worry. She has our technical staff at her disposal."

"She's never been part of a field mission. This is insane!"

The Colonel's eyes narrowed. "I have my own reasons for selecting her for this mission, soldier."

"Colonel, I fail to see—"

"I know your VR training performance in and out. But sometimes that's not enough. You're familiar with the Shadow Moses incident?"

"You know I covered it in VR."

"If there's a crucial tactical detail that case taught us, it was the power of the operative's will to survive."

"I was trained to fight. My personal feelings have no place in a mission!"

"We've learned that it doesn't work that way. And on the field, you need all the help you can get."

Rose's face replaced the Colonel's on the Codec. "Jack? You're stuck with me whether you like it or not."

"Rose . . ."

"You need someone to watch your back. But . . . Colonel, I have conditions that need to be met."

As the Colonel and Rose conversed, their images alternated on the Codec monitor.

"What is it?" the Colonel asked.

"I'll perform my duties and save the mission data. But I'm aware that technically I'm not part of the mission control team. After all, I'm just a normal girl who's worried about Jack. But that means, Colonel, that I am not required to follow your orders outside of my immediate duties. Jack is not simply field personnel for me to track. His safety comes first to me, not the mission. And because of that I will be monitoring and keeping a record of every communication you have with him, Colonel."

The Colonel smiled wryly. "Given the circumstances, you're free to do what you see fit."

"Hey, I prefer this to being kept in the dark, waiting."

"And I'd like to make a request if I may."

"Of course."

"His handle is 'Raiden.' For the duration of the mission, could you call him that?"

"Yes, sir. All right . . . Raiden. I'm here when you need me."

The pair signed off. Raiden shook his head. It was too unreal. Rose—the woman with whom he shared a bed, the woman he loved—part of the mission? Totally inappropriate. Not standard operating procedure. But then, when did FOXHOUND ever use SOP?

Rose buzzed him again. "Jack, I just switched frequencies. Jack?"

"What?"

"Do you know what day it is tomorrow?"

"April thirtieth. Is there something special about it?"

"Isn't there?"

Raiden frowned. "I can't remember. I'm sorry."

"Oh well, I'll keep trying until I hear the answer. I'm going to let you go now, Jack. Take care."

Raiden scratched his head. *What the hell was* that *about?*

One of the sentries on the floor began to stir. Raiden stood and punched the call button for the elevator. A second guard groaned and moved. No time to wait. Raiden looked for a place to hide. There were some empty cardboard boxes off to the side— they were large enough to hold small refrigerators or stoves. Raiden rushed to one, climbed inside, and pulled down the flaps. He remained silent as the guards slowly got to their feet and conversed in Russian. One of them managed to bring up the radio—someone on the other end spoke English. The guard said, "Intruder . . . Strut A . . . knocked us out . . ."

"Search the area. We've sent more men," the voice commanded.

The elevator arrived. Two more sentries stepped out of it and joined the others. The men began to search the level, knocking over crates and barrels. So far they had not noticed the cardboard boxes. Raiden remained quiet until he heard the men go through the corridor back toward the Deep Sea Dock. He quickly stepped out of the box, ran to the open elevator, and pushed the button for the top floor. The cage closed and began to rise.

The lift remained in an enclosed shaft for several levels until it reached the surface of the bay. Suddenly, bright sunlight burst into the cage, and Raiden could see out over the harbor and the Manhattan skyline in the distance. He pulled off the skullcap, revealing a long mane of white hair that tumbled out to cover his shoulders. His features were somewhat androgynous—Rose had once told him he looked like a young David Bowie.

The Colonel buzzed on the Codec. "The terrorists call themselves 'Sons of Liberty.' "

"Sons of Liberty?"

"The name of their leader is Solid Snake."

"The hero of Shadow Moses? So that's why you changed my code name."

"Right. But it can't be *the* Solid Snake. He died two years ago on that tanker after he blew it sky-high."

"Could he have survived?"

"Not a chance."

The elevator arrived at Strut A's roof and opened, startling a flock of seagulls into flight. The drone of SEAL helicopters could be heard, but they were nowhere to be seen. Raiden walked to the closest cover and crouched.

"Colonel, I'm on the roof. There are no sentries, but it would only take one to spot me in this light."

"You never had daylight VR training, after all," the Colonel agreed. "Stay extra sharp until you can find a node to log in from."

"What about the commandos?"

"SEAL Team Ten has landed on Struts B and C. They're in now."

"And the President?"

"Seems he was spotted on Strut B."

"Do we really have no line of communication with the SEALs?"

"They don't know a thing about us. You know we work in the dark, and this mission is no exception. Only a few people know about your presence here. But there's no need for concern. This operation is under the Pentagon's direct command, and the NSDD came from the Vice President and the Secretary of Defense. Your mission may be top-secret, but it's gone through the usual channels."

Raiden signed off and scanned the roof. The node was probably in the space below, inside the Strut. He sighted a stairwell, entered it, and quietly made his way down to what appeared to be a Pump Room. Sure enough, the blue node was at the north end of the space, but there were two sentries patrolling in its proximity.

He would need to distract them. There was a partition wall separating him from the node. Raiden moved swiftly to the wall and flattened himself against it. He knocked on the wall twice and then listened. The sound of the guard's footsteps approached. Raiden quickly moved around the wall in the opposite direction and emerged on the other side just as the sentry cleared. The second man was nowhere in sight. Raiden stooped by the node and went through the same procedure as he had done below. A map of the Strut appeared on the monitor, and Raiden could pinpoint the location of enemy units. There were only the two there in the Pump Room.

He avoided the guards and made his way back to the stairwell. After emerging onto the roof again, Raiden eyed the connecting bridge between Struts A and B. There were two sentries patrolling it. The best way to get across would be to use what they called "hanging mode" during VR training.

Suddenly, a small, strange device that resembled a flying life buoy drifted into view. Raiden recognized it as a Cypher. He quickly flattened himself against the stairwell wall so that he couldn't be seen. Those surveillance mechanisms were tough and tricky. It was a good thing he had snatched the chaffs. One would knock out the Cypher's circuits and not make a lot of noise. Raiden removed one from his backpack, pulled the pin with his teeth, counted to three, and tossed it at the nosy flying machine. The grenade went off and covered the Cypher with its cloud of tiny metal. The flying machine sputtered for a moment and then hung in the air. The camera no longer moved; it just stared straight ahead as if the thing were now blind and mindless.

The Colonel buzzed. "Raiden, I just intercepted new intelligence on the operation being executed by SEAL Team Ten."

"Intercepted?"

"As I said before, they need to be kept in the dark about our presence."

"So we just listen in."

"I'm patching it through."

After a burst of static the radio transmissions between SEAL team members could be heard through the Codec.

"This is Alpha Zero. We have the President."

"Is he safe?"

"He is safe."

"What about the package?"

"Tell the guys upstairs that we've secured the package. Easy money."

"Good work. Your retrieval is on the way. Come on home."

"Roger that. H-holy—!"

Sudden gunfire. Screams.

"Alpha Zero! Report!"

"Damn it! Cover the President!"

"Come in, Alpha Zero!"

"This is Alpha Zero! We're under attack!"

More gunfire. Shouting. Confusion.

"This is crazy! Is that . . . ?"

"Alpha Zero! Respond!"

The gunfire ceased. Silence.

The Colonel came back on. "Raiden! The President's life is in danger! Head to Strut B now!"

6

RAIDEN HURRIED to the A–B connecting bridge. The sentries were still there. Time for hanging mode. Without a second thought, Raiden slipped over the side of the bridge and faced the rail. Then, hanging by his hands, he slowly shimmied across, his legs dangling dozens of feet above the Hudson River. The rail was damp and cold, but Raiden's gloves were made with the standard FOXHOUND-designed texture that supported gripping maneuvers such as this one. It was hard on the upper arms, wrists, and shoulders, but it was the only way across. The trick was simply not looking down and keeping a good grasp.

It took him nearly six minutes to get across, but the sentries never suspected his presence. At the other end, Raiden carefully pulled himself up, swung a leg over the rail, and hopped onto the bridge. He then slipped onto Strut B's roof and moved down the stairwell without being seen.

He froze.

The walls in the corridor were covered in blood. It was as if a massive slaughter had taken place, but there were no bodies.

Raiden felt a strange, cold aura—someone was nearby and he

wasn't friendly. There was also a mysterious smell of . . . iron. Raiden drew the M9 and held it in front of him, alert and ready. He walked slowly to the end of the corridor, stepping over the pools of red goo, and entered the Transformer Room.

The first things he saw were the three dead, bloody SEALs on the floor. It appeared that they had been sliced up by several attackers wielding blades of some kind. One man had been completely severed in half. It was the most gruesome sight Raiden had ever encountered. It unnerved him, but he swallowed and moved on.

There was a trail of blood leading from the cadavers through the room, which was obviously an electrical control center containing generators, transformers, and other equipment that helped power the Shell. Access to the upper controls of several tall electrical banks was achieved from a catwalk grid near the ceiling that crisscrossed the room. Every light fixture in the place had been destroyed; the only illumination filtered in from a skylight. The room had an oddly solemn churchlike air, but the scene suggested a vain struggle against some gigantic creature. It was a butcher shop.

Gunfire. Up ahead.

"*Damn!*"

"*Fire!*"

"*I can't hit him!*"

"*What kind of freak is he?*"

Screams.

A radio blast: "*Alpha Zero! Come in, Alpha Zero!*"

Raiden cautiously moved forward, skirted around a large bank of transformers, and saw four Navy SEALs in combat with . . . nothing. They fired their M4s blindly. Blood spurted. Streams of it. The men fell one by one. Raiden thought he detected a whirling shape moving in and out between the bodies as they dropped to the floor. Three more SEALs rushed into the melee, but the phantom figure had disappeared.

"Where did he go?"

"What the hell was it?"

Then Raiden saw him.

The enemy was crouched on one of the catwalks above the soldiers. He had long black hair, a goatee, and narrow slits for eyes. He wore a long, dark olive drab coat, giving him a batlike appearance. The men didn't see him.

Raiden wanted to shout and warn them—but his orders were to remain incognito.

The caped figure then leaped into the air, arms outstretched. The soldiers reacted and fired wildly at him but the bullets missed their target with stark consistency. The enemy landed on the floor and, with the grace of a ballet dancer, performed a perfect pirouette. A blade in the shadowy figure's outstretched hand cut the SEALs' arms into ribbons. The men screamed in horror as blood sprayed in all directions. The enemy then aimed for the men's jugulars, slitting their throats with ease and precision. The lifeless bodies crumpled to the ground.

A radio lay on the ground sputtering. *"All Alpha! Come in! What's going on? Respond!"*

No one was left to answer the call.

The haze in front of Raiden cleared, and he saw the enemy cradling one of the limp SEALs in his arms, much like Rudolph Valentino would have held a swooned lover. Except that the man had his teeth in the soldier's neck, sucking blood. The guy was very tall, so the SEAL's legs dangled in the air, twitching involuntarily.

The man looked up and saw Raiden. Blood trickled down his chin from the edges of his mouth. The image was not unlike something from an old Hammer Horror film starring Christopher Lee. An inhumanly long, red tongue licked the blood from his mouth. And then the man bared his *fangs*.

The thing hissed at Raiden. White, opaque breath swirled from the creature's mouth. And then he smiled.

Raiden was unsettled and unsure. The surrealism of the situation momentarily deprived him of decisiveness.

"What are you?" Raiden whispered.

The unearthly enemy dropped the dead SEAL on the floor, straightened, and revealed a long knife in his right hand. The man's coat was open, revealing a bare chest with four long, bloody streaks across it. Older, similar but healed scars covered the man's torso. Slowly and steadily, the creature pointed the knife at himself and made another mark from left to right.

"Five today," the creature snarled. "Or rather, six?"

The monster completed that thought by leaping acrobatically, somersaulting in midair, and alighting on his feet directly behind Raiden. It happened so quickly that Raiden didn't know where the enemy had gone. He stood there, dazed, still shocked by the turn of events.

The vampire reached out to grab Raiden from the back.

"Get down!" a voice shouted from one of the catwalks.

Raiden reacted instinctively. He ducked, and gunfire erupted from above. Visibility was momentarily cut off due to the smoke. After a few seconds, Raiden lifted his head and scanned the room, but the vampire was nowhere to be seen. A SEAL with an M4 descended a ladder and faced Raiden. His sleeves were rolled up to his shoulders and his features were covered with a ski mask, save for piercing eyes. On his head was a large pair of radio headphones, the kind squad leaders might carry.

"Where is he?" the SEAL asked.

Raiden didn't move. The SEAL aimed his M4 at Raiden and approached slowly. But before he could reach the operative, the vampire dropped noiselessly from a perch above, knife flashing like a living thing over the SEAL's arm. Blood spurted from multiple wounds on the soldier's limb, and the M4 clattered to the floor. The SEAL fell to his knees and then attempted to crawl away, nursing the arm. The monster grabbed the soldier's neck with one hand, lifted him up as if he weighed nothing, and shoved him against a wall. The vampire studied the SEAL with detached curiosity.

Raiden stood and aimed his M9, but he couldn't get a clear shot at the creature because of the SEAL's close proximity.

The vampire leaned in to bite the soldier in the neck . . . but then he sniffed loudly.

"Hmmm," the enemy hissed. "Strange smell . . . "

Some kind of realization came to the monster, and he jerked away from the SEAL. The prey fell to the floor.

"You smell like . . . ! Are you . . . ? It has to be!"

The soldier rolled across the floor clutching his bruised throat. He managed to cry at Raiden, "Shoot him! What are you waiting for?"

Roused, Raiden squeezed the trigger. The vampire launched into another pirouette and uncannily deflected the bullets. For some reason Raiden couldn't hit him even after firing an entire clip. Raiden ejected and cast aside the spent magazine.

A radio attached to the vampire's waist crackled static. A woman's voice was heard.

"Vamp!"

The creature lifted the radio and answered. "Yeah, Queen?"

"Are you all done cleaning up?"

"Yes. But wait until I tell you what I found . . ." The vampire spoke with an Eastern European accent, of course. Most likely Romanian.

"Something interesting?"

"I'll tell you in person. Where are you?"

"In the central unit. With the President."

"Be right there."

Raiden quickly reloaded his weapon and aimed, but Vamp cried out strangely, spun around in his cape . . . and disappeared.

The only sounds left in the room were the heavy breathing of Raiden and the wounded SEAL . . . and the trickling of dead soldiers' blood as it pooled along the floor.

7

RAIDEN SWUNG the M9 over to the soldier.

"Hold on!" the man shouted. "I'm not an enemy. Calm down."

But Raiden kept the gun on him, unwavering.

"My name is . . ." The soldier imperceptibly checked himself, took a breath, and continued. "My name is Pliskin. Iroquois Pliskin. Lieutenant Junior Grade."

Raiden didn't answer. The SEAL pulled off his balaclava with one hand to reveal a man in his late forties or early fifties. Dark hair. Stubble on his face.

"Are you a Navy SEAL?" Raiden asked. Pliskin just grimaced at the operative as if the answer was obvious. "How did you get in?"

"Fast rope descent from a Navy chopper." The SEAL gazed at Raiden carefully, his reply indifferent and detached. At that moment a sea louse emerged from Pliskin's gear and crawled out onto the floor. Raiden remembered seeing the bugs in the Deep Sea Dock . . . and the intruder in the elevator.

"Have I seen you before?" he asked.

"That suit." Pliskin nodded at Raiden. "Are you . . . FOX-HOUND?"

Raiden reluctantly conceded the fact. "That's right."

"FOXHOUND was disbanded."

Raiden frowned. The man didn't know what he was talking about.

"Where were you before FOXHOUND? Delta Force?" the soldier asked.

"I was a part of the Army's Force Twenty-One trials."

"Force Twenty-One? That was about tactical IT deployment in war zones if I remember. Any field experience?"

Raiden hesitated. "No . . . not really."

"So this is your first."

"I've had extensive training. The kind that's indistinguishable from the real thing."

"Like what?"

"Sneaking Mission Sixty, Weapons Eighty, Advanced—"

"VR, huh?" Pliskin's disappointment was evident.

"But realistic in every way!" Raiden couldn't help being indignant.

"A virtual grunt of the digital age. That's just great."

"Simulated training prepares you more thoroughly than any situational exercise can! That's far more effective than live exercises."

"You don't get injured in VR, do you? Every year, a few soldiers die in field exercises."

Raiden's answer came out a little too defensively. "There's pain sensation in VR and even a sense of reality and urgency. The only difference is that it isn't actually happening."

"That's the way they want you to think to remove you from the fear that goes with battle situations. War as a video game—what better way to raise the ultimate soldier?" Pliskin shook his head.

Raiden was offended. "What, so you're saying that VR training is some kind of mind control?"

The Codec burst on. Raiden turned to accept the call.

"Raiden? What's going on?" the Colonel asked.

"The Alpha team from Navy SEAL Ten is dead—no, there's a single survivor."

Pliskin, noticing the young operative communicating quietly and looking at the object on his wrist, muttered, "The kid's wired with nanomachines . . . !"

"What about the President?" the Colonel asked.

"Looks like they took him somewhere else."

"I see. You said there was a survivor from SEAL Team Ten?"

"Yeah. Lieutenant J. G. Pliskin."

"Has he seen your face?"

Oops. "What?"

"This is a top-secret mission. No one can know that we're involved!"

"It's a little too late for that."

Raiden ended the call and turned back to Pliskin. In the meantime, the soldier had gathered his gear and walked over to the blue node in the southwest corner of the room. He had expertly bandaged his bloody arm by using his other hand and his teeth. One of the dead SEALs lay at his feet. A broken handcuff was attached to the man's right wrist, the loose end dangling on the floor. Raiden approached him and noticed the cuff.

"Take a look," Pliskin said. "A Navy captain."

"What the hell?" The officer had obviously been carrying something important—and it had been taken from him.

Pliskin suddenly put a hand to his forehead and groaned. He staggered toward the wall.

"You all right?" Raiden asked.

The SEAL dropped to a sitting position by the wall to catch his breath. "Give me a few minutes. Must have lost a few more pints than I thought."

"What was that man—just now?"

"That bloodsucking freak?" Pliskin smiled wryly. "That was Vamp. He's Romanian, a wizard with knives, as you saw."

"The way he moved. He didn't seem *human*."

"You won't see that in VR, I guarantee."

"What is he?"

"One of the members of Dead Cell."

"Dead Cell! Him?"

Pliskin nodded. "Ex-President George Sears' brainchild. Special forces to train the Special Forces. The name was originally intended to reflect its anti-terrorist functions. The unit would launch unannounced assaults on government complexes for the ultimate terrorism simulation. They were needed to show VR troopers like you how to deal with the real thing. But around the time their original leader died in prison, the unit began to unravel. They were always close to the edge, but they became more and more extreme. They began to go after U.S. allies, even civilians. We estimate that no fewer than a hundred people died as a result of 'accidents' the Dead Cell arranged on their own. They were out of control—and it all came to a head six months ago."

"What happened?"

"The unit was devastated. Their leader, Colonel Jackson, was arrested. There are only three left now—and you just saw one of them. He was Vamp. The others are a woman named Fortune and a big guy named Fatman. Colonel Jackson is Fortune's husband. Her father was Marine Commander Scott Dolph who was aboard the tanker that sank two years ago."

"Why would they go after the Big Shell?"

"How should I know? I told you they were on the lunatic fringe."

"What about the leader now? He's Solid Snake?"

Pliskin's eyes narrowed. He looked away and answered, "Snake died two years ago."

"You mean the incident that made this Big Shell necessary in the first place?"

"Right. And he was the one that sank the tanker."

"But he's a legend!"

Pliskin coughed, slightly laughing. "Legends are usually bad news. There's not a lot of difference between heroes and madmen."

Raiden was confused by the man's words. "You're saying Snake is still alive and pulled another one?"

"No, he's not involved in this one. His body was positively ID'd two years ago."

Raiden was actually sorry to hear it. He had always wanted to meet the Shadow Moses hero. "Snake is dead . . ."

"And buried."

Another thought occurred to Raiden. "What about the other terrorists? I usually don't see gear like that outside of Special Forces."

"They're former Presidential security detail just like Dead Cell."

"Pretty heavily armed for a bunch of bodyguards."

"They were officially Secret Service. But it would have been more accurate to say they were President Sears' personal army."

"They were disbanded, too?"

"When the current administration came into office."

"I saw Russian equipment, too."

"Former Soviet military. They're probably mercenaries. The Big Shell is too much ground for just Dead Cell members to hold down. Come on, you weren't briefed on any of this? And you came in alone to boot? Why?"

Raiden didn't have an answer to that. He was actually wondering the same thing.

"What are you really doing here?" Pliskin asked. "Can't tell me, huh? Fine with me." The SEAL searched through his gear and removed a pack of cigarettes. He handed them to Raiden.

"I don't smoke."

"Keep it anyway. May come in handy."

Raiden shrugged and took the pack and stuck them in his own backpack.

"Take this, too." He handed over a slightly used SOCOM pistol. Raiden was surprised. It was a terrific weapon complete with laser sighting and much better than the M9 he was carrying.

"You sure?"

"I don't need it. Looks like you do."

"Thanks." Raiden tucked it in his belt.

"The magazine's empty. Maybe you can find some more ammo around here."

"Maybe."

Raiden eyed the node. He glanced at Pliskin and thought, *What the hell? The guy knows I'm FOXHOUND already.* He went over to the node, stooped, and accessed it, palm forward. The map of Strut B appeared on the monitor.

Pliskin didn't say a word about it.

Then the radio on Pliskin's belt spit static. A voice said, *"Come in Alpha Zero! This is Bravo Zero, currently at the bridge between Struts B and C. The President is—"*

Gunfire. Shouts.

"Damn! I can't hit that thing! It's like some bad dream!"

"Alpha! Anyone! Come in, all Alpha! This is Bravo Zero!"

"Aren't you going to answer that?" Raiden asked.

Pliskin slowly reached for the radio, but it appeared to Raiden that the soldier was simply buying time.

More screams over the radio.

"The B–C connecting bridge," Pliskin said.

"We need to get there," Raiden acknowledged.

Pliskin shook his head weakly. "I need a few more minutes." He looked up at Raiden. "Remember my frequency. It's one-four-one point eight-oh. You're using nano communication, right?"

"Yeah. I can patch into your frequency."

"Better go on, then."

Raiden nodded and headed for the stairs.

"Hey," Pliskin stopped him. "What's your name?"

The operative paused and turned. "Raiden."

"Raiden? That's a strange code name."

"Makes up for the boring one my parents gave me."

"Maybe I'll find out someday." Pliskin half raised his hand in a "see you later" gesture.

Raiden turned his back on the SEAL and headed up the stairs for the roof.

8

RAIDEN WAS ABOUT to open the door from the stairwell to Strut B's roof when a Codec call came in.

"Jack, it's me."

"Everything okay, Rose?"

"Jack, do you remember what day it is tomorrow?"

That again? "I'm sorry, but I still don't have a clue."

"That's okay." Disappointment was plainly evident in her voice.

"What is it, Rose? Talk to me."

"I'd rather you figure it out. It's important."

"How important?"

"Important enough. And we'll talk about it. Tomorrow."

"Why not now?"

"Tomorrow seems more . . . appropriate. I need all the help I can get so that I won't chicken out anyway."

"Is that the reason you decided to be part of this mission?" he asked. When she didn't answer, he added, "Okay, I'm going to finish this thing by tomorrow, no matter what."

"You know I'll do everything I can to help you."

Raiden forced a change in tone. "Rose, there's something I need you to do. As an analyst."

"What is it?"

"It has to do with Solid Snake. The leader of this takeover incident is claiming that he's Snake himself."

"The legendary mercenary? Hmm."

"I need as much data on him as possible. Everything they have on him after the Shadow Moses incident."

"He's dead now, isn't he?"

"Yes. Should be a burial record somewhere, too. You should be able to request top-level security clearance from the Colonel. That should get us into the most classified material."

"I'm on it. I'll contact you as soon as I find out something."

She signed off. Raiden sighed and continued through the door to join the melee outside.

The cries of seagulls were the first things he heard. They flew around the Shell's Strut roofs, cawing mercilessly, as if they were attempting to warn the humans below that Death was on its way. The second thing he saw was the SEAL Bravo team standing on the connecting bridge between Struts B and C and its T-bridge accessing Central Core 1. Their M4 carbines were trained at Core 1's open stairwell door. A man wearing a suit lay unconscious in front of it. There was a square, black briefcase on the roof next to him.

"*Fire!*"

The SEALs shot at the darkness of the open door, but the bullets didn't appear to enter it. To get a better view, Raiden moved from cover to cover across Strut B's roof until he was nearer the edge of the B–C bridge. He could then make out a figure standing inside the Central Core's door—a sitting duck if ever there was one. But the bullets never struck the intended target.

Something very strange was going on. Raiden would have liked to use the SOCOM, but there was no ammunition. Instead, he drew the M9, checked the magazine, readied the pistol, and held it with both hands.

The SEALs continued to fire until the figure in the doorway stepped outside. Raiden gasped at yet another extraordinary turn of events.

It was a woman, tall and slender, with long, curly blonde hair. She had an almost regal demeanor and was dressed in a black leather coat as dark as her skin; the hem fluttered lazily in the sea breeze. Otherwise she was dressed in a black leather corset, something a bondage mistress might wear for an adventurous client. Her long legs were bare except for combat boots on her feet. An M9 rested on her hip, and she carried a massive, heavy weapon as if it were a feather. Raiden recognized it as a Lockheed RG-590 Experimental Aircraft Rail Cannon. Serious stuff.

The woman seemed to have no interest whatsoever in engaging the soldiers in combat. She also didn't appear to be afraid or concerned that she stood directly in their line of fire. She looked down at the unconscious man on the bridge and lightly nudged him with her boot.

My God, Raiden thought. *That's the President lying there!*

The SEALs opened up, firing on the woman once again but the bullets failed to hit her. It was as if she carried some kind of force field around her that deflected the rounds. In fact, Raiden discerned a lightly visible aura, much like pale fire, surrounding her body.

"What the hell *is* that?" he muttered aloud.

The woman called out to the soldiers, "Come on! Put me out of my misery!" There was a plaintive, melancholy timbre in her voice that indicated a very troubled soul. She spoke English with no accent. American.

More gunfire. The bullets curved around the aura, striking anything and everything but her. A flock of gulls clustered over the woman, reinforcing the illusion of peace and normalcy that the aura provided her. And yet, Raiden could feel a tangible sadness about her even from his distance across the bridge.

"This is impossible! Nothing will hit her!"

"Is she the one they call Fortune?"

Another figure slowly emerged from the stairwell. It was the inhuman fellow Raiden had encountered earlier, the one Pliskin called Vamp. The tall man stepped outside beside the woman, nodded to her, and then crouched down to pick up the President. He cradled the man like a rag doll and slung him over his shoulder. Vamp then picked up the Black Case in one hand and turned to the woman.

"Queen," he acknowledged.

Fortune nodded affirmatively, and Vamp took the President into the stairwell.

"Don't let them take the President!"

Two backup members of the Alpha team ran out of Strut B behind Raiden. His first instinct was to hide, but they had already seen him. They looked at him for a moment as if they were evaluating his threat, but then continued onto the B–C bridge. They joined the Bravo team in the middle.

"Ready grenades!"

One of the SEALs fired a grenade from the launcher built into his M4. It flew straight for the target but then stopped in midair, right in front of the woman. It dropped to the ground and failed to detonate.

"A dud!"

The SEALs moved closer. Fortune wearily raised her face as though she were surrendering to an inevitable inconvenience.

"Today is another bad day," she said.

She swung the Rail Cannon up to her hip, scattering the gulls into the air. "Is there anyone here that can give me happiness?"

The woman pulled the trigger and effortlessly mowed down the SEALs with whines of linear fire. The men screamed helplessly, jerking violently as Death struck them with decisive precision. The rifle continued to fire with a shattering sonic boom—pure overkill. The rounds cut through the metal with ease, honeycombing the bridge area where the soldiers made their final stand. The conduit creaked and tilted from the stress. A few coils of the support wires were sheared off in the middle and a section of the bridge broke away. The two new men who had brought up the rear slid uncontrollably down the destroyed, dangling platform to their deaths in the water below. One lone survivor clung desperately to the edge of the broken link, right at Fortune's feet. The SEAL struggled to retain his grip and climb to safety. He looked at the woman with a plea for help in his eyes. She ignored him and waited a few more seconds. The soldier eventually lost the battle with gravity and dropped to the water.

There was now no connecting bridge between the B–C conduit and Core 1. Raiden was cut off from the central unit.

Not a single body was left on the roof. The seabirds continued to fly around the woman and cawed again. One gull, hit by an M4 bullet, lay at Fortune's feet.

"I'm so sorry, my beauties. I'll see you again someday," she said.

She turned and walked away toward the stairwell in the Central Core. She hummed sorrowfully as her slender hips moved in a slow, dreamlike sway.

9

RAIDEN SWITCHED ON the Codec. "Colonel, the SEAL Bravo Team was wiped out!"

"I see." The Colonel didn't sound very concerned.

"What happened to the Navy's cargo choppers?"

"Both of them are at the bottom of the harbor. Looks like your new hosts have a Harrier II."

"A *Harrier*? What *is* this?"

"Calm down. It just means they anticipated the attack."

"What?"

"Besides, since the SEALs drew their fire, your infiltration went off without a hitch. On top of that, we know their defensive capabilities."

The young operative's exasperation and anger surfaced more than he would have liked. "Are you saying that this was all a feint?"

"Raiden, get a hold of yourself! The entire mission is in your hands now, do you understand?"

"But . . ."

"There's no time for questions. They could decide to retaliate for that failed assault."

"You mean the hostages?"

"They could be in danger, yes. But we have intelligence that the terrorists have wired C4 all over the Big Shell. We need to consider the possibility that they'll blow the whole plant. If that toxic spill does take place, it'll devastate not only the harbor, but also poison the coastline for generations."

Raiden groaned inwardly.

"We had to adjust the mission objectives, Raiden. The priority is now on removing those C4s. The President can wait, but this can't."

"Colonel, you know I'm no bomb expert."

"That's not a problem. The Bravo team brought an explosives pro in with them. He was supposed to stand by on Strut C according to their mission plan. You should find him there."

"Is this according to simulation, *too*?" Raiden asked sarcastically.

"What are you talking about? Get to Strut C and find him!"

"Understood. But I need to ask you something before I go."

"Make it quick."

"Who are they? Dead Cell, I mean. They couldn't hit her no matter how hard they tried. And that vampire, too. It's like . . . it's like being in a nightmare you can't wake up from!"

Rose interrupted the conversation. "Jack, snap out of it!"

"And *you*, Rose—I can't believe you're on this mission. I keep thinking I'll wake up!"

"Raiden, this is real," the Colonel said. "And that's why you won't wake up."

"But nothing *seems* real!"

Rose again. "I've made up my mind to stay with you. Whether this is real or a bad dream, I'll keep watching you until it's over."

Her voice did wonders in soothing his anxiety. "Thank you, Rose. And I won't let you be just a dream . . ."

"Are you two done?" the Colonel asked with not a little annoyance. "Raiden, you're needed on Strut C!"

The operative signed off, took a deep breath, and then gazed over the Big Shell's Struts. He was standing on B; he could barely see the farther roofs on the other side of Shell 2. The facility was overwhelmingly huge. How was he supposed to search the place for explosives? It was impossible. Nothing was going as planned. The VR training hadn't accounted for anything like what had happened to him today. Was he really ready for this mission? Why was everything so *unreal*?

Get a hold of yourself. That had been the Colonel's command. Raiden wanted to slap his own face.

Right. You have a job to do, soldier, he told himself.

He made his way quickly across the B–C connecting bridge, found the stairwell to Strut C, and descended.

From the various signs in the corridors, Raiden determined that the Strut served as living quarters for Big Shell personnel and contained the mess facilities. He stood still and listened for any signs of movement but couldn't hear anything. Raiden covertly moved down the hallway toward the Dining Hall and peered inside. No one there. The Kitchen was off to the left. He peered through a swinging door and saw an older man sitting and working at a long counter. There was an array of tools and equipment in front of him. The man was well built, African American, bald, and appeared to be in his late fifties. A leather jacket he wore was emblazoned with the legend NYPD BOMB SQUAD on the back.

Raiden entered the room, aimed the M9, and said, "Freeze!"

The man jumped and raised his hands. "Don't shoot!" A pair of pliers was in his right hand.

"You a cop?" Raiden asked.

"I'm not NYPD," the man answered. "I came in with the SEALs. The Bravo team."

Raiden's nerves were not in the best shape thanks to his encounters with Vamp and Fortune. He kept his finger on the trigger and the gun pointed at the man.

"Who are you with?" the man asked. "And what happened to SEAL Team Ten?"

"They're all dead."

"All of them?" The man winced. "That's bad . . ." He sank into thought and lowered his hands. He rose slowly from his stool.

"Did I tell you that you could move?"

The door to the Dining Hall crashed open. Raiden swung the pistol to it and saw Lieutenant Pliskin standing there. "It's all right," the SEAL said. "He's not one of the bad guys." Pliskin entered the room. An M4 was slung over his shoulder, and he looked less pale than before. "Don't go pointing that thing everywhere, kid."

The SEAL approached the older man. "What's your name?"

"My name is Peter. Peter Stillman."

Pliskin's eyes narrowed and then he nodded. "Lecturer at NAVSCOLEOD Indian Head. Also a consultant for the NYPD bomb squad. And a poor old man who got dragged along for this picnic."

The man called Stillman placed the pliers on the counter and grabbed a walking cane that had been resting against his workstation. He limped away from Pliskin, apparently not happy that the SEAL knew so much about him.

"I thought you'd retired," Pliskin said.

"I did," Stillman answered. "Can't keep up with everybody, as you can see. A famous church got wiped off the map, thanks to me," he said, sighing. "With too many lives inside. All I lost was this leg."

Raiden noted that the man's right leg must be prosthetic.

"So you're the bomb disposal guy," Raiden figured.

Pliskin gestured toward the man. "Kid, this is *the* bomb disposal guy. Open any explosives disposal textbook and you'll see his name."

Stillman shrugged. "It's just ancient history now."

"Why did they bring you out of retirement then?" Raiden asked.

"Because the terrorist group here includes one of my students." He turned back to the two soldiers. "The Emperor of Explosives—they call him Fatman. He built an atomic bomb when he was only ten. I created him in a sense."

"And that's why you're here," Pliskin said.

"Yeah. I'm pretty rusty, though. I was supposed to supervise the bomb disposal—looks like it was taken care of before I had my turn."

"I wouldn't say that." Pliskin eyed Raiden and said, "There are at least two people here who can claim to be experts at bomb disposal."

Raiden glared at him questioningly.

Stillman studied the two men. "Are you two with SEAL Team Ten? I didn't see you at the mission briefing."

"Oh, we're with another squad," Pliskin muttered. "My name is Pliskin, Lieutenant Junior Grade. Honored to meet you, sir." He held out his hand, but Stillman ignored it.

"Lieutenant J. G. Pliskin, do you have any experience with explosives disposal?"

"Don't worry about me." He jerked his head toward Raiden and added, "And he looks young, but he can do it. We need more manpower."

Raiden wanted to protest. "I'm . . ."

"What's your name?" Stillman asked him.

"Raiden."

"That's an odd name."

Raiden averted his eyes and asked, "Are there any other survivors?"

"There was another civilian—an engineer—with me."

"An engineer?"

"A skinny guy with glasses. He went in with us," Stillman said.

"Where is he?"

"I haven't seen him since that skirmish."

"Was he killed?"

"I don't think so."

Pliskin smiled to himself. "I see . . ."

"They told me he was the security systems architect for the Big Shell."

"Why would they bring a civilian along?" Raiden asked.

"Everything in this structure is computer controlled. He was supposed to get us past all the security measures."

"I never heard anything about that."

Stillman shrugged again. "He had official orders with him. He's in the Shell somewhere. But we'll leave that for later. Right now, we need to figure out how to deal with all the bombs."

"But there's no one left from the SEALs' EOD squad."

"Yep," Pliskin said. "So we have to do it ourselves."

Raiden was still uncertain. "But I've never defused a bomb before."

The Codec chirped, and Raiden turned to answer it. "Hold on a sec."

"Off to confer with the CO again?" Pliskin taunted lightly.

"Glad to hear Stillman is safe," the Colonel said. "Assist him in any way possible to clear the C4 from the structure."

"Colonel, you know I've never been trained in bomb disposal."

"It's all right. The man you're working with is the best in the field. All you have to do is follow his directions. You will, of course, keep your identity and mission objectives to yourself."

"Is it true that an engineer came in with Stillman?"

"I wasn't informed of that. It's probably something the SEALs decided on their own. There are more important issues at hand,

Raiden. The enemy may retaliate for the failed assault. Get those C4s neutralized now!"

Rose interrupted again. "Jack, you can do this. Trust me!"

The Colonel continued. "You haven't had bomb disposal training per se in VR, but you're more than capable of handling C4."

"This is a little different from *using* C4."

"You're up for this," Rose urged. "You know that."

Pliskin called to him. "How about it, kid? Are the results in yet?"

Raiden signed off and turned to the two men. He reluctantly nodded. Stillman went around the counter where his tools were displayed. "There's no need to think about this so much. You won't actually be dismantling the bomb. That's not for amateurs. What we'll try here instead is a temporary freezing measure. Here, look at this." He pushed forward a pack of C4. "This is a C4 bomb." Stillman flipped a switch and a diode glowed green. "It's live now. You can see it pulsing."

He then grabbed a canister from the counter. "Now you spray this on the sucker and . . ." He shook the canister a few times and then sprayed the contents on the C4. The mist covered the explosive with a fine, white substance. The green indicator faded. "There we go. Simple, huh? The spray freezes the detonator instantly."

"How long does the effect last?" Raiden asked.

"There's no way the thing can detonate in this condition. Even if you leave it alone, it'll stay out of commission for at least twenty-four hours."

"That's enough time," Pliskin noted.

"If we had the manpower, I'd recommend complete disposal. But this will have to do. The spray can be used from several yards away. Check the floor, ceiling, walls, under a table—everywhere. Try to imagine the locations the bomber would choose."

"That won't be easy," Pliskin said. "We don't know a thing about Fatman."

"Is there anything that'll help us locate the bombs?" Raiden asked.

"Here, take this with you." He handed each of them a device that resembled a television remote control. "It's what they call an Ion Mobility Spectrometer. It can recognize ionized gas emitted by C4s."

"The what?"

Pliskin explained, "In other words, that little gadget sniffs out C4's scent."

"That's right," Stillman said. "I've established a linkup with your radar network, so any scent detected will be represented visually. Have the sensor activated and keep your eye on the radar."

"What if he's using some other odorless substance?" Raiden asked.

"I know Fatman well. I know how into his own aesthetics he is."

"Signatures?" Pliskin asked.

"Yes. On every bomb he builds he always leaves a trace of the cologne he uses. The sensor also picks up that particular scent spectrum."

"Is that something he learned from you?" the SEAL asked.

"No, it was his own quirk. He wouldn't work by any rules except his own, and he followed them like a religion. And common sense wasn't one of his strong points. I thought I taught him everything I knew. I have no children of my own, and I thought I found a son in him. He had the right stuff, you know? There's something very unusual about an ability like that. Even at Indian Head he got special treatment. I remember some people called him one of the 'fat cats.' Maybe that's what started all this. I didn't teach him the most important thing I had to tell him. That there are some things you have to pass on. The trick is to know which one. All I taught him were . . . skills. And now I have to stop him from using them to destroy us all."

Pliskin examined the tools and said, "Let's see how well that sensor works."

"All right. Fatman would have allotted some C4s here in Strut C as well."

"Here?" Raiden asked, suddenly looking around the room.

Pliskin switched on his sensor and watched the tiny monitor. Immediately a ground plan of the Kitchen appeared, with glowing dots representing the live bodies of Raiden, Stillman, and himself. A green, mistlike grid veiled the entire area, including a washroom off to the south of the Kitchen.

"That green stuff is a visual representation of the C4 scent detected by the sensor."

"It's a pretty big area, isn't it?" Raiden asked.

"Don't complain. It's better than nothing," Pliskin retorted.

"Just activate the sensors and search the area, okay? Don't forget you need the radar to use this system. Log into the node at every Strut and turn the radar on."

"We have to keep out of the enemy's sight, too."

"Or the radar gets knocked offline if we're spotted?" Raiden asked.

"Exactly."

Stillman continued. "I know the structure of this facility. And, if he wants to take out the plant, where he would target."

"You know this for sure?"

"Of course. I taught him the techniques he uses. His ideas are based on my theories. Demolition is a kind of ideology; it makes no exceptions for time or place. Big Shell consists of twelve different Struts and two Central Cores, all connected. There should be packets of C4s on each of the vertices, or the Struts in this case. You need at least that to take a building of this integrity out."

"Six on Shell One, another six on Shell Two—a total of twelve bombs, at least?"

"Considering the Shell's architecture and composition from an engineering standpoint—that's my conclusion. And it's exactly what he would have decided as well."

Pliskin looked at Raiden. "Kid, this place is all yours. I'll take care of Shell Two."

"Wait, take this." Stillman grabbed two more items from the counter—two key cards. He handed one to Pliskin and the other to Raiden. "Security cards issued to Shell personnel. The Big Shell's security layout includes varying levels of clearance. The clearance level is identified by the number printed on the doors. Raiden, your card key can open doors with security clearance Level One. Pliskin, your card can get you into Level Three areas. You'll need it to get to Shell Two."

"How did you get these?" Raiden asked.

"That engineer I told you about gave them to me. He was supposed to program a set of all-access cards once we were on-site. Unfortunately, those cards won't get you into every area of this structure."

Pliskin shrugged. "We'll have to deal with the remaining security lockouts as they come up. Let's get going." He nodded at Stillman and added, "But you stay here."

"No, I'm going."

"The two of us can handle it. Don't worry."

"But—"

"You'll just slow us down with that leg of yours. There's a war going on here. I don't have time to babysit anyone."

Raiden could see that Stillman was hurt by the SEAL's words, so he spoke with a little more tact. "Why don't you let us handle the grunt work? You can tell us what to do over the radio like in the original mission plan."

Stillman finally nodded. "All right. I'll give you instructions from here. I may also need to prepare a backup plan just in case."

"In case of what?"

The bomb pro didn't answer. "Good luck to both of you. This is a dangerous one."

Pliskin said, "Who Dares, Wins."

Stillman registered the SEAL's words with suspicion. "Uhm, if anything comes up, let me know." He gave them his radio frequency for contact.

Pliskin nodded at Raiden. "Good luck, kid. I'll see you later." He patted the young man on the back and added, "*Semper fi.*" He then turned and left the Kitchen.

Stillman watched Pliskin go and then said, "That man's no SEAL. I don't even think he's a Navy man."

"What?"

"*Semper fi* . . . Marine Corps talk. Normally, team leaders stay in the Command Post and give orders with the kind of headphones he had on. And as far as I know, SEALs keep their officers away from the field. And 'Who Dares, Wins' is a motto of the British Special Air Service."

Raiden was confused. Again. "Is he one of the terrorists then?"

"No. Somehow, I don't think so." He turned to Raiden. "If there's someone to suspect, I'd put my money on *you*."

"I'm—?"

Stillman laughed. "Just take care of those bombs for now."

Raiden tried to laugh along with the joke, but failed. "What about you? They could be back in this area soon."

"I'll hide out in the pantry for a while." He limped over to it, opened the door, and stepped inside. "If I lock the door, it should be all right. Plenty of food in here, too, so you won't need to worry about me. I'll give you instructions by radio. Good luck . . . kid. Bomb disposal is a face-off with your own mortality. Don't let the fear get to you. When you give in to fear, the darkness comes."

Stillman closed the pantry door, leaving Raiden alone in the Kitchen with an extremely daunting task ahead of him.

10

THE FIRST TASK was to find the Strut's node, which was easily located at the far end of the Dining Hall, near the lift. Raiden downloaded the local map, and immediately his Spectrometer indicated the presence of C4 nearby on the same level. Raiden cursed silently and noted that the heaviest concentration of the green grid was just outside the Dining Hall, south of the Kitchen in a small room off the corridor. He followed the trail and found himself standing outside the Women's Washroom. Raiden didn't think it mattered if he knocked or not.

The washroom was empty. He looked under the sinks and then searched each stall around the toilets. Nothing. Raiden checked the Spectrometer again. The bomb was definitely in the washroom. What was he missing? He checked the stalls again and looked on the back side of the doors. Still nothing. Puzzled, he faced the sinks and mirrors. Then he saw it. In the mirror's reflection, the pack of C4 was clearly visible on the ceiling above one of the toilets in the stalls. He hadn't bothered to look up when he'd been in there before. As Stillman had suggested, he needed to begin to think differently about where the bomber might have hidden the explosives.

Raiden entered the stall, climbed on the toilet seat, shook the canister Stillman had given him, and sprayed the C4. As soon as it was covered with the fine, white mist, the glowing diode faded out. He got down and dialed Stillman on his Codec.

"Raiden here. I took care of the C4 in Strut C. The ceiling of the Women's Bathroom was set to blow."

Stillman grunted. "That's not like him."

"Anything wrong?"

"Maybe. Pliskin just called in, too. He's already deactivated a couple of them. He's reported other locations, too, and none of them are effective demolition points."

"What do you mean?"

"It means that they wouldn't be the best places to choose if you wanted to destroy this place."

"Are you saying they don't plan on blowing the Shell up?"

"It certainly seems that way. So far we haven't seen anything but a waste of good explosives. Unless, of course, we're missing something."

"A trap?"

"He couldn't have overlooked the fact that I would be called into this. There's something going on. Look, just keep going with what you're doing. Let's see what turns up."

"Roger that."

Raiden signed off and went for the door, but he froze when he heard the sound of boots clomping through the outside corridor. They came closer and were just outside the Washroom when they stopped. Raiden moved behind the door and flattened himself against the wall. The door started to open and Raiden realized his reflection could be seen in the mirrors! He ducked to a squatting position just as a guard looked inside. Raiden was hidden behind the door and couldn't be seen as long as the sentry didn't come all the way inside. Raiden held his breath. The guard took a cursory look at the empty Washroom and left. Raiden waited until the sound of his boots faded into the distance, and then he stood and peeked out the door. All clear.

He made his way to the roof, carefully avoided traversing through open areas, and crossed the B–C connecting bridge. Raiden figured the best way to cover the Big Shell was to move counterclockwise. Since he'd already accessed the nodes in Struts A and B, it seemed to be the logical route.

Raiden returned to Strut B's Transformer Room, where the horrid experience with the vampire had taken place. The SEALs' bodies were still there. The blood all over the floor and electrical banks was congealing. Raiden evaded the spots and checked the Spectrometer. Once again, the green grid pinpointed the location of C4—inside a cabinet housing circuitry panels. Raiden rushed down an aisle toward the destination, turned a corner, and came face-to-face with a Russian sentry.

The surprise on the guard's face was priceless. Despite Raiden's qualms about bomb disposal, he *had* gone through extensive VR training to handle a situation exactly like this one. Before the guard could react, Raiden instinctively performed a precise butterfly kick. He spun his body horizontally in a circle, jumped with one leg, and kicked with the other. The blow landed on the guard's chin. The cartwheel-like maneuver effectively knocked the man back a few feet, giving Raiden the extra second he needed to land on his feet, regain his balance, and deliver a body blow to the guard's midsection. Raiden caught the unconscious foe before he fell to the ground, dragged him off to the side, and left him there. Hopefully there wouldn't be any more of them.

This time Raiden effortlessly spotted the C4 behind the door of the circuit panel closet. He froze the device and called Stillman again.

"Okay, I've taken care of the Strut B explosive. It was in the Transformer Room."

Again, Stillman expressed doubts. "This is all wrong. This is something only an amateur would do."

"What do you mean?"

"All the bombs that have been found so far don't appear to be in the right kinds of locations. And the quantity of explosives isn't sufficient either."

"Even Fatman can make mistakes, right?"

"No. There's something else going on here! Just get a move on. I've got a bad feeling about this. You need to watch your back. I'll tell Pliskin. Just hurry."

A lone guard patrolled the bridge between Struts A and B. Raiden stood just outside the sentry's line of vision and waited until he turned to walk the other way. As he had done on the earlier trip, Raiden slipped over the rail, hung by his hands, and shimmied across the bridge to the other side. He climbed up, peered over the rail to make sure the guard wasn't looking, and quietly jumped onto the bridge. Within seconds he was in Strut A's stairwell.

The Pump Room was just as Raiden had left it. At first, the Spectrometer didn't indicate the presence of C4, so Raiden made his way to the lift. Perhaps the explosive had been placed on a lower level where Stillman had predicted. He crept from cover to cover, not wanting to repeat the recent experience with the guard in the Transformer Room. He was almost to the elevator when he came across the body of a SEAL who had been shot to death. His backpack had been flung open and the contents had spilled over the floor. Raiden paused long enough to see if there was anything useful. He found a couple of chaff grenades, three fragmentation grenades, two stun grenades, and a cartridge of darts. On closer examination, Raiden determined that the darts were tranquilizers. He pocketed all of the items; the tranquilizers would fit his M9 and might come in handy for subduing enemies silently. Finally, Raiden reached into the bottom of the pack and found two boxes of SOCOM ammunition. Perfect. It was his lucky day.

Raiden took the few moments to replace the SOCOM's magazine and store the rest of the ammo in his pack. He positioned the M9's holster on his back and stuck the SOCOM on his belt so that it would be his default weapon. Somehow, he felt a little more confident with the extra armaments.

Before entering the elevator, he checked the Spectrometer one more time. Now the green grid appeared at a corner of the monitor toward the south. Raiden followed the "scent" and soon found a door marked with a 1. Level 1 Security. The PAN card Stillman had given him came in handy.

The room had a low ceiling and was filled with pipes of all sizes. Raiden figured these were water, steam, A/C, and heating conduits for the Shell. Following the map on the Spectrometer, Raiden dropped to his knees, crawled under the conglomeration of pipes, and snaked along until he found the box of C4 stuck on the floor beneath a heavy steam pipe. He quickly used the coolant, confirmed that the explosive was deactivated, and then wormed his way out of the room.

Raiden returned to Strut A's roof and scanned the sky. He spotted several police and military choppers in the distance, keeping the vigil on the plant as before. The sun was not much higher than it had been when he was last on Strut A. It seemed as if a lifetime had passed since he had infiltrated the Big Shell, but in reality it wasn't midday yet.

Another Cypher was buzzing along the A–F connecting bridge. It bobbed gently as it hung in the air, waiting to spot an intruder and broadcast the information to whomever was watching. Raiden scrutinized the roofs and bridges within his range of vision to confirm that he was alone. He drew the SOCOM, aimed at the spy-bot, and fired. The Cypher exploded into a hundred pieces, leaving behind a small puff of black smoke. It was now safe to cross the bridge.

Raiden reported back to Stillman.

"You're doing well, Raiden," the older man said. "Three

down, three to go. But I still don't like what I'm hearing about the placement of those bombs. Pliskin's nearly done—and he hasn't found a single one in a place where I suspected it might be."

"I'm at Strut F now. Should I continue?"

"Of course! But I have to figure out what Fatman's up to. Let me know if you have any problems."

Strut F's stairwell led to a two-level warehouse that was full of boxes, crates, barrels, and unused machinery. Upon entering, Raiden immediately heard voices. At least three men were in the vast space, but he couldn't see them. He continued down the stairs to the lower level and slipped inside. He immediately pressed his back against a stack of crates to avoid being seen by one of the guards, who happened to be a mere ten feet away. Raiden waited until the man walked in the opposite direction before he moved around the crates and into a passageway lined by heavy machinery. The node was straight ahead. Raiden shot for it, stooped, and accessed the map. The Spectrometer indicated that there was indeed a bomb planted in the warehouse, somewhere in the middle of the room. Raiden skirted away from the node and hid behind another stack of boxes. He removed the tranquilizer darts from his pack, emptied the M9, and loaded the magazine with the darts. He didn't want to kill anyone if he didn't have to. Putting an enemy to sleep was good enough for him.

Raiden emerged from his hiding place with the M9 in hand and then crept along the aisle to the middle of the room. The Spectrometer pointed to a large grouping of boxes, arranged in a square and stacked almost as high as the ceiling. Obviously a forklift was needed to access the top. Raiden eyed a catwalk over the B2 level of the warehouse and got an idea.

The operative made his way back to the stairwell and climbed to the upper level. From there he could look out over the Warehouse. He spotted another guard patrolling near the fortress of boxes, so he took aim with the M9 and fired. The man went down quickly and silently. Raiden found the rung ladder leading to the catwalk, scaled it like a monkey, and positioned himself on the grid directly above the boxes. He swung down and hung onto the catwalk with his hands, feet dangling. It wasn't a long drop to the top of the boxes—maybe seven feet. He released his grip and landed lightly on top of the arrangement. Raiden quickly scanned the room to make sure no one had seen him, and then climbed down into the fortress of boxes. The C4 was on the floor. He quickly sprayed the explosive, scaled the boxes to the top again, and then simply ascended the outside of the configuration to the B1 floor.

The guard he had tranquilized lay there in the aisle, so Raiden picked him up underneath the arms and dragged him out of sight behind some barrels. But the man's radio spurted, *"Four five two, respond!"* Raiden froze. *"Sending reinforcements. Over."*

Great. Time to leave.

Raiden rushed to the stairwell but heard the sound of running boots. He ducked back into the Warehouse, looked frantically for a place to hide, and then scampered to an alcove with a closed door marked ARMORY—3. He tried it, but of course it was locked. It was a number 3—which meant he needed a Level 3 security card to get inside. Pliskin had one, but the soldier was in another part of the building. Raiden heard the footsteps rushing closer, so the operative skirted across the floor to an array of heavy machinery. A forklift with a large open crate atop its fork sat in the middle of the aisle. The crate was full of straw. Raiden climbed onto the vehicle and eased himself into the crate. As the guards poured into the Warehouse, he quickly covered himself with straw and waited.

The men called back and forth to each other. Raiden heard them running up and down the aisles, overturning boxes and smashing crates. At one point, a few pairs of boots ran beside the forklift. Raiden figured as long as they didn't find the tranquilized guard, he'd be okay.

It took nearly ten minutes, but the men finally gave up and

left the warehouse. Raiden waited another sixty seconds to be sure and then he emerged from the straw. The place was quiet. He climbed out, hit the floor running, and made his way to the stairwell.

Strut F's roof was empty. Raiden moved cautiously to the E–F connecting bridge, saw no guards or Cyphers, and began to cross.

The Codec burst on. "Be careful!"

It was a voice Raiden didn't recognize. The Codec's monitor was blank.

"Who is this?"

"There are Claymore mines on the bridge. Stealth-equipped Claymore mines. Invisible to the naked eye." The voice was modified by a device that disguised it electronically.

"Identify yourself!" Raiden demanded.

"Just call me . . . 'Deepthroat.' "

Raiden blinked. "Deepthroat? You mean from Shadow Moses?" He had studied the files from that incident and knew that Deepthroat was the code name used by a cyborg ninja— Gray Fox—who had helped Solid Snake accomplish his mission.

"Call me 'Mister X,' then."

"Mister X now, is it? Why would it matter if I called you Deepthroat?"

"Never mind about that."

"Why did you contact me?"

"Let's just say I'm one of your fans."

The Codec went dead. Raiden immediately buzzed the Colonel. "Someone calling himself Mister X just contacted me, Colonel. Do you know anything about it?"

"No," the officer answered. "Whoever it was, it wasn't a burst transmission. The transmission was sent from within the Big Shell."

"He called himself Deepthroat at first. Do you think—?"

"I caught that part, too, but the possibility of it being true is none. Gray Fox was the one who used that alias in Shadow Moses, and he's dead."

"Is it an enemy trap?"

"Could be. Exercise extreme caution."

Raiden signed off and scanned the E–F bridge. If there really were Claymores, he wouldn't be able to see them. He dug into his pack for the thermal goggles and put them on. His surroundings immediately appeared filtered through an infrared field. The idea was that electronic and living materials would be displayed brightly as solid images. He began to cross the bridge and instantly spotted a Claymore. He had been trained to disable landmines of that type; they used a directional sensor that exploded when an upright target entered its forward field of vision. What was particularly handy about his training was that he could disarm it with the flick of a switch and then pick up the mine, carry it, and use it elsewhere on the enemy. Raiden did so with three Claymores that he found on the bridge. He didn't have room in his pack to carry more, so he simply deactivated the remaining two and tossed them off the bridge into the water.

Rose called him on the Codec. "Jack, do you remember the day we met?"

What now? Raiden asked himself. *What's her game?* "I'm kinda busy right now, Rose."

"You're right. Sorry."

"But I do remember. It was right after I was transferred to New York. There were all these tourists around you. In front of the Federal Hall."

Rose giggled. "A group of middle-aged Japanese ladies came up and asked me which building it was that King Kong was climbing in the movie."

"You pointed out the World Trade Center."

"But the ladies weren't convinced."

"The tourists were talking about the black-and-white King Kong."

"I said it was the Chrysler Building."

"You hadn't seen the black-and-white original."

"I just vaguely remembered the pictures. And then you showed up and started mouthing off. You were like, 'No, it's the Empire State.'"

"I said the Chrysler Building was in *Godzilla*."

She laughed. "We started arguing and I forgot all about the tourists. I was insisting that I was right and you were doing the same. The next thing we knew, the Japanese women had gone away. And we ended up going to the Skyscraper Museum to see who had the better recall."

"We argued all the way to Battery Park."

"And for nothing!"

"—since the museum was closed! We went our separate ways from the museum. And then I found you again by coincidence in the FOXHOUND base corridor."

"An amazing coincidence that we were actually working at the same place!"

"That night we went up to the top of the Empire State."

"It was so beautiful. I could look down on the Chrysler Building from a hundred and twenty stories above ground."

"I felt . . . overwhelmed. I didn't care anymore who was right."

"And that was our first date."

"We watched *King Kong* in your apartment a bunch of times that night. Didn't sleep until morning . . ."

Rose sighed audibly.

"If it weren't for that coincidence, we wouldn't be together," Raiden noted.

"I know." Rose quickly changed her tone. "I'm sorry, Jack. I'm taking up your time again."

"What?"

"Take care."

She signed off. Raiden shook his head. Every guy he ever knew had said women were impossible to understand. He now counted himself as a member of the club.

The roof of Strut E was a heliport. Raiden emerged from the connecting bridge and heard voices not far away. He hugged the stairwell structure and inched his way to the corner to get a better view of the space. A woman dressed in tiger-stripe camo stood near the railing on the roof. She had a radio in her hand and was in the middle of a conversation with a man. The woman had short blonde hair, was fit and muscular, and spoke with a Russian accent. The man on the other end of the radio sounded American.

"I've taken care of that annoying fly," the man said. "What's the situation over there?"

"Puzzling," the woman answered. "I saw a man dressed like a ninja just now."

"Ninja?"

"It's the only way to describe it. A kind of cyborg ninja complete with a sword."

"What?"

"Are you hiding something from me?" she asked.

"Olga, are you sure it wasn't an Arsenal Tengu?"

"Don't be a fool. Think I wouldn't know the difference? I've never seen field gear like that, ever."

"All right. We'll intensify patrols. Anything else?"

"Actually, one more thing. You'll find it hard to believe, though. I saw a man hiding under a cardboard box."

"Where?"

"On the connecting bridge to Shell Two."

The man grunted.

"So you believe me this time?" she asked, almost taunting.

"I've seen someone use that box trick before. We'll lay a trap on the Shell Two connecting bridge."

"Over and out then."

The woman the man called Olga shut off her radio. Raiden drew the SOCOM and stepped out in plain view. "Freeze!"

Olga didn't flinch. She turned toward Raiden and gazed at

him as if he was a curious specimen in a zoo. They were about ten feet apart.

"You must be one of Dead Cell," Raiden said, the gun trained on her.

"Of course not," she answered. "What a thing to say."

"Put your weapon on the ground."

The woman smiled widely. "Not a chance."

With that, she leaped over the railing, Arabian style. It happened so quickly that Raiden was unable to react. He rushed to the spot and peered over the railing, but there was no trace of the woman in the water below.

Who was she? And where the hell did she go?

11

FOR THE FIRST TIME, Raiden felt more comfortable reaching Pliskin on the Codec instead of the Colonel. He punched the SEAL's frequency and spoke. "I saw a female soldier. Russian."

"Uh-huh. Must be Olga Gurlukovich," Pliskin answered. He seemed very sure of himself.

"How do you know?"

"Unlike you, I've been briefed."

"She's not a Dead Cell?"

"No. She commands a Russian private army."

"They must be the ones patrolling the Big Shell."

"That's right. She's led the group ever since her old man, Colonel Gurlukovich, died. Watch yourself with her. She's a tough one."

Raiden signed off and took another look over the rail. There was still no sign of the woman. Either she was a magician, or she was incredibly agile. Raiden figured she must have swung beneath the rail, under the roof, and entered Strut E by some other means.

He made his way to the stairwell and descended a flight to

what appeared to be a Maintenance Room for the heliport above. The node was next to the elevator, just as he expected. There was no one around, so he quickly accessed the map and checked the Spectrometer. The green grid pointed to the upper level—the C4 was somewhere on the heliport. Raiden crossed the room to the other stairwell and began to ascend but stopped when he found one of the Russian guards sprawled out on the steps. Raiden examined him and determined that the guy had been knocked unconscious. Who could have done it? It couldn't have been one of the SEALs—they were all dead! The Russian woman wouldn't have taken out one of her own men. Had Pliskin come this way? Was it the work of the mysterious Mister X?

Never mind. Stay on task.

Just to be prudent, Raiden dragged the man off the stairs and tucked him away in the Maintenance Room behind a generator. He then ran up the steps and peered out the stairwell door. A magnificent, fully-equipped Harrier II sat on the heliport, patrolled by one solitary Russian guard. Raiden checked the Spectrometer again—the bomb was somewhere on or inside the aircraft. How the hell the terrorists got hold of an AV-8B Harrier II was indeed a puzzle. As far as Raiden knew, only the United States, Britain, and a couple of allies owned and operated Harriers. It was an impressive gunship, one of the best in the world for light ground attacks.

Raiden crouched and moved quickly to a grouping of oil barrels. He waited until the guard was on the other side of the Harrier and then ran to the side of the aircraft. He ducked and slipped under the fuselage. Raiden remained low and watched the guard's legs. The man approached and then walked past. Raiden sprang out behind the guard and executed a choke hold that subdued the sentry swiftly and quietly. Raiden pulled the limp soldier beneath the Harrier and stuffed him next to one of the wheels. He checked the Spectrometer again and pinpointed the location of the C4 at the rear of the craft. Raiden crouched and found the explosive tucked in the landing gear. He shook the canister and sprayed the C4.

Raiden ran back to the stairwell and buzzed Stillman. "I've taken care of the C4 on Strut E. It was on the heliport, right beneath the Harrier."

"Good work," Stillman answered. "Only one more left to go."

Pliskin burst into the conversation. "Do you read me, Pete?"

"I'm here. What's up?"

"Raiden, you need to hear this, too."

"I'm listening," Raiden said.

"I checked out the bottom of Strut H for you, Pete."

"Wait," Raiden said, "What's this about?"

Stillman answered. "I asked Pliskin to look around. Knowing Fatman, I can't shake the feeling that all the bombs so far were just wrong."

"So did you find anything?"

"A hell of a lot of C4 packed into the bottom of the Strut," Pliskin replied. "Pete called it right."

"I knew he had the real thing up his sleeve!"

"So all the other ones were dummies?" Raiden asked.

"No, they're a threat all right," Stillman said, "even though the detonation wouldn't be enough to destroy the entire Shell. But the C4 Pliskin found would inflict *serious* structural damage."

"That's not the bad news, either," Pliskin continued. "These are sensor-proof."

"What?"

"New model, I guess. The ionization sensor can't detect them. The whole thing is sealed tight to prevent vapor leak, and there's no trace of that cologne signature. Pete, looks like he fooled you."

"But you managed to find the thing anyway?" Raiden asked.

"It was sheer luck. Any ideas, Pete?"

"Are there more out there?" Raiden asked.

"I'll go see for myself," Stillman announced.

"But you can't move fast enough."

"He's right," Pliskin said. "I can try to spray them from a distance."

"Hold on," Stillman barked. "There's something not right about this one, I can feel it!"

"Well, Pete?" Pliskin asked. "Should I come back and get you?"

"No, there's no need. Raiden, you have one left to go, correct?"

"Right. Except for those scentless ones."

"How about you, Pliskin?"

"I have two left, not counting this one," the SEAL answered.

"Okay. It'll have to be me. I have the Level Four card that'll get me into Shell Two in any case."

"You'll never make it," Raiden said. "With that bad leg of yours, they'll spot you for sure."

"That won't happen. I—I can walk just fine," Stillman admitted hesitantly. "I can even run."

"What do you mean?" Pliskin asked.

"That bomb five years ago. I messed up. Even with all my experience, I lost it. And a church was lost in the explosion. All those kids playing nearby, too . . . These past five years, I've lived a lie."

"Lied?" Raiden asked.

"Yes, lied. I didn't lose my leg in the explosion." Both Raiden and Pliskin waited for the bomb pro to explain. "So many dead . . . all because of my mistake. All I could think about was hiding from the crime, shielding myself from the public outcry. I wanted people to be sorry for me, for my weakness. I faked being a victim myself because I couldn't bear to face the families of the real victims. This is no prosthetic. I can keep my footing on catwalks and hike over deserts. I lived my lie so well I haven't even answered to myself for my sins . . . It was supposed to be a shield. And it's become a shroud instead. I've killed my soul playing the victim. Instead of protecting me, it's made my life even more hellish."

"What good can that do the victims?" Pliskin asked.

"I know," Stillman murmured. "I'm a coward."

"Hey, Pete . . ."

"God forgive me . . . I can walk with my own two feet. And I need them to stop Fatman. His crimes are also mine—one of omission and arrogance. No one should teach the skills I taught him without a clear conscience. This is the only way I can defuse my own sins."

"I get you, Pete," Pliskin said. "This one's all yours. You got it, Raiden?"

"I understand," the operative answered.

"Pete, I've taken care of the guards in Struts G and H of Shell Two. I wouldn't recommend you go into any of the other Struts."

"I owe you one."

"I'll get back to freezing the baby bombs then."

"You do that, too, Raiden."

"I'm on it."

"I'll have the radio with me," Stillman said. "If you need to get in touch, just don't ask for 'Peg-Legged Peter.' He's gone for good."

He signed off. Pliskin raised his eyebrows at Raiden and also cut transmission. Raiden took a breath and then set out for Strut D.

12

THE BRIDGE CONNECTING Struts E and D was vacant. Raiden
rushed across, quickly scanned Strut D's roof for enemy combatants, and then entered the stairwell. The floors below the
roof consisted of a two-level Sediment Pool, and the place certainly smelled like one. Raiden winced as he crept inside the
upper level, eyed the murky liquid in the pool, and hoped he
wouldn't have to get in it. Luckily, the Strut's node was adjacent
to the entrance, so it was no problem accessing the map and activating the Spectrometer. The green grid covered the space's
entire southwestern section. A catwalk encircled the pool, so
Raiden hopped onto it and made his way around—and then saw
the guard on the lower level. The man stood near a hatch in the
floor; in fact, the floor was covered in hatches. According to the
Spectrometer, the bomb was located under one of the hatches
near the guard.

Once again, Raiden retrieved the M9, checked to make sure
it was loaded with a tranquilizer dart, and aimed at the guard
from his high vantage point. He squeezed the trigger—and
missed! The dart made a noisy *ping!* that echoed throughout the

chamber. The guard flinched and immediately pulled his AKS-74u from his shoulder and let loose a stream of spray fire at the upper level catwalks. Raiden barely had time to jump out of the way and hug the wall. Bullets zipped wildly just in front of him, almost two feet away. The ceiling became riddled with holes.

The Russian soldier then got on his radio and alerted his mates. No time to lose. Raiden squatted and then lay forward on his belly. He inched back onto the catwalk, the M9 ready. Prone, he carefully moved to a position where he could see the portion of the lower level where the guard stood. The man hadn't seen Raiden, so he wasn't sure where the dart had come from. At the moment, the guard was concentrating on a section of the catwalk a few yards to Raiden's right. The operative quickly pushed forward, aimed, and fired. The guard simultaneously saw Raiden and swung his assault rifle over. The dart struck the sentry's neck just as the trigger was pulled. Raiden ducked back into cover as a short burst of gunfire clattered around him, but then it ceased. Raiden looked again. The man was down.

Once he was on the lower level, Raiden used the Spectrometer again to pinpoint exactly where the C4 was located. He opened the hatch, found the explosive, and sprayed it with the canister. When the glowing diode faded, he ran as fast as he could back to the upper level and stairwell. He paused just long enough to witness three more guards enter the Sediment Pool's lower level to investigate their fallen comrade's distress call. Raiden disappeared through the door, climbed the stairs, and hid beneath a ventilation duct on the roof.

He made a call to Stillman on the Codec. "I have the last C4 frozen. There's nothing showing up on the sensor now."

"Good work, Raiden."

Pliskin joined in. "You're way ahead of me, kid. I still have one to go."

"How's your bomb, Peter?" Raiden asked.

"It's a bomb all right. Sealed C4, and in huge quantities."

"You think there's another one in Shell One?"

"For sure. Somewhere at the bottom of Strut A."

"Why are you so certain?"

"If this bottom section of the Strut is demolished, Shell Two will be well on its way to destruction."

"You mean Shell Two will actually sink?" Pliskin asked.

"Not immediately. There'll still be five Struts left. But if Shell One loses a Strut at the same time, it'll be a very different story. The Big Shell's structural integrity depends on a very exact balance. If both Shells lose a Strut each, the whole structure will tear itself apart under its own weight."

"What do we do?" Raiden asked.

"I have a sensor that can locate even those scentless C4s. It makes combined use of a neutron scintillator and a hydrogen bomb detector."

"You brought that stuff with you?"

"Of course. I made the calibrations while I was in the pantry."

"Does it work?"

"I just tested it, and it definitely responds. But the best I can do is a sound beacon, not the radar."

"Sound?"

"The shorter the interval between beacons, the closer the target."

"I get you."

"There's another one in the pantry I was in. Sensor B. You can go back and get it."

"It's all yours, Raiden," Pliskin said.

"I'm going to study it some more and see if the freezing process will work. Don't touch the other one until I say so," Stillman said.

"Okay," Raiden acknowledged. "I'll stand by until you radio in."

At least he wasn't very far from Strut C, where the Kitchen

was located. He had to wait, though, because the responding guards from the Sediment Pool appeared on Strut D's roof to have a look around. Raiden remained where he was, silent and still. Thankfully, the guards didn't perform a very thorough search. One man muttered that "there was no one here" and they went back inside. Raiden waited another minute to be certain, and then he dashed across the bridge to Strut C.

The Kitchen was empty. He entered the pantry, examined the various items Stillman had left behind, and picked up what he thought might be the sensor. He punched a button and the sound beacon beeped once. It chirped again after a few seconds.

He called Stillman. "Peter, I have Sensor B."

"Good. Head to Strut A and go all the way to the bottom."

"How's your invisible bomb?"

"I'm looking at it, but I'm keeping my distance. How's Pliskin doing?"

The SEAL burst on the line. "A few more minutes. I just got to the last Strut, but there are a few enemy sentries I have to take care of."

"Does it look bad, Peter?" Raiden asked.

"Maybe. It's an odd one. The detonator hasn't been activated."

"What?"

"But the sensors are live . . . which means . . . hmm . . ."

Raiden set off for the roof. There was a clear path to Strut B. As he ran across the bridge, Pliskin made another transmission.

"I've located the last C4."

Stillman suddenly gasped. "No. Is that it?"

"I'm about to freeze it. Then—"

"Wait!" Stillman shouted. "Pliskin!"

Raiden heard the *hiss* of spray, followed by a new sound—a ticking countdown.

"Damn! That *was* it!"

"What's going on?" Pliskin shouted.

"The detonator just woke up! It's counting down!" Stillman cried.

"What happened?" Raiden asked. He reached Strut B and continued across the next bridge to Strut A.

"The big ones were rigged to be activated when all the baby C4s went offline!" Stillman explained breathlessly. "Raiden, the one on Shell One should be counting down, too! Hurry!"

"What's the remaining time?"

Stillman paused to make a quick calculation. "Four hundred seconds! Raiden, move! Get to the bottom of Strut A *now!*"

The operative cranked up the effort. He ran top speed across the roof to the stairwell. As soon as he opened the door he was confronted by a guard. The momentum with which Raiden was moving hit the sentry full force, knocking the man down the flight of stairs. Raiden didn't stop. He jumped over the unconscious man and made it to the Pump Room. The elevator was sitting there waiting for him. He jumped in and pressed the button to descend to the bottom.

The Codec burst on. "Raiden, Pliskin," Stillman said. "Listen carefully."

"What is it?" Raiden asked.

"I fell for it."

"Fell for what?" Pliskin asked.

"Fatman has my number. A proximity trigger. Microwave. With an eight-foot range. It's not a technique I taught him. Neither was that multi-bomb booby trap. Looks like he's far surpassed me as far as explosives technique goes. As for the rest—"

"Pete, get the hell out of there!" Pliskin shouted.

"There's less than thirty seconds left. It's too late."

"No!" Raiden cried.

"Pliskin, get away from Strut H as fast as you can."

"Pete—"

"Raiden, keep your distance! When you find the bomb in

Strut A, use the spray from as far away as possible! You can do it. I know that!"

Just as the elevator reached the bottom of Strut A, the Codec's transmission went to static. Raiden heard Stillman just beginning to shout in terror as the bomb exploded. In the distance, far away, there was a low rumble. Even there, at the bottom of the water in Strut A, Raiden felt a tremor.

He had no time to grieve for Peter Stillman. Raiden stepped out of the lift and turned on Sensor B. The intervals between beeps were much shorter than they had been in the Kitchen. Raiden moved across the upper storage area, which was still filled with crates and boxes, and into the corridor that led to the Deep Sea Dock. The hatch was open. Raiden went through and Sensor B went crazy. It beeped constantly, faster and faster as Raiden approached the infiltration pool. The small deep-sea submarine hadn't been moved since he was last in the room. Raiden walked around the perimeter of the pool and noticed that the beeping was at its fastest when he aimed the device at the sub. The bomb was somewhere on it. Raiden moved to the far side of the pool to keep his distance as instructed, slipped on his goggles, and slid feetfirst into the cold water. He ducked his head and examined the submarine—sure enough, there was an abundance of C4 packs attached to the underside of the vehicle. He swam forward until he was just about eight feet from the explosive, shook the canister, and sprayed. Even underwater the coolant managed to coat the C4 and deactivate the detonator.

Peter Stillman, you're a genius. May you rest in peace.

Raiden got out of the water and removed his goggles. He stood and tried to contact Pliskin on the Codec. Nothing but static. So he tried the Colonel.

"Raiden here. I've neutralized the bombs."

"Good work, Raiden," the Colonel said.

"Colonel, any damage report on the explosion?"

"Seems that the duct for diverting the contaminated seawater was destroyed. And the central section of Shell Two is flooding. And the explosion's ignited the oil slick on the surface."

"What about the toxins?"

"The chemicals stayed in containment. There's no immediate danger."

"Is the Big Shell stable?"

"Shell One was unaffected. The price was high, but the threat of the bombs is over for now."

"What's the next objective?"

"Rescue the President. Get back to the upper level."

"Roger that."

He walked through the corridor toward the elevator. "Raiden, the terrorists have retaliated for our bomb neutralization."

"What?"

"A hostage has been killed—shot in the head. They shot one of them on the roof just to make sure we caught it. One of our satellites captured it, clear as day."

"Damn!"

"They announced that they would kill one every hour from now on."

"What are my orders? What should I do?"

"Stay with your mission objective. Rescue the President!"

"What about the other hostages?"

"President Johnson is your first priority."

"Priority my butt! They're all in danger!"

Rose interrupted. "Jack, be reasonable. I know what you're feeling, but you can't save them all."

"No, not by myself."

The Colonel said pointedly, "Are you expecting Pliskin to come through? Looks like he's turned his radio off, too."

"I can't complete this mission by myself," Raiden said.

"That man was not included in the simulation. He is not a factor in this mission."

Simulation? Huh? "What do you mean by that, Colonel?"

"Your mission must remain a solo effort!"

"What about the SEALs? No second attempt?"

"They haven't even gotten to planning that. All we can do is wait. In the meantime, you're our only hope."

Raiden sighed. "I understand."

"Raiden, go and rescue the President. You can start off by getting to the upper level of Strut A."

He signed off and then noticed that the elevator had been called up while he was in the infiltration pool. Now it was on its way back down—and he hadn't called it. Someone was coming! Best to find a hiding place. Raiden scampered to a grouping of crates, flattened himself behind them, drew the SOCOM, and waited.

The lift stopped and the cage opened. The woman known as Fortune stepped out and into the room, her long, linear rifle in hand.

13

As BEFORE, she was wearing a black leather corset-like leotard. Her long legs and arms were still bare. The water lice that covered the floor were oddly attracted to her and swarmed close to the woman's feet—but they didn't touch her. They separated to form a clear path in front of her.

Fortune scanned the room and then focused her gaze in Raiden's direction.

"I can't tell you how happy I am that you are alive after all," she announced. "I knew this moment would come."

Raiden didn't make a sound.

"Show yourself and finish me—like you finished my father!"

Huh? Her father?

"Otherwise, you'll be the one to die."

To emphasize her point, she fired the rifle three times, blasting away the top several crates from Raiden's hiding place. One of the shots blew away a pipe at the top of the door to the infiltration pool area, bringing down a shower of rubble. That way out of the room was now blocked.

Raiden cursed to himself, prepared, and performed a forward

roll out from behind the boxes. He landed in a crouch, aimed the SOCOM at Fortune, and emptied several rounds. As before, the bullets veered away from the woman and struck the back wall, as if deflected by an invisible force field. Again Raiden was dumbfounded by his lack of ability to hit her.

Fortune frowned when she saw the young operative. "That's not . . . him?"

Raiden completed another forward roll and stopped behind the cover of another stack of crates.

"This could be interesting," Fortune muttered. She then called to him, "You've seen the fires of hell, haven't you?"

Raiden blinked. *Fires of hell. Could she mean Liberia? The civil war? How could she know about that?*

"Maybe *you* can give me death," she proclaimed.

Behind her, the elevator suddenly engaged and rose. Someone had called it.

"My name is Fortune. Lucky in war and nothing else. And without a death to call my own. Hurry, kill me, please!"

Once again, she swung the Rail Cannon in Raiden's direction and fired. The blasts destroyed the crates, forcing Raiden to retreat. He paused long enough to fire a few fruitless shots at the woman and then ran to the other side of the room. Fortune aimed the gun just ahead of him and blasted a group of barrels, igniting them. Raiden leaped for cover, managing to avoid the serious effects of the explosion. Nevertheless, the heat was intense, and he was sure that some of the white hair on his head had been singed.

He scrambled back and slipped between a rack of diving equipment and a supply cabinet. Raiden ran out the other end and jumped over a stack of empty SCUBA tanks. He continued to move farther away from the woman. If he could spend at least a minute hiding somewhere safe, perhaps he could figure out what the hell he was going to do!

The Codec chirped. It was the Colonel.

"Colonel, I'm a little busy right now."

"Raiden, Fatman just contacted us directly!"

Raiden stopped and caught his breath. "Fatman called *us*?"

"Yes. Looks like he placed a bomb on the heliport. He specifically asked for you, Raiden."

"What?"

"He's killed off Peter Stillman. Now he's after you."

"Why me?"

"How should I know?"

A blast from Fortune's rifle was too close for comfort.

"Look, this is really not a good time for this."

"The countdown's already begun, Raiden!"

Raiden wanted to scream in frustration. *What is this? Give me a damn break, already!*

But he got hold of himself, gritted his teeth, and said, "Great. How much time do I have left?"

"I'll show you the count."

A digital timer popped up on the Codec's monitor. "Five hundred seconds?" Raiden gasped.

"It looks like he has a different agenda from that of Dead Cell," the Colonel said.

"He's planning to take out the Big Shell. What about backup?"

"None. There's no time."

"What type of explosive is it?"

"He didn't say."

The elevator descended to the floor, and the cage opened. The being known as Vamp stepped out and joined Fortune.

"I'll take over, Queen," he said.

"What is it?" she asked him.

"It seems Fatman is out of control."

She nodded as if she'd known it all along. "He'll actually try to destroy this place."

"Yes. This could unravel everything we've planned."

"But why would he do such a thing?"

"Who knows? But he's nothing more than a stereotypical

mad bomber now. He's completely lost sight of our ideals. And with it, his loyalty to Commander Jackson."

"All right. I'll take care of the wayward soul." Fortune indicated the area where Raiden was concealed. "It wasn't him."

"Unfortunate."

"I expected more from this one, really."

"But he couldn't kill you, I see."

"Completely useless."

Vamp smiled. "Then he's all mine."

Raiden had heard it all, watching from a perch atop metal shelving. Fortune returned the linear rifle to her back, so he risked aiming the SOCOM at the pair.

"Now!" he shouted, mostly to himself.

The SOCOM recoiled another three times. The bullets bounced off Fortune's unseen protection and ricocheted in various directions. For a moment nothing happened. And then Vamp wavered. One of the rounds had struck him in the middle of the forehead. An incredibly lucky shot.

The vampire grunted as blood trickled from the hole. He then toppled into Fortune's arms. She caught him and laid him on the floor. His side was bleeding as well—one of the other stray bullets had caught him there.

Raiden jumped down and ran for another stack of crates. Fortune paid him no mind—she simply crouched beside Vamp and held the creature's head in her lap.

"Vamp? Are you gone?" she asked him.

His eyes were closed. He didn't move.

"No," she whispered. "No! That death was meant for me!"

Raiden reloaded and stepped into the aisle. The SOCOM pointed at her head, he slowly approached the woman.

"Why am I the only one who can't die?" she wailed to the ceiling. "Alone again! Cheated out of death again! How long will you force me to live?" She wept hysterically. "How much longer, Dad? You've punished me enough!"

Raiden was uncertain. Fortune's weapon was not in her hands. He couldn't shoot an unarmed, crying woman. Nevertheless, he kept the SOCOM's barrel trained on her head as he moved directly behind her.

"I thought you could give me peace," she said, still looking at Vamp but addressing Raiden. "But you couldn't kill me, either."

Raiden continued to move toward the open elevator. Fortune seemed to have no interest in stopping him. The operative reached the cage, entered it, and pushed the button for the top level. The door slid shut with a *clang*. Fortune stroked Vamp's head as the elevator rose.

Vamp's eyes opened. After a few seconds, he said, "There's no need for sorrow, Queen."

Fortune gasped. "Vamp?"

"I died once already. I can't die twice."

14

RAIDEN RUSHED CARELESSLY out of the lift when it reached the Strut A roof. He ran to the A–F connecting bridge without taking precautions against patrolling guards or floating Cyphers. Miraculously, he was alone. The readout on his Codec told him he had 205 seconds left to find Fatman's bomb. He hurried across the bridge and then traversed Strut F's roof. Raiden spotted a guard on the F–E connecting bridge; but as he ran closer, the operative saw that the guard was dead—he was still standing, leaning against the bridge railing like a scarecrow. As Raiden sped past him, whatever freak balancing trick nature had played on the man collapsed—the guard fell to the bridge with a *splat.*

The heliport on Strut E's roof was empty. In fact, the Harrier was gone. No one else was in sight.

Now what?

He grabbed the two sensors Stillman had given him and turned them on. The green grid displayed prominently over the map of the entire roof. Raiden blinked and wanted to sock himself. The bomb was sitting on the center of the helipad in plain view. He scampered to it, sprayed it with the freezing solution, and successfully disarmed the C4 with thirty seconds to go.

That was too easy. What the hell is going on?

"So you're the one!"

It seemed that the voice came from the air around him. Raiden looked around and saw nothing.

"You're right on time, I see. I like a punctual man."

Is he Dead Cell?

"I am Fatman," the voice replied, as if answering Raiden's unspoken question. "I am the greatest that humanity has to offer . . . and the lowest!"

Raiden detected the thrill of pride in the man's voice. But where was he?

A flash of movement behind him.

Raiden swirled around but only caught the image of a large man running—no, *gliding*—past and disappearing behind a structure that was part of the roof. Raiden ran to the edge of the structure, his SOCOM ready to fire.

And then he heard it. A faint *tick-tick-tick*. Like a clock.

"Hear this rhythm? It's the rhythm of time. And life!"

Another flash of movement. This time Raiden saw a little more. The guy was indeed overweight. The gliding effect was accomplished by wheels on his feet—he was wearing Rollerblades! Despite his size, Fatman was surprisingly agile and adept at using them.

"Don't you love the sound? I used to hang around department store clock counters."

The bomber's swift movements and ethereal, mocking voice disoriented Raiden. The operative whirled on his feet to get a clear shot of the skating figure, but the man was too quick. Raiden ran forward to the end of a large shipping container and still couldn't find the Dead Cell member.

"Life is short."

Raiden turned around again. Fatman stood behind him at

the other end of the container. He was dressed in a green blast suit, the high "shield collar" hiding his chin and mouth. Only his piercing eyes were uncovered. Fatman's head was bald and shiny, but the scalp was burned in a map of scar tissue. In his hand he held a cocktail glass filled with red wine. The hand that held the glass was as white and slender as a ballerina's, every nail painted with scarlet fingernail polish. An Uzi was slung over his shoulder, and he wore a stuffed backpack. Probably full of bombs.

Raiden held his fire but kept the handgun trained on the man.

"Bombs tell the time with every moment of their existence. And nothing else announces its own end with such fanfare." Fatman raised his glass. "Glad you could make it. The party's about to start." He sucked the wine through a straw that was bent over the restricting collar. "Yum. A good year! Let's drink to Stillman, shall we?"

Raiden wanted to shoot him but sensed that the man was hiding something. "If you destroy the Big Shell, you'll never collect your ransom."

Fatman wrinkled his brow. "Ransom? What are you talking about?"

"Thirty billion dollars in cash!"

There was a beat of silence and then the Dead Cell member burst out laughing. "So *that's* what's going on, huh?"

Now Raiden was really confused. "What the hell are *you* talking about?"

"Oh, you'll know soon enough. And I could care less what they plan to do. My ambitions are much more simple. To be the most famous bomber of them all."

"You're nuts. No one's going to give a damn about you."

"Oh, yes they will! I'll go down in history—as the man who beat Peter Stillman! That's the only reason I assisted them."

"Like hell you beat Stillman. He had your number!"

"What did you say?" There was anger in Fatman's voice.

"You have nothing of his courage or—"

Fatman cut off Raiden with sneering laughter.

"What are you laughing at!?"

"That crock died a dishonorable death six months ago."

Six months ago? "The decimation of Dead Cell?" Raiden asked.

"Call it what you want. Only the right stuff survived that hell. It set me free, you know. Opened the way to a new dimension . . . so that I could become the emperor among detonation devotees!"

"You're nothing but a common criminal! And that's the only way people will ever remember you."

Fatman flung his glass to the roof, shattering it into pieces. "How dare you! I'm an artist!" He then whisked away on the Rollerblades, moving swiftly behind the container. "This is why I dislike boorish military types!" He stuck his head out and announced, "It's time to start the party. This is how it works. I plant a bomb and it explodes soon after that. If you prefer to stay in one piece, you'll have to disable my bombs. Laugh and grow fat! Let's move!"

He bellowed huskily and then skated away from the container. Raiden fired the SOCOM at him, but Fatman's blast suit deflected the bullets. Raiden cursed and ran to the spot where the bomber had just been. Sure enough, he had left a pack of C4, ticking away. Raiden quickly grabbed the coolant, shook it, and sprayed it on the explosive.

By then, of course, Fatman had already planted another bomb. "Here's one for you!" he laughed. He skated away from a ventilation duct. Raiden tried to shoot him again—the exposed bald head was perhaps the only viable target on the man's body. But the bomber was simply too fast on the Rollerblades.

Raiden rushed to the ventilation duct and sprayed the coolant on the C4 there. He then twisted around in time to see Fatman place two bombs side by side at the edge of the roof. "Next up, the happy couple!"

But instead of skating away, Fatman pulled the Uzi off his shoulder, aimed it at Raiden, and fired. A wave of bullets sprayed across the area where the operative stood, forcing him to leap up and over the ventilation duct. He barely avoided the deadly barrage. Fatman laughed again and rolled away. Raiden bolted to his feet and raced across the roof to the edge. He sprayed the coolant on the two bombs just as the digital readout next to the diode displayed 0:03. Fatman was setting them to explode even earlier than before.

"How do you like it in three?" Fatman shouted. He waved at Raiden from across the roof, and then he skated across the heliport out of sight. Raiden took off toward the spot, worried how long he would be able to keep up this "game." He reached a trio of C4 bundles just as their readout indicated 0:04 seconds left. Thank goodness there was still coolant in the canister . . . but how much more was there?

Time to deploy offensive tactics. Raiden skirted across the helipad and stepped up and onto the ventilation grill he had utilized earlier. Using that as a stepping-stone, he climbed on top of the adjacent metal container. Now at a higher vantage point, Raiden could see the entire roof—as well as the skating Fatman—from above.

Raiden pointed the SOCOM at the shiny bald head . . . and squeezed the trigger.

The Dead Cell bomber jerked as a red puff burst off the side of his head. He screamed in agony and lost his balance. He fell to the roof hard, rolled, and landed on his back. Raiden jumped off the container and ran to him, the handgun ready for another shot.

It wasn't necessary. Fatman was mortally wounded. The side of his scalp was a mangled mush of blood, tissue, and bone. The blast suit collar was already soaked in redness.

The man's eyes opened and focused on Raiden. "My suit . . . I've nothing to wear . . . to the party . . ."

"The party's over for you," Raiden said.

"That's . . . what you think."

"What do you mean?"

Fatman extended one hand and pressed a button on a small device that he was clutching. An electronic *beep* sent a chill down Raiden's back.

"What did you just do?" he demanded.

There was glee in Fatman's dying eyes.

Raiden pried the device from the man's fingers. "What is this?"

Fatman weakly held his hand in front of his face. "I have beautiful hands . . . don't you think? The hands . . . of a true artist. These delicate hands can craft . . . works of art."

Raiden dropped to his knees and grabbed Fatman by the collar. He shook the bomber. "Answer me! What the hell is this?"

"It's the switch . . . for the biggest bomb . . . in this entire place! And it's no use . . . once it's activated . . . there's no stopping the count."

"Where did you plant it?" Raiden looked around but the roof was empty. "Where is it?"

"Somewhere in this area . . . don't worry . . . it's very close by."

Raiden put the SOCOM's barrel against Fatman's forehead. "Where is it?"

"Go ahead. Shoot me. I'm already dead . . ."

"Damn you!"

"Think you can . . . find it? When it goes off . . . it'll take the Big Shell with it." He smiled broadly. "This is the highlight . . . of the party. Bring it on . . . I say. They'll be happy, too. I die here. And start . . . my legend. Too bad you won't be around . . . to see the movies . . . laugh and . . . grow fat!"

With that, the bomber exhaled heavily, shut his eyes, and went limp. His head flopped to the side.

Raiden lost it. He grabbed the corpse by the suit collar and shook it violently. *"Where is the bomb? Where is it? Don't you die yet! Don't you—"*

He stopped. Just under the man's shoulder was a faint red light. Raiden pulled the heavy man up and then pushed him over onto his side. The backpack—and everything in it—was set to explode. Raiden gasped and grabbed the coolant. He shook it and sprayed the explosives. He covered the entire thing with the fine, white foam until the canister was nearly empty.

The glowing diode faded away.

Raiden breathed a sigh of relief and stood.

The Codec buzzed.

"Good work, Raiden," the Colonel said. "Looks like all the bombs are neutralized. One of their main leverages is now gone. That leaves—"

"Colonel, Fatman didn't seem to know about the ransom demands."

"Intentionally kept in the dark, I'd say. He seemed to be coming from a very different place from the other terrorists."

Raiden wasn't satisfied with that answer. But what could he say?

"Raiden, a lot of hostages—our President included—are still in danger. Keep your mind focused on protecting them."

"What are my orders, then?" Even he could hear the sarcasm in his own voice. Not good.

"Rescue the President!"

"We have no idea where he is."

"You haven't been in the Central Core yet. I suggest you start there."

The Colonel signed off as another call came in. "How are you doing, kid?"

"Pliskin! Is everything all right?"

"Could be better. Looks like I was out cold for a while."

"How did you manage to stay alive?"

"Had a little help from a friend."

"A friend?"

Pliskin didn't explain. "What about the bomb?"

"Defused. And Fatman, too."

"That's good news."

"How's Shell Two?"

"It's a mess. The bomb crippled Strut H."

"What about the toxins?"

"The what?"

"If the Big Shell blows up, the explosion is expected to produce massive amounts of toxins."

"Never heard anything about that," Pliskin said.

"Huh?"

"Well, looks like there's not much danger of that in any case. But the Central Core is starting to flood. It won't last much longer."

"What about the President and the other hostages?"

"They weren't in Shell Two. They're in Shell One."

"We need to get the hostages out of here now."

"It's too far from Manhattan for a swim."

"What about lifeboats?"

"There doesn't seem to be any. Doesn't make sense."

"So a chopper is our only extraction?"

"Right. And it comes with a passenger limit. Intel has it that there are about thirty hostages."

"It'd take more than a single trip."

"We'll have to come back, then."

"Can you pilot a chopper?" Raiden asked.

"No, but I brought a gearhead with me. He's a good guy. I'll introduce you later."

"Pliskin, I'm on the heliport right now, but I don't see their Harrier. It's out somewhere."

"We'd better move now. Our chances with a Harrier after us are close to nothing."

"Do you know where the President is?"

"No. That one's all yours."

"The President is at the top of our rescue list. These are our orders, Lieutenant J.G.!"

"Your orders. Not mine."

"What?"

"See you later, kid."

The SEAL signed off. If he *was* a SEAL. Now Raiden had doubts about the guy, too. The man was clearly on his side—more or less—but he was an enigma. He didn't seem to belong to any particular outfit. Was he a loner? What was he doing on the Big Shell in the first place? And who were these "friends" he mentioned?

Raiden wiped the sweat from his forehead, shook his long mane of white hair, and proceeded to head for the E–F connecting bridge and the T-section pathway to Core One. But the silent and sudden appearance of a bizarre and menacing figure blocked his way.

"Wha—?"

The figure was dressed in ninja clothing—except the suit appeared to be made of metal and was robotic. It held a long samurai sword pointed directly at Raiden.

"You passed with flying colors," it said. The strange electronic voice was the same as that of the mysterious Mister X.

No doubt about it. Mister X was a cyborg ninja.

15

"IDENTIFY YOURSELF!" Raiden shouted as he aimed the SOCOM at the figure.

Mister X's helmet had no facial features. It was a plain white face mask, similar to what one might wear to a fencing match. As the being spoke, the front plate illuminated.

"I'm like you. I have no name."

As Raiden gazed upon the figure, he discerned that the thing wasn't really a robot. A real person stood before him. The ninja moved far too gracefully to be wearing anything truly metallic; instead, the exoskeletal suit was made of a sleek material that *resembled* metal. Raiden assumed it was bulletproof.

"You're Mister X," he said.

"If you like." The ninja let down its guard and returned the sword to the sheath. "Come. Let's get out of the open."

Raiden hesitantly relaxed and then put away the handgun. He followed the ninja into the stairwell, down one floor, and out onto an open balcony level just below the heliport. It was relatively protected from surveillance. The ninja rested its hands on the railing and looked at the water.

"Are you with FOXHOUND, too?" Raiden asked.

"Neither enemy nor friend." The ninja turned to him. "Just a messenger from the *La-le-lu-le-lo*."

The what? *What did he say?*

The ninja tapped its neck. Raiden's Codec burst on and transmitted Mister X's voice. "This is safer, I think."

"Safe from what?"

"Eavesdropping, of course."

The thing has nanomachines, Raiden thought. "All right. Why did you contact me?"

"I've been ordered to give you backup, including the relaying of necessary intel."

"Ordered by whom?" The ninja didn't answer. "Why won't you identify yourself?"

"There is no need for you to know."

"I'll decide whether I need to know."

"You are not yet trusted to make such decisions. But I'll tell you something you do need to know instead. The current location of the President."

"What?"

"Or rather, the person who knows the current location of the President."

"Who is it?"

"A Secret Service agent named Ames, currently being held with the other hostages."

"Secret Service, huh?"

"The head of the President's security detail. Ames has been fitted with the same type of VIP nanomachine system as the President. If you're within range, you should be able to communicate."

Raiden narrowed his eyes. "Why are you telling me this?"

"Do I need to repeat myself?"

"There's no reason to believe any of this! You understand that?"

"Of course. But you also have no choice but to believe. Do you have any other leads?"

The ninja was right.

"Where are those hostages?"

"They are being held in the B1 Conference Hall in the Shell One Core. You'll find Ames there."

"What does he look like?"

"We don't know if Ames is indeed a 'he.' I've never met this person, either."

"How am I supposed to look for someone without even a description?"

"Use your ears."

"What's that supposed to mean?"

The ninja shifted its weight and looked out toward Manhattan again. "Ames has a pacemaker. You'll be able to hear the machine sound in the heartbeat."

Raiden wanted to laugh. "You expect me to walk up to these hostages and listen to every one of their heartbeats?"

"The sound is too minute to detect unamplified. You'd be captured immediately."

"So what am I supposed to do?"

"Use a directional microphone. There's one somewhere in the Core. Try the Computer Room."

The ninja turned back to Raiden, reached into a utility belt, and handed over a card. "Take this." It was a PAN security card, similar to the one Stillman had given him. "This will unlock all Level Two security doors, including the one into the Core. It works together with your body's own electronic field. But watch yourself. The Core is more heavily guarded than any other section in the Big Shell. You'll get nowhere dressed like that. Try this instead."

The ninja reached into a backpack and removed a bundle of clothing and a helmet. It was the same camo gear worn by the Russian militia.

"One of the terrorists?" Raiden asked.

"The surveillance camera won't let you get in the elevator without the right uniform."

"You want me to disguise myself?"

"Men assigned to the Core and those on perimeter duty are given different colors to wear. Your new outfit will work in some areas, not others. And the uniform alone won't fool them, either."

"You're talking about weapons."

"Right. You need an AK."

"But I saw them carrying an AN-94."

"All men assigned to the Core section carry AKs."

"So without an AKS-74u, someone will see through me really quick . . ."

"You can take care of the weapon issue yourself. One other thing—"

"There's more?"

"You'll also have to pass a retinal scan to get into the Conference Hall."

Raiden grunted. "Biometrics. Crap."

"Nothing but the real thing will suffice. Deception is not an option here. I suggest you hurry. They have the nuke on their side."

Raiden blinked. "The nuke? They have a nuclear weapon *with* them?"

"You didn't find their continuing presence here unusual? Even with the President as hostage, this is an island—and they have no visible means of escape."

"Even if they do have a nuke, the warhead is no good without an access code. The security lockout can't be bypassed."

"They don't need to. They have the code. You saw it, too, I believe. The Navy man with the handcuff. The other half of it is on the football—or the Black Case, if you like. The nuclear button. And now they have it."

Raiden recalled the case Vamp had retrieved from the President during the battle with the SEALs. He should have known . . .

"Why did they have to bring the football along?" Raiden asked. "To a decontamination plant of all places!"

"But they did have to. Because, after all, the Big Shell is the farthest thing from a cleanup plant there is."

"What?"

"Dead Cell didn't have to bring a nuke along with them. It was right here to begin with. Nothing in this affair is what it seems."

"A cover-up? But why? For what?"

"For Metal Gear. It is housed here."

Raiden felt a rush of adrenaline. "Metal Gear?"

"The very same. Bipedal nuke-capable vehicle of Shadow Moses infamy. This place is the R and D center for its newest incarnation."

"What the hell is going on?"

The ninja chuckled at the operative's exasperation and said, "Better ask Ames the rest." It dug into the backpack once again and handed Raiden a cellphone.

"What's this for?"

"You might be glad you have it. Keep the vibration function on."

Raiden examined the device. It appeared to be an ordinary mobile phone. He saw that it was already set for vibration. "What do I need a cellphone for?" he asked, looking back up at the—

—but the ninja was already gone.

This mission just gets weirder by the minute, he thought. He punched a frequency on the Codec.

"Colonel, who was that man just now?"

"He's not one of ours. We have no one like that in our unit."

"He said the Big Shell was housing a new model of Metal Gear!"

"First I've heard of it."

"Colonel, what are you not telling me?"

The CO did little to hide his annoyance. "I've been completely open with you, Raiden! I've told you everything."

"Is that everything you know—or everything I *need* to know?"

"Snap out of it, Raiden! I'll have the Metal Gear rumor looked into. You need to make contact with this Ames."

"So you believe that ninja?"

"Since we have no leads on the President's current location, we have no other alternatives. Right now, collect as much data as you can, including anything on Metal Gear."

"Are those my orders?"

"Yes, they are. Disguise yourself as an enemy soldier and infiltrate the Shell One Core."

"Understood."

Raiden signed off and sighed. He would have liked to stay there and gaze upon the Hudson. Despite what was happening on the Big Shell, the waters were calm and peaceful. The seagulls still hovered over the structure, cawing plaintively.

He couldn't help but think the birds were telling him, *Get out! Get out!*

16

TIME TO MOVE. Raiden decided against donning the enemy uniform until he was actually inside the Core. Besides, he needed to get hold of an AKS-74u to complete the disguise. Hopefully he would come across an incapacitated guard; worst-case scenario — he'd have to incapacitate a guard himself.

Raiden sprinted to the E–F connecting bridge, which was also the east entrance to the Shell 1 Core. A guard was on lookout duty just outside the door. Raiden crouched at the connecting T on the bridge and kept out of sight. He drew the M9 and checked to see that it was loaded with a tranquilizer. The guard eventually leaned lazily against the rail to gaze at the water and light a cigarette. Raiden lifted the weapon and aimed. The range was farther than optimal, but he had to give it a try. The operative held his gun hand with his left, kept it steady, and squeezed the trigger. The guard jerked, looked around in surprise, and then crumpled to the floor. Raiden holstered the gun, stood, and prepared to run to the Core — but a Cypher appeared from under the bridge. The spy-bot was an armed "Gun Cypher" — it would fire at anything it perceived to be an enemy. Raiden instinctively drew the

SOCOM and aimed at the Cypher's camera before the thing saw him. He fired once and blew the lens to bits. The Cypher went haywire, attempting to compute what had just happened to it. The machine wavered unsteadily over the bridge and spun around as if it were trying to locate its eyesight. Raiden rushed forward to get a better angle. He fired at the Cypher's dead center. The machine burst into flames, lost its ability to fly, and plummeted to the water below as if it were a meteor.

Raiden entered the Shell Core and found himself in a room marked 1F. Before he could venture deeper into the structure, the Codec buzzed. It was Rose.

"Got a minute, Jack?"

"Yeah?"

"I found some information on where Solid Snake is interred."

"Great. Shoot."

"I've located the grave site."

"And the body?"

"Exhumed for DNA testing."

"Well? Do you have the results?"

"The right arm was missing, but there was no doubt that it was him. That body belongs to Solid Snake."

Raiden sighed. "Hmm. So the head of the terrorist group must be—"

"An imposter."

"Right."

"You sound disappointed."

"I guess . . . I guess I was kind of hoping to meet the legend in the flesh."

"I get you. But it looks like he's not behind this incident."

The Colonel interrupted. "Raiden, the President needs you, I think!" Raiden winced. "Disguise yourself as enemy personnel and infiltrate the Core section. Your priority is to contact Agent Ames!"

Raiden signed off without acknowledging. There was something about the Colonel that wasn't right, and frankly, the guy was getting on his nerves. Raiden moved into the shadows and studied his surroundings. At the end of a corridor was an elevator, in front of which patrolled a guard. A security camera was mounted on the ceiling at the head of the corridor. Without the AK, he wouldn't be able to pass beneath the camera. He'd have to take it out. First, though, he quietly and quickly changed into the BDU. A balaclava fitted over his head and face, revealing only his eyes and nose. Raiden then readied the SOCOM, aimed at the camera, and fired one round. After making sure the camera was disabled, he stepped in front of the corridor and waved at the guard at the other end; the man, alerted by the gunshot, was already coming toward him with his AK pointed forward. Raiden beckoned him, as if he needed help with something. He turned the SOCOM around in his hand so that he was holding it by the barrel.

The sentry approached Raiden. "What was that?"

"Look at this," Raiden said, doing his best to speak Russian with the proper accent. He pointed toward the shadows where he had changed clothes. The guard moved past Raiden and walked toward the corner. Raiden raised the pistol and slammed the butt into the back of the guard's neck. The man fell and rolled forward. Raiden quickly dragged him into the dark corner and relieved the unfortunate sentry of his assault weapon.

Carrying the AK and dressed like any other enemy soldier, Raiden rushed down the corridor to the elevator and called it. When it arrived, he stepped inside and punched the button for B2. The next order of business was to find the node for the Core so that he'd have Codec access to maps of all the levels.

The elevator doors opened and Raiden was immediately confronted by two enemy sentries. They barely glanced at him. They pushed past him into the lift as Raiden stepped out. He didn't look back at them. The doors closed and he breathed easily—the disguise apparently worked.

The main point of interest on the B2 level was the Computer Room, which was manned by two guards sitting at workstations and intensely watching monitors. A large green parrot occupied a cage hanging from the ceiling. The Core's node was right there in the space with them. Raiden stepped into the room. One of the men casually turned toward him, didn't say a word, and went back to his monitor. The parrot squawked. Raiden pretended to be one of the guys by standing behind them and taking a look at the monitors. The images were views from various security cameras in the Core. One was obviously in the Conference Hall on B1. Several blindfolded and gagged people were sitting on the floor with their hands tied behind their backs. Men and women. Hostages.

The parrot squawked again.

Raiden grunted and moved away from the monitors. He casually stepped to the node, squatted, and placed his hand on the panel. The two guards didn't notice.

The operative stood and studied the newly drawn map of the level on his Codec. A storage space was connected to the Computer Room. Raiden looked up and saw the door.

"They keep extra camera lenses in there?" he asked one of the men.

The guard barely acknowledged Raiden. "I guess so."

Raiden opened the door and stepped inside. It was a typical supply closet, full of electrical equipment and spare parts for computers and surveillance cameras. He scanned the boxes and finally found what he was looking for. The directional microphone was clearly labeled and appeared to be brand-new. It was long, like a rifle barrel, and not very conspicuous. Nevertheless, he took it out of the box and stuck it in his backpack. He then grabbed a box of camera lenses, walked out, and shut the door.

"Find what you were looking for?" the guard asked.

"Yeah. Thanks."

The parrot squawked, "I miss you . . . !"

Raiden ignored the bird, left the Computer Room, and headed for the elevator. On the way, he dropped the box of camera lenses in a garbage can.

The lift doors opened on the B1 level, and Raiden stepped into a foyer. A door marked Conference Hall was straight ahead, but the retinal scanner the ninja had warned him about was plainly in view. How the hell was he going to get past it?

A guard appeared from a hallway, approached the retinal scanner, lowered his face against it, and peered into the lens. The lock on the door clicked loudly and a computerized voice intoned, "Retinal pattern recognized. You are cleared to enter." The man straightened, opened the door, and went inside. Just from the brief glimpse of the interior, Raiden saw one of the hostages on the floor.

The operative moved down the hall and found himself in a break room. Two guards sat at a table eating rations. There were several food and drink vending machines, as well as a refrigerator and sink. Raiden acted as if everything was normal. He went to the sink, washed his hands, and dried them with a paper towel. He then stood in front of one of the vending machines and studied the contents.

"Don't you have your rations?" one of the men asked.

"Huh? Oh. Yeah," Raiden said. "I just thought that candy bar looked pretty good."

"You're not carrying change, are you?"

"No. Of course not."

"Then how you going to buy one?"

"I was just looking."

The guard finished his meal and threw away the trash. "I have to get back inside."

Raiden said, "I'll come with you."

He followed the guard into the hallway and toward the retinal scanner. Just as the guy was about to lean forward to look into the machine, Raiden grabbed him in a choke hold. He had to be careful and not kill the man—the scanner wouldn't work on a dead eyeball. The guard struggled fiercely, but Raiden held him firm. He then shoved the man's face forward and used his left hand to open the guard's eyelids wide.

The lock clicked. "Retinal pattern recognized. You are cleared to enter."

Now it was okay to snap the man's neck.

Raiden dragged the limp body into an alcove near the elevator and moved a potted plant in front of him. He then rushed to the door and opened it before the lock re-engaged.

The Conference Hall was huge. At least three sentries patrolled the room. The hostages—all thirty or so of them—were scattered about sitting on the floor. They were blindfolded and had tape over their mouths.

Which one was Ames?

Raiden slipped the directional microphone out of his backpack and held it along the side of his AK. As subtly as he could, he placed the earphones in his ears, and then began to "patrol" the space. As he came near a hostage, Raiden pointed the gun at him or her. The microphone was amazing. He really could hear the person's heartbeat. It took a few minutes for Raiden to get the hang of pointing the mike in the exact direction in order to capture the sound. He also had to avoid being too obvious about it. The other guards would surely raise the alarm if they suspected he was up to something out of the ordinary. But so far the plan was working. The ninja was right. If Ames was in the room, Raiden was going to find him.

But he broke into a sweat by the time he'd moved past the twentieth hostage. What if Ames *wasn't* in the room? What then? Was the ninja's information about the pacemaker correct? Every heartbeat sounded pretty much the same. The women's were a little faster. Nothing unusual so far.

And then he heard a tiny electronic beep accompanying a heartbeat. He was a middle-aged man dressed in a brown suit with his tie loosened. Raiden moved closer and listened carefully to the sound until he was absolutely certain he'd found the right guy. Raiden watched the other three guards and then squatted beside the hostage.

. . .

THE MAN DRESSED in a duster and carrying a six-shooter at his side sat in the Conference Hall Control Room. He could see the entire floor through a large etched glass window.

Revolver Ocelot noticed the new guard squat by the hostage named Ames. Thinking quickly, he turned to a surveillance monitor on a workstation, fiddled with the controls, focused on the two men, and pumped up the volume.

"YOU MUST BE Ames," he whispered. The man cocked his head, startled. "Keep still and listen to me." He moved closer to Ames' ear. "I'm not a terrorist. I got in here using one of their uniforms. I'm taking off the tape. Stay quiet."

The man nodded slightly. Raiden silently and slowly pulled the gag off the man's mouth. Ames took a deep gulp of fresh air and then asked, breathlessly, "Who told you about me?"

"An informer calling himself Mister X. He was dressed like a ninja."

"I see." Raiden noticed that the man relaxed somewhat when he heard the words *Mister X.* "Take this thing off me, will you?"

Raiden removed the blindfold. He looked at the operative, eyes narrowed against the sudden brightness.

"I'm Richard Ames."

"Secret Service?"

"No. I was sent in by the *La-le-lu-le-lo,* just like you."

"What?" Those words again! The same gibberish the ninja spoke.

"You're here to find out where the President is. We have little time, so I'll be brief. How about switching to nanocommunications first?"

"Nanocommunications?"

"Right. Silence beats talk when it comes to safety."

• • •

THE VOICES suddenly ceased. Ocelot watched the two men on the monitor and saw that their lips weren't moving.

"What the . . . ?"

He jiggled the controls to make sure there wasn't a malfunction, and then sat back in frustration.

"ARE YOU ON?" Ames asked.

"Right here," Raiden replied. "Do you really know where the President is?"

"Almost certainly. He was moved to the first floor of Shell Two's Core section."

"Is he still there?"

"I don't know. I can't get a response. He has nanocommunication ability, too."

"You don't think he's been . . . like some of the other hostages . . . ?"

"Huh?"

"A hostage was killed in retaliation after the SEAL Ten disaster, remember?"

"What are you talking about?" The confusion in Ames' voice was real. He didn't know about the murder.

If there really was a murder, Raiden thought.

"Regardless of what they do to other hostages, they won't touch the President," Ames said.

"What makes you so sure?"

"The case."

"You mean the nuclear button they took?"

"Right. And the case won't do a thing by itself. That case may be the single most advanced example of a weapons fail-safe system. The password is nothing less than the physiological data of the U.S. President."

"You mean—?"

"The President's own vital signs—heartbeat, brainwave pattern, blood pressure, and so on—are constantly monitored and relayed by his internal nanomachines. This information along with the DNA pattern serve as a biometric password, unbreakable even by the latest parallel-processor supercomputers. The password entry itself cannot be performed unless brainwave patterns and heartbeats fall within normal parameters, rendering chemical and other forms of coercion impractical. In other words, the login must be made of the President's own free will. As a fail-safe, the input must also be reconfirmed hourly, even after the initial login. If a valid confirmation is not forthcoming, the system will automatically cancel the login."

"And that's why they can't harm the President."

"At least until the bird flies."

"Is there really a new model of Metal Gear here?"

"Absolutely. The Black Case serves as the launch key to Metal Gear as well."

"Why would they hide a Metal Gear in an offshore plant?"

Ames furrowed his brow and looked at Raiden with renewed suspicion. "Haven't they told you anything?"

"What?"

"The entire thing was planned—the oil spill, the tanker accident that caused it, everything. The Big Shell was built specifically for the development of a new Metal Gear model. The inspection tour was to check its progress."

What? Raiden's anger and frustration resurfaced. "What's going on around here?"

"Wait!" Ames nodded toward the big window across the room. It was difficult to see clearly through the etched glass, but Raiden made out two blurry figures.

"There's Snake now. In the Control Room," Ames said.

17

ALL RAIDEN COULD SEE was the bulky silhouette of a man wearing a coat. "That's him?"

One of the figures shut the Venetian blinds on the window. Now it was impossible to see anything except for gray silhouettes. Raiden cursed silently but then remembered he had a very useful tool. He pointed the directional microphone at the Control Room window.

The other man addressed the one Ames referred to as Snake. "King. Fatman is dead."

"It doesn't matter," King/Snake answered. "Saves us the trouble of getting rid of him ourselves."

"Why did he betray us?"

"Who knows? They're a band of lunatics to begin with. Nothing they do should come as a surprise."

"I'll have his background rechecked, just in case."

King paused. "You think he was working for *them*?"

"We can't discount the possibility. Especially with that intruder still at large."

"Yes . . . the man in the sneaking suit."

"You know more about those suits than I do."

"But FOXHOUND disbanded four years ago. So it must be . . . the Patriots?"

Huh? Raiden thought. *The Patriots? Who the hell are they?*

"What about the damage to Shell Two?" King asked.

"The circulation system for the contaminated water has been damaged. The water being drawn in is overflowing, and the lower block of the central section is flooding."

"Then seal the connecting pathway between Shells One and Two."

"The Semtex and IR sensors are already in place."

"Any effect on . . . *it?*"

"No."

"What about the President?"

"The password entry has already been made to the Black Case. In one hour, we'll need confirmation from him. His work is done after that."

"Make sure you keep him alive until then."

"Yes, I know."

Ames was right, Raiden thought. *They only need the President for his vital signs until the nuke is launched. After that, he's expendable.*

"What about the unit's activation?" King asked.

"Almost complete. The code has already been entered. All we need now is for the girl to start the system."

"The usual method, I assume?"

"No. The drugs took care of everything."

"Hmm . . ." King turned his back on the other man. "Only a few more steps to Outer Heaven!"

Outer what? Raiden thought. *Who are these guys? And what girl are they talking about?*

He heard the sound of a door opening. Someone else entered

the Control Room, casting a thinner shadow on the blinds. More curves. A woman.

"Who is that cyborg ninja, Shalashaska?" she asked with a heavy Russian accent.

"I cannot even guess."

"What about you?" she asked King.

"I'm having the matter looked into."

"Olga!" the other man said. "Don't cast suspicion where it isn't due!"

"Where it isn't due?" she asked with venom. "When you watched my father die and did nothing?"

The man called Shalashaska sighed. "It's been two years, Olga. Let it go."

"I read the file on Shadow Moses, by the way," she said with sarcasm.

"Olga, how could you suspect me?"

"You're Revolver Ocelot! You think I can trust *you*? I know that the ninja is not one of *my* men."

"How meaningful you make that sound," Ocelot said. "If Sergei were still alive—"

"If the old man were still alive, I wouldn't need to take orders from you!" Olga announced.

"Olga, Sergei was my best friend—"

She interrupted him with a cold whisper. "If you sell us out, Ocelot—I'll kill you myself."

Raiden heard a pistol cock. Ocelot had drawn a gun on the woman.

"Listen, daughter of Sergei. Don't ever let me see your gun pointed at me again."

Olga just chuckled lightly. "If you wish. I'll put a bullet in your back instead."

"Stop this fighting!" King demanded. "I took you both in when no one else would! You think any government would have you as irregulars in this political climate? The worst kind of wet-works, maybe. But even that's doubtful."

It was obvious that King was the leader, for the other two im-mediately stopped their bickering. But whether or not he really was "Snake," as Ames had said, was still a question in Raiden's mind.

"I'd recommend against switching camps," King told the other two. "You've nowhere left to go."

Raiden heard the woman grumble under her breath, and then there were some quick footsteps and the sound of the door opening. She had left the room. All at once the man called Ocelot started moaning as if he were in pain. He grunted through his teeth.

"It's happening again?" King asked.

"This damn right arm—Liquid!"

Raiden heard Ocelot attempt to restrain whatever was hap-pening to his arm, and then something very curious occurred. The heartbeat he had pinpointed as Ocelot's was joined by a sec-ond rhythm! Was he interpreting the sounds incorrectly? The man couldn't have *two hearts*, could he?

"It's almost as if it's having its revenge!" Ocelot shouted.

"How much do you think we spent on that arm in Lyon? The best transplant surgery team in the world!"

"I never trust a Frenchman."

"Well, shut up and give yourself the injection."

"I'm trying."

Raiden heard some fumbling, a couple of snaps, the ripping of a paper strip . . . Ocelot was using a hypodermic on himself. After a few seconds, his protestations diminished.

"There's something going on," he said. "The incidents are be-coming more frequent. Maybe that intruder's presence . . . ?"

"Ocelot, I'll leave this place in your hands. I'll take care of the intruder."

"Yes, King."

The door opened and "Snake" left the room. The conversation was over. Raiden lowered the directional mike and turned back to Ames. "Is that really Solid Snake?"

"That's what he claims," Ames answered.

"I thought Snake was dead."

"Solid Snake did die. But he's also here in the Shell. Either he survived, or there are two of them."

"Two of them?"

"And that's impossible." Ames peered at the Control Room to make sure they were safe to talk. "Anyway, what did you manage to catch?"

"They said password input was complete."

"I thought so."

"You said the password entry into the Black Case had to be made by the President willingly."

"That's right."

"So this means the President is cooperating with them?"

"It would have to be, yes."

"Why?"

"Probably tired of being a puppet. But it wasn't a smart move to betray us . . ."

"A puppet? What do you mean?" Raiden asked.

"We're running out of time. They *will* fire a nuke. You know what you need to do before then." Ames looked hard at Raiden and nodded slightly.

Raiden blinked. *He wants me to assassinate the President! Hold on . . . I'm no assassin . . . what's going on here?* "What do you mean, 'fire the nuke'? The nuke is nowhere close to the ransom deadline."

"Ransom?"

"Thirty billion dollars in cash."

"What are you babbling about?" Ames shook his head in disbelief. "The nuclear strike is not a threat—it's been the objective all along!"

"What? They plan to slaughter millions of people?"

"No. A high altitude detonation. You've heard of the Compton Effect?"

"Yeah. Total disruption of electronic equipment caused by EMMA pulse."

"Textbook answer. When an average nuclear warhead goes off within the atmosphere, the result is an electromagnetic pulse of up to fifty billion megawatts. The EMMA field can reach tens of thousands of volts per meter, and most electronic equipment will be toast in an instant. And this is what they plan to do right over Manhattan."

Raiden felt a surge of adrenaline. "The New York Stock Exchange—"

"—will suffer the same fate."

"If one of the key movers of world economy stops functioning, it could mean the beginning of a global depression. Black Monday will look like a picnic in comparison."

"But that isn't their aim. What they plan to do is 'liberate' Manhattan, pull it offline, and turn it into some kind of a republic. Hence 'Sons of Liberty,' I suppose."

"Sons of Liberty?" That's what the Colonel had called them.

Ames looked beyond Raiden and his eyes widened. "Ocelot is coming! I'm going offline. Search my right pocket. Hurry!" Raiden did so and found a PAN card. "You'll be able to unlock doors of up to Level Three security with that. Use it to get to Shell Two. Take care of the President before they launch that nuke!"

Ames switched out of nanocommunication mode and then averted his eyes. Raiden stood and readied his AK, just as Revolver Ocelot approached them. His spurs clinked as he walked. The man was truly an imposing figure—tall, with long golden locks, and a duster coat that was right out of a spaghetti Western.

"Who are you?" he asked Raiden.

An enemy soldier heard Ocelot and ran forward. He pointed his AK at Raiden and commanded, "Show your face!"

Ocelot gestured toward Ames, indicating the missing blind-fold and gag. "What do you think you're doing?"

Ames answered for the operative. "I asked him to remove these. I'm ill, you see."

Ocelot smiled. "I always knew that the DIA turned out second-rate liars."

"Wha-what are you talking about?"

"No need for denials. We know what you are . . . Colonel Ames."

Ames' mouth dropped open. Apparently he thought his cover was foolproof.

Ocelot drew his revolver and pointed it at the man's head. "They knew that the President was planning to betray them. So they sent you in to keep tabs on him, am I right?"

"You—!"

"Sorry, Colonel. You failed to carry out your duties."

Ames sputtered, "You'll never escape the *La-le-lu-le-lo!*"

Ocelot spun the revolver in his hand. "Is that so?" He caught the six-shooter by the grip and pointed it once again at Ames. But before he could pull the trigger, Ames suddenly clawed at his chest in agony. He cried out in pain and convulsed.

"What the . . . ?" Ocelot said, stepping back.

"You . . . tricked . . . me!" Ames managed to gasp. "I . . . un-derstand . . . now . . . *you're* . . . !" But whatever was gripping his heart made a decisive final squeeze. Ames choked and fell over. Dead. It had happened in an instant.

Raiden stood there stunned. His instinct was to step forward and examine the man, but Ocelot turned to him with the revolver pointed at his chest. "You—which team are you with?"

Raiden remained silent.

"Show me your face!" The other militia man raised his rifle. Ocelot addressed the soldier, "You know who he is?"

"No. He's not one of mine," the guard answered.

"Identify yourself!"

Raiden reluctantly removed the balaclava. His long white hair fell to his shoulders.

Ocelot's eyes sparkled and he nodded. "Hmm, we meet at last . . . !"

The villain raised the handgun to Raiden's forehead. The operative stared ahead stoically, resignation in his eyes.

A clatter above them. Movement. A flash of silver.

The cyborg ninja materialized from overhead, his sword almost on Ocelot's left arm before the killer managed to swing it out of the way. The newcomer stood in front of Raiden and pushed the operative back. The militia man fired a burst at the ninja with his AK, but the ninja's superfast blade deflected the bullets. The rounds ricocheted away—and several of them found hostages. The unfortunate victims cried out in surprise and pain.

"Hold your fire!" Ocelot shouted. The militia man stopped. "We need the hostages alive!"

The ninja looked at Raiden and said, "Hurry. Get away! Leave this to me!"

Ocelot tilted his head as he gazed at the warrior. "You? But you died!" Ocelot took a step back as an assault team rushed toward them from the back of the hall. Raiden turned and ran for the security door. Gunfire erupted behind him. As he slipped safely out of the room, he stole a glance back. The cyborg ninja was holding his own, defending himself against a hurricane of gunfire with a single samurai blade. The figure jumped about swinging the sword with precision and speed. Raiden had never seen anything like it before.

That guy really is *on my side,* he thought. His inclination was to stay and help, but he knew that this was his only chance to get out of there and continue his mission—whatever the hell it was now.

18

RAIDEN MADE IT to the Core elevator just as a Shell-wide PA announcement bellowed loudly and clearly, *"We have an intruder in Shell One! All personnel, we are on red alert! Begin Caution Mode protocol. Search every section of the structure! The intruder may be dressed in our own colors. Face check all personnel encountered! I repeat—"*

The elevator doors closed. As the lift rose to F1, Raiden made a call on the Codec.

"Colonel, Ames is dead," he said when the officer answered. "Looked like a heart attack."

"That's unfortunate," the Colonel replied. "However, we do at least know where the President is."

"So there really is a new type of Metal Gear in this place?"

"Apparently. We're still looking into it."

"I've also been told that the nuclear strike was what the terrorists were after from the start. *Not* the thirty billion dollars!"

"Chri—it was a cover-up all along . . ."

Raiden was really angry now. "Colonel! What are you keeping from me?"

The officer flared up as well. "I am not keeping back anything! It's not as though I'm told all the facts, either! I'm pulling in all the favors I can to look into all this. Just be a little patient. Our priority should be with the President right now. We can take it that they've completed the password entry and are preparing Metal Gear for nuclear strike. Get to the President as soon as possible!"

Raiden shook his head in frustration. "But the President is cooperating with them!"

"According to Ames, yes. But it's also true that they're about to get rid of the President. There's something else going on here, and the President may be able to tell you what it is when you see him in person."

"What?"

"Once they get the confirmation for nuclear launch, they'll do it. You need to rescue the President before then."

Rose interrupted the conversation. "Jack, I agree with the Colonel. You need to protect the President for now."

Raiden took a deep breath and tried to calm down. "All right." He signed off as the elevator doors opened on F1. He was back at the entrance to Core 1. An enemy sentry was in the corridor where Raiden had knocked out the surveillance camera. Before the guy could turn around to see who was in the elevator, Raiden ducked to the side of the lift so that the cage would appear empty. He put his finger on the DOORS OPEN button; hopefully the guard would take the bait. The approaching soldier's footsteps grew nearer.

"Who's there?" the man asked in Russian. Raiden remained silent.

Finally, the soldier stepped into the lift. Raiden knocked away the AK with his left hand and then delivered a powerhouse punch to the man's face with his right. The soldier lost his balance and fell into the elevator. Two swift kicks were all it took to send the guard to dreamland. Raiden looked out of the elevator to make sure no one else was around and then dragged the body into the hallway. A large covered waste basket stood at the side of the lift. Raiden removed the lid, picked up the soldier, and dumped him unceremoniously into the trash. The lid fit perfectly on top. Raiden brushed his hands together and moved on.

He emerged into sunlight and came face-to-face with another guard on the E–F connecting bridge. There was nothing for Raiden to do except act on instinct. He drew the most accessible weapon—the SOCOM—and fired before the sentry could react. The round caught the man in the chest. He whirled around and slammed against the bridge railing, then slid to the ground. Raiden didn't like having to kill anyone—he was trained to incapacitate them if possible and only use deadly force when absolutely necessary. Raiden told himself that this had been one of those compulsory cases.

He made it onto the roof of Strut E and continued toward Strut D. The bridge between Struts D and G was the only way to get to Shell 2. He would then need to go around the structure to either Strut L to the right or Strut H to the left in order to gain access to one of the 'I'-connecting bridges to Core 2.

The Strut D roof was curiously vacant. After the Caution Alert had been announced, Raiden expected the place to be crawling with enemy soldiers. Apparently there just weren't that many of them to cover an edifice as large as the Big Shell. They were probably still scampering through Core 1 trying to find him.

The Codec buzzed. It was Pliskin!

"Raiden, can you hear me?"

"Pliskin! Where have you been?"

"Checking around. I'm in Strut H right now. How's the situation over there?"

"We have a lead on the President's location."

"Where is he?"

"Shell Two Core, the first floor."

"I'm cut off from the Core where I am. It's a mess here."

"All right. I'm on my way to Shell Two right now. I'm about to cross the bridge between Struts D and G now."

"Wait! There are IR sensors in place on the connecting bridge! If you break the beams, the Semtex will go off."

"I heard them talking about that."

"Target the control units and destroy them. Make sure you don't shoot the Semtex."

"What do the controls look like?"

"Take a look with your binoculars."

Raiden grabbed them from his pack. He noticed the packs of Semtex attached to rails and other surfaces. Near each explosive was a small box with a red indicator light.

"How am I going to shoot those tiny things from here?" Raiden asked.

"Can't help you there, kid. Got a sniper rifle?"

"No."

"Better find one. Quick."

Raiden rubbed his chin. He remembered something he had seen earlier. "I think I know where to get one. Later."

He signed off and reversed his tracks back to Strut E. But before he could cross the E–F bridge, another Gun Cypher appeared. It sensed movement in his direction and began to turn its camera toward him. Raiden went down on one knee and released a burst of fire from the AK he was still carrying. The rounds blew the Cypher to bits.

Raiden crossed the bridge, made his way into the stairwell and then down to the Warehouse. The cavernous space was quiet, but to be safe he kept to the walls and moved swiftly and silently. Finally, he found the alcove where the door marked AR-MORY 3 was located. Using the security card Ames had given him, Raiden opened the Level 3 door.

Inside was a treasure trove of weapons and ammunition, a regular candy store for gun enthusiasts. Raiden stocked up on SOCOM bullets, took a few frag grenades, chaff grenades, and a couple of Claymores. Then he found what he came for—a PSG-1-T, a compact, long-range sniper rifle with zooming scope sighting and a standard crosshair aim. Boxes of ammunition for the weapon were in plain sight. Raiden felt as if he'd eaten a couple of power bars.

It took him ten minutes to travel from the Warehouse back to the Strut D roof, and he encountered no enemy personnel along the way. Raiden crouched at the entrance to the bridge and used the PSG-1's scope to evaluate the targets. One IR sensor was attached to a small, white-striped pump a few feet beyond the midway beams. Raiden loaded the rifle, readied it, and took careful aim. One shot did the trick.

Two control boxes were nestled on the left side of the bridge among the C4 packs and IR beams. These shots were trickier—he had to blow off only the tops of the boxes to avoid hitting the C4. Raiden steadied himself and pulled the trigger. A miss—the bullet zoomed way out over the Hudson.

Concentrate! he ordered himself. *And relax!*

The second and third tries were successful.

At first he couldn't locate any more targets, but then Raiden noticed a Sons of Liberty flag flapping in the breeze. As the flag fluttered, he could see a control box behind it on the railing. Raiden took aim at the flag—which consisted of a spotted snake on top of red and white stripes—and fired. Not only did he destroy the control box, but it was gratifying to blow a hole in the flag as well.

A group of seagulls had gathered in front of another box. Raiden fired a warning shot just over their heads. The birds cawed and flew away, revealing the target. Another shot, another one down.

Raiden studied the bridge with his binoculars to make sure he hadn't missed any. Sure enough, there was a control box on the floor of the bridge at the other end, just at the entrance to the Strut G roof. He took care of it with a single shot.

It was now safe to cross the bridge. For the first time since the mission began, Raiden left Shell 1 and made his way toward Strut G, the first stop on Shell 2. As he moved, Raiden wondered how stable the structure was. The entire side containing Struts H, I, and J leaned inward and was surely unsafe. Struts G, L, and K, plus the Core, seemed to be all right. When he was halfway across, the Codec buzzed again.

"Raiden, I found us a ride," Pliskin said.

"I'm all ears."

"One of the enemy's Kasatkas."

"Is it in good shape?"

"Full tank. I'm heading for Shell One now. What about the Harrier?"

Raiden peered back to Strut E and didn't see it. "It's not on the heliport."

"Good. I'll set this one down there then."

"Can you cover the hostages? They're being held on the first floor of the Core."

"Will do."

"You didn't happen to find any other places where hostages were being held, did you?"

"No. Nothing like that."

"Okay." Raiden's suspicions that the Colonel was either lying or keeping facts from him were growing stronger.

"How many hostages are there?" Pliskin asked.

"A few short of thirty. One dead and several wounded."

"The Kasatka's cargo area will hold thirteen max."

"What about the other Kasatka?"

"I sabotaged it. It can't come after us if it can't get off the ground."

"Oh."

"We'll just have to make two trips."

"Can you fly a Kasatka?"

"I have a pilot who's flown the civilian model, the KA-62, in

VR. There's not a whole lot of difference between the military KA-60 and the civilian model."

Raiden heard another voice. "Cleared for takeoff."

"Who's that?"

"Raiden, let me introduce you to my partner—Otacon," Pliskin said.

"Otacon?"

The newcomer's face appeared on the Codec. He was younger than Pliskin, wore glasses, had longish hair, and might have been considered a nerd in some circles. Was this the *civilian scientist* that Peter Stillman had mentioned?

"Hey, Raiden," Otacon said. "Nice to meet you."

Raiden heard sudden gunfire through the Codec.

"Damn!" Pliskin shouted. "Otacon, get us out of here! Raiden, I'll talk to you later!" With that, he signed off.

Raiden couldn't help smiling. He *liked* Pliskin. Even if the Colonel had doubts about the guy, Pliskin was okay in Raiden's book. And now he had the civilian pilot with him, another fellow who seemed all right.

He made another Codec call.

"Colonel, I need some answers from you. Who exactly is Pliskin and his partner?"

"I know what you're thinking," the man said defensively.

"It keeps coming back to Shadow Moses. And now this Otacon . . ."

Rose got on the line. "AKA Hal Emmerich, Ph.D. A Shadow Moses survivor. Snake and Otacon both became fugitives after Shadow Moses, wanted for acts of terrorism."

"An anti–Metal Gear organization."

The Colonel said, "They sabotaged and destroyed countless Metal Gear units throughout the world."

"And were responsible for the incident two years ago that necessitated the construction of the Big Shell," Rose added.

"Snake and his partner aren't terrorists!" Raiden insisted.

"Jack, why are you defending them?"

He wasn't sure how to put it in words. It was mostly a feeling. "I look back on what I've done here so far, and things like training and sense of duty alone won't get you through a sneaking mission like this."

"Jack, are you okay?"

"You need something *higher*. I can't think of the right word, but . . . it has to be pure will, backed up by . . . by courage, or ideals, or something like that. I'd stake my life on it. The Solid Snake that saved Shadow Moses couldn't turn into a terrorist."

The Colonel said, "Maybe that's true, but they went down with that tanker two years ago. We even recovered Snake's body."

"And the DNA test results on that body say it's him," Raiden repeated, not believing a word of it.

"Jack, I know what you're saying, but Snake is dead. He can't be here, not even as this Doctor Hal Emmerich."

"But that also means that he can't be the terrorist leader behind this thing!" Raiden reasoned. Simple as that.

He signed off and continued across the bridge toward Strut G as the sound of a chopper grew near. Raiden looked up and saw a Kamov Kasatka rising skyward from behind the bulk of Shell 2. The chopper hovered over the bridge. Pliskin was in the doorway—he waved at Raiden. The operative saluted him and then the Kasatka headed for the Shell 1 heliport.

Raiden turned back to continue his journey across the bridge only to see a large man standing in front of the access door on the roof of Strut G. He wore a long leather coat, had blond hair, a mustache and goatee, and appeared to be quite physically fit.

"I've been waiting for you!" the man shouted. "A messenger from the Patriots!"

That voice. Raiden knew it. The man in front of him was the one Ames had referred to as "Snake." The one the other two terrorists had called "King."

19

KING NARROWED HIS EYES, taking a closer look at Raiden. "Where do I . . . know him from?" he muttered to himself.

Raiden wasn't intimidated, even though the man exuded powerful charisma. "So you're the boss around here."

The man boasted, "No, not just around here. I'm the boss to surpass Big Boss himself! Solid Snake!"

"No!" Pliskin shouted from above. The Kasatka had returned and Raiden had been too distracted by the appearance of the terrorists' leader to notice.

Both Raiden and King looked up.

"That is *not* Solid Snake!" Pliskin called.

King gazed at the soldier in the helicopter for a brief moment . . . and then he smiled. "What a pleasant surprise . . . brother!"

"Save it," Pliskin yelled. "You're no brother of mine."

Raiden stood dumbfounded, listening to the two men shout. *They* know *each other?*

"Don't say you've forgotten me, Snake," King said.

This time it was Raiden's turn to narrow his eyes and peer more closely at the terrorist leader. The man really did resemble *the* Solid Snake! Quite a lot, in fact. But there was something else. Another set of traits Raiden recognized as someone equally legendary—the soldier whom King had mentioned—a resemblance to Big Boss.

"Snake?" he asked. He looked back up at Pliskin. Again, Raiden was dumbstruck by the striking similarity between the two men. They really could be . . . brothers!

Pliskin—or Snake—or whoever he was, shouted, "Raiden! Take cover!" Then, as Raiden hit the deck, the soldier leaned farther out of the chopper and fired a burst from his M4 at the terrorist.

Raiden's jaw dropped when he saw King activate a hidden control beneath his coat and *in an instant* transform his clothing into a highly sophisticated suit of armor—designed with a look similar to Fatman's blast uniform, only leaner, streamlined, and more maneuverable. The bullets from Snake's M4 deflected off the suit in a hail of sparks.

"Stop impersonating him!" Snake yelled to King.

"Brother, I'm a whole different game from Liquid!" King taunted. "I am Solidus Snake! Doctor Clark secretly created me out of the same batch that produced you and Liquid. Didn't you know?"

Snake disappeared from the chopper door for a split second, returned with a grenade launcher, and fired. His target jumped to the side so that the grenade struck the door to Shell G. The blast was concussive enough to knock Raiden to the ground—but Solidus withstood the shock and remained standing.

"That the best you can do, Snake?" he called to the Kasatka.

Snake followed the attack with a second grenade, hoping to catch the enemy off guard. But Solidus jumped off the bridge just before the explosive destroyed it. The airspace was immediately blanketed in black smoke. Neither Snake nor his pilot, Otacon, could see anything.

"Did I get him?" Snake called.

It took a few moments before the smoke cleared enough to see through. There was no sign of the villain, but Raiden was hanging on for dear life to a girder from the demolished D–G connecting bridge. His feet dangled precariously over the water—but being trained in hanging mode, Raiden was perfectly capable of saving himself from the situation. The operative used his abdominal muscles to raise his legs and clutch the girder with them. He had just about swung himself up and over so that he was on top of the girder when the sound of another helicopter came dangerously close.

The AV Harrier II rose from below on a steep ascent, and on its nose cone stood none other than Solidus. The exquisitely designed aircraft hovered steadily so that Solidus could walk to the cockpit and set himself inside.

Raiden stared in awe. *Oh my God . . .*

"Otacon," Snake shouted to his partner, "we're in trouble! It's the Harrier!"

The Kasatka swung around quickly.

Solidus raised a fist in the air. "The world needs only one Big Boss! I'll drown you fools for interfering!" With that, he closed the cockpit door and took the controls. Before a second had elapsed, the Harrier had fired a missile at the Kasatka. Otacon managed to dodge the projectile, but just barely. The armament destroyed the door to Strut D instead, cutting off Raiden's retreat in that direction. The Harrier swooped over the strut and turned around to face the Kasatka, which had flown over the D–G connecting bridge. Raiden had managed to get to his feet—on the Shell 1 side of the burning bridge.

Snake called to Raiden. "This is a Stinger missile launcher!" He dropped a case from the chopper. It fell heavily on the bridge near the operative. "The Kasatka can't stand up to the Harrier!"

The enemy aircraft sped forward, forcing Otacon to ascend rapidly. The two steel warriors soared into the sky above the Big Shell ready to do battle. Raiden looked at the Stinger case. He knew what he had to do, but he had no experience in firing a Stinger.

It can't be that different from a grenade launcher! he told himself.

He stooped to open the case as a cacophony of explosions filled the air. The surface-to-air, electronically targeted guided missile launcher was one of the most technically sophisticated portable weapons imaginable. Using the same principle as a bazooka gun, a user could knock entire aircraft out of the atmosphere provided that he could accurately program the targeting function.

The Harrier, of course, was equipped with AIM-9 Sidewinder missiles, an assortment of air-to-ground weapons, and AGM-65 Maverick missiles. A GAU-12 25-mm six-barrel gun pod was mounted on the centerline under the nose. Raiden knew the weapon had a three-hundred-round capacity and a lead-computing optical sight system.

The aircraft had moved away from its skirmish with the Kasatka and was now attacking him! An explosion on the bridge rocked Raiden. He fell over as debris showered his body, but he clutched the Stinger launcher as if it were a lifesaver. As soon as the shock wave had passed, Raiden stood and ran back to the roof of Strut D. Part of it was on fire as well, due to the destruction of the stairwell door. Raiden crouched behind the railing and held the launcher to his shoulder. He got the Harrier in sight and switched on the targeting system.

The Harrier fired a Sidewinder directly at Raiden. He reacted quickly, leaping forward and landing on his feet running. The missile devastated the section of the roof, but at least two thirds of it was still intact. Raiden just made it to a stable area and repeated the Stinger preparation. The Harrier rose for another go at the operative, but the Kasatka came swooping down. Snake fired another grenade at the Harrier—and it hit. The aircraft wobbled and spun for a few seconds but quickly regained its equilibrium. The damage was minimal.

Get out of the way, Snake! Raiden willed. He had the Harrier in his sights and turned on the targeting system, but it was still a tricky shot. The chopper and the gunship were so close together that the Stinger sensors could mistakenly target the Kasatka.

Wait! Raiden thought. *The Soliton Radar!*

He had the satellite maps of Shell 1. They could be of some assistance in the targeting procedure. Raiden pulled up the view on the Codec. The fighter jet was represented by a big red arrow and the Kasatka was a small red dot. By keeping one eye on the radar and another eye on the Stinger's scope, Raiden found that keeping track of the Harrier's position in relation to the other chopper was much easier. Feeling renewed confidence, Raiden fired the missile. It struck the Harrier in its underbelly, causing a huge, dynamic explosion over the Big Shell. Heat and burning fragments enveloped Raiden, but he covered his head with his arms. The sneaking suit beneath the enemy uniform protected him.

The aircraft began a free fall, completely out of control. First it struck Strut G with a ferocious impact. The Harrier seemed to hang there for a moment as the Strut creaked and sagged to the left, and then the fighter continued its descent. As it plummeted past Raiden's eyes, he could make out the rage-filled face of Solidus in the cockpit. There was blood all over him. In the next couple of seconds the aircraft crashed into the water.

Nothing happened for some time. Raiden looked up, decided it was safe to stand, and got up. The Kasatka hovered above him. Snake continued to lean out of the door, but his face registered shock and surprise.

"There's something coming up!" he shouted.

Raiden peered down over the rail. Sure enough, a giant shadow under the surface of the water was growing larger. It suddenly broke through the waves and continued to rise—until it was *flying.*

"That's Metal Gear!" Raiden cried in horror. "It's already active!"

The thing was huge. It resembled what Raiden could describe only as the result of breeding between a gigantic, mechanized bird and a monstrous, metallic sea mammal. And it *roared* like a beast from hell.

In its beak was the Harrier. And Solidus, still alive, was already unbuckling his safety harness and climbing out of the cockpit. He looked up with his right eye—for the left one was gone—and shouted at the figure at Metal Gear's controls.

"Vamp! Go!"

The vampire was indeed in Metal Gear's cockpit. The cover flipped open and its unearthly pilot grinned. He stepped out of his own harness, stood on the hovering mecha battlestation, and faced his leader. As soon as Solidus passed him and got into the cockpit, Vamp leaped off the fuselage and landed on the water— on his feet. And then he began to run toward Strut L. On top of the water.

Raiden's jaw dropped.

Otacon, at the Kasatka's controls, gasped. "What's that—?"

"It's running on water!" Snake proclaimed.

Raiden couldn't believe it. The guy still had a hole in his forehead where the operative had shot him earlier.

He's supposed to be dead!

But it got better . . . or worse, as the case might be.

Vamp reached the bottom of Strut L and continued to *run* up the side of the structure. Like a human insect. Like a spider speeding up a wall.

It took only a few moments for the vampire to reach the roof. He leaped over the railing and ran through the door. Gone.

Raiden swung his head back to look at Metal Gear. Solidus was now completely at its controls. The metallic beast stopped hovering, spread its wings, and made a slow, graceful dive into the water.

20

PLISKIN/SNAKE CALLED on the Codec. "Raiden, you all right?"

"Yeah. How about you guys?"

"Barely managed, but we're all right."

"The chopper?"

"We need some time for repairs."

"Oh." Raiden sighed with disappointment.

"The President's all yours."

"Okay." Raiden hesitated for a second. "Can I ask you something?"

"What?"

"Are you *the* Snake?" The man in the chopper merely grunted, not knowing how he should answer. For Raiden that was plenty of confirmation. "They said you were dead!"

"No, not me," Snake answered. "There are too many things I still need to do."

"Snake, you're a legend! And that's why I need to ask you this."

"Legend? A legend is nothing but fiction. Someone tells it, someone else remembers, everybody passes it on."

Raiden shook his head. "I'm here because I was assigned to

this mission, not because I want to. If I could, I'd be out of here in a second. Look—how could you come back to all this? Why keep fighting?"

"There's something my best friend said to me once . . . we're not tools of the government or anyone else. Fighting was the only thing I was good at, but . . . at least I always fought for what I believed in."

That was a good enough answer for Raiden. "What about . . . what about the DNA results from that body I had exhumed?"

Otacon interrupted, his face appearing on the monitor. "That was Liquid's body. He and Snake are identical on the genetic level. A deception—for our own protection. We stole his frozen body from some organization. Kind of a hassle, though . . ."

Snake added, "That's all there is to it."

"Are you two really an NGO?" Raiden asked.

Otacon fielded that one. "Insofar as we're a nonprofit organization of civilians advocating a cause, yes. The cause happens to be the eradication of Metal Gear."

"We work on our own," Snake said. "But it's a cause worth fighting for."

"Why would you stick your neck out for something this risky?"

"That's the way I used to look at it four years ago. I was holed up in the middle of nowhere in Alaska drinking too much."

Otacon clarified, "We have a responsibility to the coming generations, to the world."

"What responsibility?" Raiden asked.

"To keep track of the mistakes we've made as a species."

"We need to remember," Snake said, "to spread the word, to fight for change. And that's what keeps me alive."

"You think you can change the future?"

"I'm not as arrogant as that."

Raiden was conflicted by the words he was hearing. "What you do isn't grassroots activism. It's more like terrorism."

"I admit that," Snake said softly.

Otacon came to his defense. "But our group, Philanthropy, received some information. A new Metal Gear prototype was being developed here, and terrorists were planning to raid the facility. The information came from a very reliable source."

"So you're here to—?"

"We're here to stop all that, but I also have a personal motive," Otacon said.

Snake explained, "Looks like the terrorists have his sister in the Big Shell. We're here on our own, not under anyone's orders. We have our own battles. Otacon's here for someone—I'm not."

"This is a military mission!" Raiden said, a little annoyed at Snake's cavalier attitude toward the whole thing.

An incoming call from Rose was a welcome excuse to change the frequency.

"Jack? Are you all right?"

"Just barely."

"You almost gave me a heart attack . . . those explosions . . ."

"Sorry. Wasn't intentional." Raiden waved at Snake as the Kasatka flew away toward the heliport.

"I know that. And I know I need to stay stronger," she said.

"Say a prayer for me, Rose. So I can come back."

"You will make it back. I'm with you all the way, remember . . ."

"That means a lot to me, you know." He switched frequencies to talk to his boss. "Colonel, Metal Gear's already gone active."

"It's not too late," the man said. "You can still prevent a nuclear strike by securing the President and preventing password confirmation from taking place. Get to the President. He's in the Core section of Shell Two."

"I'm checking the satellite images," Rose said. "Looks like you can get to the Core from Strut L."

"The Core hasn't gone under yet from what we can tell," the Colonel explained. "Follow the railings down, then jump onto the pipes."

Raiden looked out from Strut D's railing. The D–G bridge was in pieces and still on fire in some places—but Raiden thought he could utilize a "stepping-stone" method of crossing it safely. The large pipes the Colonel was talking about ran underneath the G–L connecting bridge, which had been demolished by the Harrier. Raiden figured they were exhaust pipes for the climate control within the Big Shell.

"The only viable Strut in the outer perimeter is Strut L," Rose said. "That attack just now doesn't make any sense. It's like they have no more use for this place."

"Colonel," Raiden said. "You were monitoring the Codec calls. That man was the real Snake all along."

"Maybe," the Colonel answered.

"Maybe?"

"Don't let your guard down with him."

"Why do you say that?"

"Because they were never a part of the simulation. They're an unknown factor."

Raiden exploded. "You can take your simulation and—! We're out here, we bleed, we die!"

Rose urged him to calm down.

"Even if that is Snake," the Colonel continued, "that has no bearing on your mission."

"Colonel, you and Snake used to be on the same side. I don't understand. I read about you and Snake in *The Darkness of Shadow Moses . . .*"

"I don't give a damn what that piece of trash said. Do you get me?"

The Colonel signed off, leaving Raiden with the unenviable task of crossing two incomplete bridges to his next destination.

Might as well get going.

Raiden left the Stinger on the roof and made his way out on the girder that he had hung from earlier. The wind had become more forceful. Raiden chose to play it safe and crawl to the end on his hands and knees. From there he had to make a short leap to the other half of the busted girder, which was still attached to what was left of the bridge. Luckily for Raiden the girder had broken away from the unreachable bridge and jutted toward him. He just had to make a five-foot leap over empty space without a net.

He checked his belongings to make sure nothing was carelessly dangling. Raiden concentrated on the end of the other girder and *willed* himself over. He then closed his eyes and saw in his mind an image of himself safely on top of it. Opening his eyes once again, he was ready.

Raiden leaped like a toad and landed on the other girder with ease.

He crawled to where the piece of metal met with the unsteady bridge. The structure rocked when Raiden climbed over the rail and hopped onto it, so he ran quickly to Strut G's roof and skirted around the burning rubble that was once the stairwell entrance. Raiden avoided more debris and made it to what was left of the G–L connecting bridge. Much of it had fallen into the ocean. Only the large exhaust pipe still held and connected the two Struts. It began about ten feet below the roof railing, so the challenge was climbing down, keeping one's balance, and not letting the strong breeze have any detrimental effect on movement.

Seagulls circled over his head as he swung his leg over the rail and prepared to descend a trellis of cables to the pipe. The friction gloves improved his grip for the shimmy down. He took it nice and slow. Hand over hand just like in the gym where he trained for real. Snake was right—VR training had nothing on the real stuff.

Raiden reached the pipe, kept his body low, and grabbed the circumference for support. Indeed, the wind had picked up. Raiden looked at the clouds. They were big and billowy—and moving—but there didn't appear to be any chance of rain.

He moved along the pipe toward Strut L. At one point he came across a large mass of bird droppings. There was no way around it—he would simply have to crawl through it. Raiden winced as he did so . . . and quickly discovered that the stuff was extremely slippery.

He slid to the right . . . ! He was falling . . . !—and would have gone completely over had he not clutched a rivet sticking out of the pipe.

Raiden latched on to it with three fingers until he managed to pull himself back to the top of the pipe. He continued his crawl through the droppings and onto dry metal once again. He took a moment to wipe the filth from his gloves and the parts of the enemy's clothing that had come into contact with it.

As he approached the bottom of Strut L, he heard voices. Two Russian sentries had come to the roof for a smoke. They walked over to the railing and leaned against it. Raiden quickly ducked directly beneath the edge of the roof, still on the pipe . . . but he had to get to a ladder that was attached to the railing farther along the wall. The only way to do it without the soldiers seeing him was to go into hanging mode again. Raiden grasped the cables that ran along the outer wall of the Strut and pulled himself up. The muscles in his arms ached from all the dangling he was doing, but he was nowhere near giving out. He had trained and worked hard on developing the muscles in his body. His heart would have to fail before his muscles would.

When he was within inches of the railing bottom he had a sudden curiosity as to what the time was. He glanced at the Codec—the digital readout indicated that it was just around two o'clock. He'd only been at the Big Shell for a little over half a day. It seemed like forever.

Raiden grasped the bottom rail and performed the hand-over-hand maneuver that he did so well. But as he was moving beneath the two soldiers, one of them decided to answer the call of nature. The man unzipped his pants and did his business over the side of the Strut. The stream splashed down directly in front of Raiden, forcing him to halt his progress until the man finished.

First bird poop, and now this? he thought.

There was tremendous strain on his wrists and shoulders, and Raiden had to close his eyes and grit his teeth while he waited. Finally, the man zipped up and walked away. Raiden shook his head—no one would believe the things he had to do and witness as a FOXHOUND operative—and then he moved on to the safety of the ladder.

21

RAIDEN WAITED until the two sentries were back inside the Strut and then climbed the ladder to the roof. Drawing the SOCOM, he covertly crept to the L–K connecting bridge, searched carefully for signs of Cyphers or planted explosives, and made his way across to the T-connector for the Shell 2 Core. The pathway was clear of obstacles—probably because the terrorists needed the bridge themselves. He moved quickly over the bridge, listened at the door for signs of activity, heard nothing, and slipped inside.

Unbelievable, he thought. *I'm in Core Two.*

Not having access to the Central Core's maps—he needed to find a node—Raiden blindly followed the entrance passageway into a large room marked 1F. It was full of air purification equipment and was a maze of pathways and blocked off machinery. On the east side, Raiden found a long corridor that led to a sealed door marked with security Level 3. A woman stood before it talking on the radio.

The Russian—the woman he had heard in the Control Room with Solidus Snake and the man called Ocelot.

Raiden quickly ducked out of sight. It was possible that the

President was in that sealed room, so the operative flattened against the wall, remained still and silent, and listened.

"My father had some unfinished business with him!" the woman said.

Solidus' voice — on her radio — answered, "Olga, Snake is definitely here. He's in Shell One. Calm yourself."

She turned and moved toward Raiden. The operative slid along the hallway, turned a corner, and waited.

"We will not change the plan because of your personal feelings," Solidus said.

"Then screw your plan! I've been waiting for this day for two years, and I *will* send him to the bottom of the ocean, right next to my old man!"

"The launch comes first."

"Damn it!" She slammed her fist into the wall. "Where's Ocelot?"

"Not here."

"I don't trust him."

"Don't talk that way about one of your own."

"He's *not* one of my own. He left my father to die, remember?"

"Olga, we'll talk later. We need to get started on the final checks for the unit."

"All right. I'm headed back there."

"The upper connecting bridge to Shell One is down."

"What about the chopper?"

"One of the Kamovs is out of action, and the other one was *stolen*. Take the oil fence from Strut L."

"I'll tell my men to start pulling out."

"Not yet. Their retrieval comes last — the intruder's still at large."

Olga said his name with spite. "Snake . . ."

"What about the other man?"

"He's got luck on his side, certainly."

"He survived the explosion . . . Listen, Olga, the code confirmation is in one hour. Keep the President alive until then."

"I know. No one gets in here. Turn the current on to be sure."

"Of course."

There was the sound of a switch. Raiden heard a crackling sound. He dared to peer around the corner. Olga stood several yards away from the sealed door, her back to Raiden. She watched the floor in front of her as a trace of blue plasma rolled over it.

"High voltage current on," Solidus announced.

"The door stays shut unless the President manages to take out that circuit panel from inside the room. And it's no job for bare hands."

"All right. Come back immediately."

"One more thing . . ."

"What?"

She turned and walked toward Raiden. He moved quickly down the hall and slid into an alcove. She went the opposite direction, so he stepped out and followed her around the perimeter of the floor. She eventually reached an area that was too far away for him to properly hear the conversation. He still had the directional microphone in his backpack, so he dug it out and moved parallel with her in another part of the Air Purification Room. He aimed the mike at a partition separating them. Reception wasn't great and he had to keep adjusting the microphone's position, but he could hear.

"We leave for Russia when this business is done. I want half the money for that," the woman said.

"Of course. That was part of the agreement."

She moved again and stood next to an elevator. Raiden ducked behind a cargo box and continued to use the mike.

"We start living for ourselves after this. If there's anyone who wants to stay there, I want you to take good care of them."

"Gladly. Gurlukovich soldiers are the cream of the crop."

"It's time they went free."

"What happened to the building of 'Mother Russia'?" Solidus asked with a little sarcasm.

"The old man is dead. The world is a different place now."

"It's your life."

Olga started walking again. Raiden followed her past the elevator—and another door marked 3—to the far north side of the room. He crouched behind another partition and continued to listen.

"Just a reminder. I'm going to say this again, one last time. Don't try anything on us."

"The feeling is mutual, Olga."

Raiden heard her switch off the radio. Her footsteps grew fainter down the corridor and a hatch opened and closed. She was gone. Raiden quickly made his way back to the head of the electrified corridor and then called the Colonel on the Codec.

"Yes, Raiden?"

"I'm in front of the room where they're keeping the President!"

"Everything all right?"

"No sign of flooding, but I can't get close to the door. The floor's electrified."

"Don't test it. You'll be bacon."

"Any suggestions?"

"Remember the Shadow Moses training."

"Take out the circuit panel?"

"Right."

"But there's no way into the room."

"Try ventilation ducts."

Raiden scanned the hallway and brightened. "Yeah, I think I see one!"

"Look for a remote-control missile launcher. You can guide it through the duct into the room."

"And then target the circuit panel! Got it."

"Right. Just make sure you don't hit the President!"

"The President is wired with nanomachines. If we know the frequency, I can raise him . . ."

"We've tried that repeatedly, but there's no response. It looks like the walls have a built-in radio shield."

"So that's why Ames lost contact with him . . ."

"If you need to confirm his position you can log into the node."

"Understood."

"But locate the missile launcher first."

Easier said than done. Raiden signed off and called Snake.

"What's up, Raiden?"

"Snake, do you know where I can find some remote-controlled missiles?"

"Hmm. I saw a Nikita in a busted-up supply room on B1 in the Core of Shell Two."

"Really? That's perfect!"

"But be careful. Contaminated seawater's broken out of the tanks thanks to that explosion. Most of B1 is probably flooded by now."

Great.

Raiden rubbed his brow and signed off. The only way to get to B1 was to go down. He retraced his steps to the elevator. He swiped the security card on the door marked 3 and started to look inside; but a sixth sense that he had relied upon so many times in the past kicked in. Raiden halted himself . . . and barely opened the door—just far enough to peer through. There appeared to be armaments in there, as well as a pair of gun cameras mounted on the ceiling! Raiden breathed a sigh of relief. He readied the SOCOM and shot both cameras to bits. *Now* it was safe to enter.

There was no remote-controlled rocket launcher inside, but there was a small supply of Nikita rockets themselves. Where was the firing mechanism? Snake said he had seen it on B1. Raiden prayed that the elevator wasn't damaged from all the explosions. All he needed was to step into a lift with a disabled shaft, and he was a dead man.

Raiden called the elevator, and it arrived with no problems. If he had been superstitious, he would have crossed his fingers when he stepped inside and pressed the B1 button. But the ride was smooth all the way down. The doors opened and he cautiously looked for signs of trouble before stepping out onto the wet floor. He was alone.

The Central Core's node stood right there next to the elevator. Even though there was an inch or two of water covering the floor, Raiden stooped, placed his hand on the panel, and accessed the maps. It was like growing another pair of eyes. He didn't have to fumble his way through unknown territory. Unfortunately, the plans didn't reveal the extent of the flooding. Raiden stood and moved away from the elevator—and directly in front of him was a stairwell that was full of water. It was the only way to the rest of the floor, which was obviously submerged.

Raiden searched his pack for the oxygen module he had used during the swim to Big Shell. It was almost empty—there was enough air for a few minutes' time. Probably not enough for the round-trip. He put it in his mouth anyway and resolved not to use it unless he had to.

He dived into the water and swam down the stairwell and into the Central Core's Filtration Chamber. The map on his Codec indicated the direction he should travel, as long as his breath held out. The problem was that he had to take the time to search the floors, cubbyholes, and alcoves for the supply closet Snake had mentioned. Floating litter and debris from the explosion also made it difficult. Raiden passed damaged equipment and an overturned electric cart. It was hard going, and the only way Raiden found it bearable was to concentrate solely on the search and not the pain in his lungs.

After a couple of minutes of holding his breath, Raiden spotted a vertical shaft of light in the water ahead. That meant there was an air pocket on the surface! He swam toward it, ascended, and gasped lovely oxygen when he broke the water. There was an eight-inch space between the water level and the ceiling. He breathed normally for a few moments and then went under once again.

The map denoted an L-jog in the corridor ahead. Raiden followed it and kept going. Another minute or so passed and he felt his lungs crying for air again. There were no light shafts in sight, so he allowed himself a breath through the oxygen module. It was enough to sustain him a little farther.

The supply cabinet was at the end of the corridor. The Level 3 door had been blown off. Raiden swam inside, took another breath from the module, and looked around. Sure enough, a Nikita launcher lay on one of the shelves. He grabbed it and swam back, retracing his route.

He reached the L-jog when his oxygen module ran out. Raiden took one last breath, spit out the contraption, and continued. He was fine for the next minute or so—he no longer had to take time to search for the weapon—but it was still a long way to the air pocket. His lungs began to ache during the third minute of swimming. He saw the light shaft up ahead but the weight of the missile launcher slowed him down. His chest was in agony. Raiden pushed himself to swim just a bit farther and ascend to the surface. Another few yards. He felt dizzy. Almost there. Hold it . . . hold it . . .

Raiden gasped the sweet air before he passed out. He treaded water for a full minute, resting his lungs and diaphragm. Then it was back to the elevator.

AFTER RETURNING TO 1F, the first thing Raiden did was to grab the Nikita rockets out of the Level 3 room next to the lift. He then made his way back to the electrified corridor. The Shadow Moses VR training scenario had required him to guide a remote-controlled missile through a jogging corridor and hit a target in a completely different room. It's what he would have to do in this real-life case, only through a narrow air duct instead of a hallway.

Raiden grabbed a crate and placed it beneath the vent in the hallway next to the electrified corridor. He stood on the box and smashed the mesh grill off the vent with the butt of his SOCOM. He then stuck the barrel of the Nikita launcher into the duct, turned on the targeting guidance system, and set his Codec for the appropriate map. A heat dot represented the President's position in the locked room. According to the map blueprint, the electrical circuit panel was located on a wall to his right, directly across from the exit vent. He was safely out of the way. The duct itself had three sharp jogs in it.

Here goes nothing, Raiden thought as he re-checked the controls and prepared to fire.

The Nikita jerked—but smoothly, as it was a beautifully designed precision instrument made for ease of use on the battlefield.

The missile moved quickly, of course, so Raiden had to be on top of the controls and operate them with split second reaction. *Straight. Turn. Straight. Straight. Get ready. TURN. Straight. Straight. Get ready! TURN! And . . . out!*

The missile broke through the exit vent, soared across the President's chamber—probably scaring the executive half to death—and exploded into the circuit panel. The lights in the corridor immediately extinguished. Raiden jumped off the crate, stored the launcher in the hallway, and gingerly tested the corridor leading to the chamber.

The voltage was off.

Raiden rushed to the door, used the Level 3 security card to open it, and stepped inside to meet the President of the United States.

22

RAIDEN PROCEEDED CAUTIOUSLY, the SOCOM drawn and ready. After walking through the first small room, the President approached him. Smoke was still drifting from the destroyed circuit breaker behind him. Raiden recognized the man—he'd seen him on television—and put his gun away.

"President Johnson," he said.

"So you're finally here . . ."

"You've been expecting me?" Raiden asked.

"Your equipment—that Skull Suit isn't exactly standard military issue."

President James Johnson was a man in his late fifties, handsome, charismatic, and physically fit. He didn't appear to have been harmed.

"Are you all right, sir?"

Johnson seemed surprised by the question. "Is this some kind of sick joke?"

"Huh?"

"I thought you came to kill me!"

Raiden shook his head, but the President stepped closer.

There was a plea in his eyes, a subtext that eluded Raiden for the moment. "I'm prepared to face the consequences of my betrayal," the man said.

"What are you—?"

The President suddenly pulled Raiden close to him and reached between his legs. The operative jerked away, startled by the man's intimate intrusion.

"You're . . . a man!" Johnson said. Apparently he had been confused by Raiden's androgynous appearance. Or perhaps he had been expecting a female assassin? At any rate, the President was embarrassed by his mistake—obviously Raiden had not been sent to kill him.

"Well, who *are* you?" he asked.

"FOXHOUND, sir."

"FOXHOUND!" Johnson nodded, turned, and walked a few steps away. "I see. Now things are starting to make a little sense." He sneered at himself with despair and abandon. The man took a moment to consider the situation and then turned back to Raiden.

"Switch over to nanocommunication so nobody can listen in."

"Yes, sir." Raiden went to Codec, and the two men communicated silently. "Do you read me, sir?"

"Uh . . . yes." The President wasn't used to speaking through Codec.

"Mister President, it's my understanding that the terrorists have managed to input the code sequence necessary for launching a nuclear strike."

"That's correct. I punched the sequence in myself."

"You're working for them?!"

"If you had asked me two hours ago, my answer would have been 'yes.' Right now, they're keeping me alive until my vital signs are reconfirmed."

"They betrayed you?"

"I wouldn't put it that way. We had a conflict of ideals . . . and I lost. I wanted power. They sought destruction."

Raiden was struck by the absurdity of the man's words. "Ideals? What kind of *ideals* can justify terrorism?"

"Any movement is driven by an ideal."

"But why stoop to terrorism?"

"I wanted absolute power."

"But you're the President! You have power!"

"No, I'm just a figurehead."

"Huh?"

"I don't have any control. The real power is in the Patriots' hands."

The Patriots. Solidus Snake had mentioned them. "Who are the Patriots?"

"The power controlling this country. I'm not surprised you've never heard of them. Very few are aware of their existence, even among those with maximum security clearance. Politics, the military, the economy—they control it all. They even choose who becomes President. Putting it simply, the Patriots rule this country."

Was this guy crazy? Raiden wondered.

"Hard to believe, isn't it?" Johnson asked. "But it's the truth. The Space Defense, income tax reduction, and the National Missile Defense programs—every policy that's been credited to me was actually done according to their instructions."

"Wait a second. Space Defense was initiated by Congress!"

"That's what the Patriots want the country to believe. It's all a show. 'Democracy' is merely filler for textbooks! Think about it. Do you actually believe that public opinion influences our government?"

Raiden had to admit it. "No."

"This country is shaped and controlled as the Patriots see fit. The people are shown what they want to believe. What you call government is actually a well-staged production aimed at satisfying the public." Johnson grimaced. "Don't look at me like that— I'm legally sane, you know."

"It's not your sanity that worries me."

The President allowed himself a smile, nodded, and then continued. "The Patriots—even I don't know who the actual members are. Are they financial, political, or military leaders? No one knows. Even my instructions come from a cutout. All I've been told is that every key decision is made by a group of twelve men known as the Wisemen's Committee."

"But your office . . . ! The White House . . . ?"

"Merely puppets. Pawns in a game. By pledging my loyalty, an insignificant son of a senator was awarded the Presidency. Of course, that wasn't the only price I had to pay."

"What do you mean?"

"Even if a pawn becomes a queen, it is still just a playing piece. I wanted to leave my own mark in history. But my ambitions were . . . used . . ."

"Huh?"

Johnson looked away. "You'll understand someday." After a moment's pause, he went on. "I wished to be a member of the Patriots. I wanted to wield the power of a king, instead of being an expendable pawn."

"And that justifies acts of terrorism?"

"Yes. I'd intended to use the new Metal Gear as a bargaining chip."

"*Bargaining chip?*"

"But I underestimated Solidus. He actually wants to challenge the Patriots—even if it means the destruction of the world!"

"What are you saying?"

"Whether you believe it or not, the balance of power rests in the hands of the Patriots. They regulate the country's various interests through controlled presentation, staging a 'drama' that is palatable to the general masses. Can you imagine what would happen if they ceased to function? Picture a massive political vacuum, a space that every power monger will try to fill for their own greedy ends. I'm talking about an unregulated power struggle—panic, civil war, chaos . . . Like it or not—the Patriots is an organization that must continue to exist."

"So you changed your mind because you wanted to avoid global chaos?" Raiden asked.

"Exactly. When I told Solidus that I wished to prevent disaster, he replied that pawns can never become players."

"And who is this . . . Solidus?"

"My predecessor. The forty-third President, George Sears! That was the name the public came to know him by. I knew him by his code name, 'Solidus Snake.' He was the third Snake, preceded by Solid and Liquid . . . a survivor of the *Les Enfants Terribles* project. Neither Solid nor Liquid, he was a well-balanced masterpiece that the Patriots saw fit to entrust with the Presidency. However, he fell out of grace with the organization four years ago when, acting on his own, he started an incident."

That rang a bell for Raiden. "Four years ago . . . Shadow Moses?"

"That's right. At the time, the DARPA chief, Donald Anderson—together with certain influential parties—initiated the development of Metal Gear REX and an advanced nuclear warhead. However, this did not fall in line with the Patriots' plans. What's more, Solidus decided on his own to send his most trusted man, Ocelot, to provoke Liquid Snake, bringing about the said incident. As a result, he succeeded in obtaining REX and data on the warhead. But in doing so, he ended up revealing the existence of both REX and the genome army—a blunder that earned him the wrath of the Patriots. Shortly thereafter, Solidus was removed from the Presidential Office."

"I thought he resigned."

"That's the story given to the general public. Following his 'resignation,' the Patriots selected me—their new pawn, for the Presidency."

"But that would mean that the Presidential race was—"

"That was quite a show wasn't it? It was a well-scripted drama staged by the Patriots for the benefit of the public. Even the Democrats and the Republicans were dancing to the Patriots' tune. Everything went according to plan, but for one exception. Following his resignation, Solidus' 'health' was scheduled to fail him, bringing about his untimely death."

"Capped?"

"Correct. But before the Patriots could execute their plot, Solidus went underground with the help of Ocelot. As he avoided pursuit, Solidus gained control of Dead Cell, winning over Colonel Gurlukovich's outfit. From there, he bided his time, knowing that his opportunity would soon arrive."

"What opportunity?"

"The completion of the new Metal Gear project—an opportunity that would even his odds against the Patriots. By stealing the Patriots' most valued project, he would be able to place them in a very uncomfortable position. It's the only chance he has for survival. Once he has the new Metal Gear, he'll declare war against the Patriots. Needless to say, he must be stopped."

"And Metal Gear is already operational . . ."

"No. Not yet."

"Huh?"

"What you saw was Metal Gear RAY—hijacked two years ago from the Marines by Ocelot. That was not the new Metal Gear."

"Then where's the new Metal Gear?"

"Right here."

"What?"

The President gestured around him. "You're standing in it. To be more precise, this entire Big Shell facility is the new Metal Gear."

"What'd you say?"

"No, I'm quite serious! The upper structure that you've seen is camouflage—designed to represent an offshore cleanup facility. The main structure extends from the foundation all the way down to the ocean floor. The connecting elevator is located on the B2 Shell One Core. 'Arsenal Gear' . . . that's the code name for the new Metal Gear."

"Arsenal—?"

"That's right. Arsenal. We're talking about an impregnable fortress carrying a load of a couple of thousand missiles, including nuclear warheads—all protected by a horde of mass-produced Metal Gear RAY units!"

"Mass-produced?"

"The RAY unit was originally designed for the Marines to be used as a countermeasure against the Metal Gear variations popping up throughout the world. The Patriots had RAY redesigned to protect the new Arsenal Gear."

The concept was mind-boggling. "So now anti–Metal Gears are *protecting* a Metal Gear?"

"Ironic, isn't it? That's not all. Arsenal Gear has full access to the military's tactical network, giving it the ability to exercise absolute control over our nation's armed forces, not to mention our nuclear armament. In short, Arsenal was created to be the core of our country."

Raiden was flabbergasted. "What kind of idiotic weapon—?"

"Weapon? No, you're not seeing the full picture. Arsenal Gear is more than just a military tool. It is a means to preserve the world as it is. It will establish a new form of control. The Patriots will use it to keep their place as the country's true rulers . . . Right now they feel pressured and threatened."

"By what?"

"They fear an overabundance of digital information. The world will drown in the coming flood of information, and they along with it."

"I don't get it."

"The Arsenal plans include a system to digitally manage the flow of information, making it possible to shape the 'truth' for their own purposes. In short, the Arsenal's system is the key to their supremacy."

"The key?"

"Yes, the 'GW' system. Short for George Washington. GW is the Patriots' trump card. Arsenal Gear will be fully operational when GW is successfully integrated. Once operational, it will be a completely new form of power for the Patriots to wield. I had hoped to seize the project from them so that I would be in a strong bargaining position."

"Bargain for what?"

"I'd hoped to trade my way into their ranks. But Solidus preferred rebellion. Outer Heaven—his plan to unleash a nuclear blast over the skies of Wall Street to break the Patriots' control over the business community—is also a key factor in his offensive effort."

"Outer Heaven . . ." Raiden remembered hearing Solidus mention the words.

"Listen. There isn't much time. The 'football' served as the key for activating Arsenal Gear. I've already input the necessary code sequence. It won't be long before GW begins to establish connections with other external systems and Arsenal Gear becomes fully operational. Stop them before that happens. That is your role."

"My *role*?"

"You've got to find Emma Emmerich. She's the only one who can stop that thing once it's been activated."

"Emma . . . *Emmerich*?" *I know that name*, Raiden thought.

"She's the system programmer for Arsenal Gear. I believe she's somewhere on Level B1 in the Central Core of this building."

"I thought the levels below us were flooded."

"I'm sure they won't let her die just yet as she's the only remaining programmer for this project. According to Ocelot, she was being held in a locker room located in the northwest part of Level B1. Cut transmission and get moving!"

Raiden nodded, but he was stunned by everything he had just

heard. The nanocommunication ceased and President Johnson handed him a PAN security card.

"This is a Level Four card. It'll give you access all the way to Emma's location." He then reached into the pocket of his trousers and removed a disc. "Give this to her when you find her."

Raiden took it. "What is it?"

"On that drive is a program for disrupting the control functions between GW and Arsenal Gear. Take Emma to the Computer Room on Level B2, Shell One Core. She'll know how to load the program into the main system."

"A virus?"

"That's right. Modeled after FOXDIE, a biological weapon designed to selectively eliminate personnel with a specific genetic code. The Patriots had it engineered as a fail-safe should anything go wrong with the project."

"But why do you have it?"

"Ocelot forgot to search me! Now, you've got to hurry. That disk is the only way you're going to stop Arsenal."

The President sighed heavily, as if he'd just relieved himself of a tremendous burden. He cocked his head slightly at Raiden and said, "Well, I've told you everything you need to know. There's only one thing that remains to be done." Johnson then took Raiden by surprise and seized the SOCOM from the operative's holster. He pointed the gun at his own chest just as Raiden grabbed the butt and the man's hands.

"Kill me!" Johnson shouted. "Now!"

"What the—!"

They grappled with the weapon.

"There's no time to argue! The final check for my vital ID will start any second! If you kill me now, you'll at least prevent the nuclear strike!"

Raiden attempted to pull the SOCOM away from him. "Cut it out!"

"Do it! That's your role!"

Raiden managed to pry the weapon from the man's hands—
and a shot rang out! Raiden heard it and saw the look of shock
and pain on the President's face. He was hit—but the SOCOM
had not discharged!

A familiar voice boomed behind Raiden. "That's abusing
your right to free speech, Mister President!" As Johnson fell to his
knees, clutching his bloody chest, Raiden whirled around and
saw Revolver Ocelot standing ten feet behind them, the six-
shooter raised and smoking. "Or is it . . . ex-President?" Ocelot
chuckled slightly, spun the revolver in his hand, and holstered it.

Raiden raised the SOCOM and pointed at the terrorist. "The
President! Why did you—?"

"Alas, my finger must have *slipped.*" He grinned, seemingly
unconcerned by the weapon pointed at him. "I'll see you around
. . . 'Carrier Boy.'" With that, Ocelot turned and walked away.

Shoot him! Raiden ordered himself. *Shoot him in the back!*

But he couldn't do it. Something—he didn't know what—
told him that it would do no good at this point. Besides, the President was still alive. He had to tend to the man.

Raiden knelt beside Johnson. The President clutched the operative's arm. "Forget him . . . he . . . did us a favor," the man gasped.

"Sir!"

"Everything I did . . . I thought I was in control . . . but it was
all an illusion. My feeble attempt at rebellion . . . I played right
into their hands. I've served their purpose . . ." He coughed up
blood. Raiden felt helpless—there was nothing he could do.
Johnson continued weakly, "Without free will, there is no difference between submission and rebellion. My only real choice is to
put an end to this charade . . . let me at least have the freedom . . .
to end it myself."

"What are you—?"

"Find Emma. Stop Arsenal. That is my last order—as your
Commander-in-Chief . . . I'm counting on you . . . !"

The man went limp as he exhaled a long, final breath.

23

RAIDEN STOOD AND shook his head. The mission was rapidly becoming a nightmare of epic proportions. He placed a call to his superior.

"Colonel, the President is dead."

"I see . . ." The Colonel sounded mystified by the development. "I'm sorry to hear that."

"Where do we go from here?"

"Your mission was to rescue the President and eliminate the terrorist threat. However, given the recent turn of events, we will honor the President's last directive. You must put a stop to Arsenal Gear once and for all."

"Do you actually think there's any truth to his story about this Big Shell facility being a front for Arsenal Gear?"

"I don't have the security clearance necessary to verify the facts. However, he *was* the President. I'm sure he knew what he was talking about."

"Aren't you forgetting that he was part of the terrorist plot?"

"All the more reason why I believe his information is reliable. We're talking about a man who chose to die rather than risk a nuclear holocaust. Thanks to his sacrifice, the nuclear launch authority has shifted to the Vice President, effectively eliminating the terrorist threat."

"Colonel, when you put it like that, it almost sounds like I should've assassinated the President to 'eliminate the threat.'"

"That was not my intention. I was trying to point out that there is certainly some credibility to the words of a man who chose death to protect the innocent."

Rose's face appeared on the Codec monitor. "The Colonel has a point, Jack."

"What about the information he gave me on the Patriots?"

The Colonel admitted, "That's a new one on me. I'll see what I can find out."

In response, Raiden simply made a grunt of frustration.

"Raiden, we're running out of time. Find Emma. She's supposed to be located on Level B1, in the Core of the building you're in, right?"

"Yes, sir."

"You've got to find her before Arsenal becomes fully operational."

"Hurry, Jack!" Rose pleaded.

"It's up to you to make sure that the President didn't sacrifice his life in vain," the Colonel added.

"Understood . . . Raiden out."

He signed off and stood there for a moment, staring at President Johnson's lifeless body. The secrets behind the mission were puzzles within puzzles. It was as if a godlike puppet-master was controlling the events, and Raiden felt as if he were merely one of the marionettes. But exactly who was the puppet-master? The so-called "Patriots"? Solidus? Someone else?

If you're just a puppet, why the hell should you know all the facts? Raiden asked himself. *You might as well get going. Find the woman and get on with the new mission objectives.*

He turned and walked out of the room, through the door, and

back into 1F. As he approached the elevator, a call came in on the Codec.

"What's your status, Raiden?"

"Snake! The President . . . he's been assassinated!"

"What?"

"There was nothing I could do . . . !"

"What about the nuclear strike code sequence?"

"He died before his vital ID could be reconfirmed."

"Then the enemy's lost their nuclear strike capability."

"But that Ocelot guy obviously killed the President on purpose."

"Why?"

"It doesn't make any sense. They had to know that they couldn't launch the nuke if they killed the President."

Otacon chimed in. "Maybe there's a way to launch without reconfirming the vital ID?"

"Or maybe they've found a more effective weapon within Arsenal Gear," Snake said.

"You knew about Arsenal Gear?" Raiden asked.

Snake sighed. "Yeah."

Is everyone on this mission keeping things from me? "Then why didn't you tell me about it?"

"You never asked."

"Am I correct in assuming you also know that the Big Shell is a front for the project?"

"You mean, did I know that the Big Shell, a fully functional environmental cleanup facility, was designed to camouflage Arsenal Gear? Yeah, I did. It's exactly that . . . a massive cover story. The good news is that it hasn't really done much in terms of cleaning up the environment, so we won't have to worry about any toxic gas being released if we have to blow the house down."

Raiden couldn't hide his irritation. "Right. And *when* did you find all this out?"

"It took a while, but we uncovered the info around the time

you took out that mad bomber. There's no doubt that Arsenal Gear is being built here . . . and it was all set up two years ago on that day—all of it."

"Two years ago . . ." Raiden said. "What really happened here?"

The Codec monitor displayed photos of Metal Gear RAY, one after the other.

"I took these photos two years ago," Snake said.

"I know these pictures. They were on the news and on several websites. If I remember right, the reporters blamed you for sinking the tanker."

"That's right. Otacon . . . me . . . we were used."

The photos vanished and Otacon appeared. "We'd hoped that by going public with photos of the new Metal Gear we could persuade the government. At least that was the plan at the time."

"Two years ago, on the Hudson River," Snake continued, "we had learned that a new Metal Gear model was being secretly transported. When I think about it now, we should've known better than to trust the information."

Raiden recalled key points of the tanker incident VR training simulation that he had gone through as Snake described them. Snake's version of the events was, of course, different.

"I'd infiltrated the dummy tanker to obtain proof that a Metal Gear was under development. Shortly after I made it aboard, an armed group led by Colonel Gurlukovich raided the ship and gained control."

"Olga and Ocelot were among the raiding party," Otacon added.

"Yeah. And *him*."

"Who're you talking about?" Raiden asked.

"A man that was supposed to be dead."

Otacon continued, "Their target was also Metal Gear RAY. But Ocelot eliminated Colonel Gurlukovich and Marine Commander Scott Dolph—and he hijacked RAY."

"So he betrayed them."

"I don't know what kind of deal was going down," Snake said. "All I remember is what Ocelot said at the time—'I'm taking it back.'"

"Ocelot then sank the tanker along with the soldiers of the Marine Corps," Otacon said grimly.

"How did you manage to get out?" Raiden asked.

"Otacon had a small boat ready for me."

Otacon laughed wryly. "That was the easy part. The tough part was not getting dragged down with the sinking tanker—small miracle when you think about it. It turned out that the whole thing was a setup to lure us. Photos of Snake—taken by a Cypher—were released to the public. In turn, we became the world's most wanted environmental terrorists."

"It was definitely a move aimed at putting a stop to our anti–Metal Gear activities," Snake said.

"But why did they choose Snake?"

"Since the Shadow Moses incident Snake became sort of a hero," Otacon said. "I think the Patriots weren't too happy about that."

Raiden gasped in frustration again. "You knew about the *Patriots*?"

"Well, yes . . . to a certain degree."

"It seems like everyone knows about them except me!"

"They didn't choose Snake to be a hero . . ."

"So they decided to do a smear campaign?"

"I think the Patriots wanted to make an example of him so everybody would think twice before opposing them."

"That's it? They set all this up just to nail you guys?"

"No, there's more to it than that. The Marines' Metal Gear RAY project headed by Commander Dolph was carried out in opposition to the Navy's Arsenal Gear project. To be more precise, the Patriots considered Metal Gear RAY to be a thorn in their side. Hence, they attacked the dummy tanker and stole RAY.

They followed this up with the perfect plan. They immediately sent a fully loaded tanker to the same location and sank it, then set up the facility to camouflage the development of Arsenal Gear."

"And we fell for it," Snake said. "Two more puppets in their show."

"Colonel Gurlukovich . . . and his daughter Olga?" Raiden asked.

"Both fell victim to Ocelot's plot," Otacon answered.

"Was Solidus behind all this? He used Ocelot to get hold of RAY?"

"No. He was underground, keeping a low profile at the time."

"Then it must be the Patriots."

"If that's the case, what's Ocelot doing alongside Solidus?" Otacon asked, mostly to himself.

"Forget it," Snake said. "We're wasting time. We can figure this out later. The nuclear strike's been prevented, but Arsenal still has a massive payload of missiles to deal with."

"Right," Otacon said, "if the opposition gets control of them . . ."

"Raiden, you've got to find Emma."

"Wait a second," Raiden said. "Isn't Emma Emmerich—?"

"My sister," Otacon answered with a sigh.

"What's she doing here?"

"You got me. She's a computer whiz who specializes in neural-AI and ultra-variable volume data analysis using complex logic. How she got involved in weapons development is beyond me."

"Whatever the reasons, we need her in order to stop Arsenal," Snake added.

"Raiden, find her," Otacon said quietly.

"I'm on my way."

He signed off and called the elevator. While he waited, he contacted his boss.

"Colonel, I want some background information on Emma Emmerich."

"I've got it right here," the Colonel said. "Direct from the National Security Agency's personnel files. Apparently she was involved in some sort of high-level project, but there are no details on that. Her record shows that she resigned from the agency two years ago. Emma Emmerich. Full name—Emma Emmerich-Danziger. Members of her family call her 'E.E.' Hal Emmerich's father married Emma's mother when Hal was a teenager and Emma was much younger, so Hal and Emma are step-siblings. After divorcing Hal Emmerich's father, Emma's mother took Emma to England and raised her there. Danziger is her mother's maiden name, but she prefers Emmerich. After returning home to England, her mother married a man named Robinson, a businessman. The following details are from a report filed with the NSA when she joined the agency.

"Just before graduating from high school, Emma injured Robinson in self-defense during an alleged assault on her person. As a result of this incident, she followed in the footsteps of her stepbrother, Hal Emmerich, and left home to enroll at Oxford. It is believed that at this particular point in her life, she was extremely angered by the fact that her brother failed to protect her. Consequently, she severed all family connections and is very resentful. She seems to believe that her brother is to blame for everything. While attending Oxford, she was noted for her success in a deciphering event sponsored by British GCHQ."

The elevator doors opened and Raiden stepped inside. "They may not be blood-related," he said, "but she sure sounds like Otacon's sister." He pressed the button for B1.

"There's more. Raiden, do you recall a certain situation that's more or less become a legend among hackers? To refresh your memory—at the time, just about all of our nation's communications and information resources were concentrated at NSA, in Fort Meade. In fact, NSA's basement facility operated round-the-clock to amass data obtained not only from public communications, but everything from satellite to wiretap operations as well. I don't think I'm exaggerating when I say that whoever controlled the NSA facility could move the world. On January 24th of 2000, the facility suffered a total system shutdown for a seventy-three-hour period."

"Did they ever figure out the cause?"

"It's believed that a small group within the government had arranged the incident with the assistance of a notorious group of hackers. The result was a full review of NSA's safety measures, which in turn led to the decision to shift the data-gathering operations to an isolated location that would be safe from physical attack as well as cyber-terrorism."

"And where might that be?"

"My security clearance couldn't get me that information. But I did find out that one of the key members of the hacker group was none other than Emma Emmerich. Although she started off as a specialist in artificial intelligence and complex logic, Emma is now regarded as a computer genius."

Raiden wondered if that "small group within the government" was the Patriots. "That would make her a prime candidate for recruitment in the intelligence community, wouldn't it? And knowing most of the intelligence agencies, I doubt fair play was a major concern in their recruiting efforts."

The elevator arrived at B1. Raiden carefully looked out the doors before leaving the lift. He was alone.

"Your assumption's correct. The government played on her weakness—her strong hate for Hal Emmerich, the brother who left her when she was six years old."

"She hates him that much?"

"When she was six, Emma and her father were involved in a pool accident. She survived, but her father drowned."

"What did the police have to say about that?"

"Their report states it was an accidental death."

"Isn't that about the time that Otacon left his home and family?"

"Exactly. But I don't have any idea why he chose to do so."

"Does Emma blame Otacon for her father's death?"

"I don't think so. Her hate seems to stem from the fact that she believes Otacon abandoned her. You see, although the two weren't directly related, they were said to be very close. It's rumored that sibling rivalry was what launched her career as a hacker. Four years ago the government leaked her the details of the Shadow Moses incident. In doing so they were able to recruit her for the NSA. I have little doubt that they also used the NSA hacking affair as a means to 'convince' her to cooperate."

"You think that her hate drove her to frame Snake and Otacon?"

"That I don't know."

Raiden signed off.

The mission just kept getting more dramatic by the minute.

24

THE CODEC buzzed again.

"Jack?"

"What is it, Rose?"

She hesitated. "I've always been alone."

"Huh?"

"I'm so lonely."

"Lonely? Rose, we've always—"

"Not always."

"What do you mean?"

"You've never slept beside me."

"What are you *talking* about?"

"After we've been together in my room . . . you stay awake all
night or you head for the door."

Raiden rubbed his brow. "Is this really the time to bring this
up?"

"Why, Jack? Why?"

"Listen, Rose, "I'm right in the middle of—"

"Why? Why can't you relax when you're with me?"

"Look . . . the mission . . . !"

"Why don't you open up to me?"

"Rose! I . . . I . . ." He gave up trying to avert the conversation. He stopped moving and leaned against a wall. "I just can't."

She went on. "All I ever wanted was to share your dreams— to spend a meaningful evening with you. I just wanted to find you by my side when I woke up. Is that asking too much?"

Raiden fumbled for words. Then he just came out with it. "It's the night. I'm scared of the night. It's got nothing to do with you."

"Scared of the night? What's that supposed to mean?"

"I can't relax when I'm with someone . . ."

"Jack? You wouldn't even let me into your room!"

"I need privacy. I just can't be bothered."

"Bothered?"

"Wrong word. What I wanted to say was that there are certain things that I have to keep to myself."

"Do you remember that time I forced my way into your room? We'd known each other for almost a year . . . and you blew up! It was the first time you ever raised your hand against me."

Raiden saw on the monitor that she was crying. *What brought this on?*

"I was so worried about you . . ." she sniffed.

"Look . . . I'm sorry . . . !"

"It wasn't your violent nature that scared me. It was your room . . . your heart . . ."

"Stop it . . ."

"There wasn't anything in your room—only a bed and a small desk. It looked like a prison cell."

"Rose?"

"No television set . . . no family pictures . . . not even a poster . . ."

"Rose, I only use that room for sleeping."

"A lifeless room . . . almost like your empty heart . . ."

"That's why I tried to keep you out."

"I thought I was beginning to understand you—until I saw that room."

He couldn't help being sarcastic. "Would you've been happier if I had a picture of you hanging on the wall?"

"That's not what I was trying to say."

"Enough, Rose. We'll talk about this later . . . after the mission."

"Right. After the mission. I understand."

And she signed off.

What the—?

Never mind. He couldn't deal with her at the moment. Time to focus on his surroundings. B1 was much more flooded than it had been when he had been there earlier. Now the water was up to his thighs. He waded toward the stairwell entrance to the underwater corridor. Emma was supposed to be in a locker room on the northwest corner of the floor. That was back through the passage where he had found the Nikita. All he remembered was the L-shaped hallway and the supply closet at the end. Raiden studied the Codec map and determined that there was indeed another corridor leading off from the L toward the northwest. It must have been blocked or something and he hadn't noticed it before. He hoped it wasn't covered by anything he couldn't move.

No more wasting time. Raiden took a deep breath and dived in.

The water seemed murkier. Perhaps more junk from the Hudson had seeped in. Raiden paused long enough to put on his night-vision goggles, which he had forgotten to do. This helped considerably, but visibility was still subpar. Nevertheless, he continued to stroke forward until he came to the L-jog. He didn't stop. Raiden swam on, hoping that the air pocket he had used for a breather was still there. It wasn't too far ahead.

The blocked passage was to his left, closer than the air pocket. He took a moment to evaluate the situation. It didn't appear to be a big deal—the hallway entrance was blocked by a disabled maintenance vehicle—something like a golf cart. Raiden had simply not noticed it as anything significant during his first trip through the aquatic corridors.

He ignored it for the moment and swam on until he saw the blessed shaft of light, which was still there. He ascended to the top, broke the surface, and breathed. The ceiling was now a mere inch or two from his face. After adequately filling his lungs, Raiden dived and swam back to the maintenance cart. Thanks to the water, the vehicle had enough buoyancy that Raiden could push it out of the way easily. He then went on into the unexplored hallway.

The layout of the level made sense to Raiden now. The map showed that the filtration floor was divided into chambers. He had been in only one of them. There was a hatch at the end of this corridor that would lead to another chamber. The northwest section was beyond that. Raiden swam easily, conserving his strength and oxygen, but it wasn't long before he needed to fill his lungs again. The distance seemed much farther than it appeared on the Codec map!

He came upon a shaft of light just as he was becoming un-comfortable. He rose to the surface and found himself just be-neath an air vent. It was a nice place to park for a moment and recharge.

The Codec buzzed.

"Raiden, are you reading me? This is Otacon. What's your sit-uation?"

"Wet and miserable. This place is flooded. The seawater that's been pumped up is pouring into the building."

"I see. Listen, there's something I have to tell you about E.E."

"Don't worry about her. I'll get her out—"

"She's afraid of water."

Raiden wasn't sure he heard the man right. "What?"

"Yeah. When she was six years old, she almost drowned with my father in our swimming pool."

Uh-oh. "She can't swim?"

"Well, yes and no. We used to swim a lot together when we were kids. In fact, she swam like a fish until that day when she almost drowned."

That pretty much coincides with what the Colonel told me, Raiden thought.

"When the accident happened, I was in my room. I learned later that E.E. was calling me for help. She didn't doubt for a minute that I'd be there. You could see the pool from my room . . . but I didn't realize at the time that she needed me."

"What were you doing?"

"I . . . I was . . ."

Otacon obviously didn't want to elaborate. "So Emma survived the ordeal," Raiden said.

"Yeah. But my father didn't."

"So you blamed yourself and left your family?"

"No. E.E. seems to believe that was the case. The fact is . . . I betrayed her."

"And you think that she can't swim because of the traumatic experience?"

"I haven't seen her since that day . . . but yes, I think so. I got a letter from Julie, her mother, after they moved back to England. In her letter, she mentioned that E.E. couldn't swim anymore. She refused to even wear a bathing suit."

"Damn! If she still can't swim, we're in trouble. Level B1 in the Core is pretty much flooded."

"Look . . . maybe you can help her overcome the trauma."

"You want *me* to help her get over it?"

"It's still going to take some time to repair the Kamov."

Snake busted into the conversation. "Sorry, kid. Emma's rescue is up to you."

Raiden snorted. "Thanks. An underwater mission." He hadn't done that in VR training. "Look—I'll see what I can do."

"I suggest you drum the map of the building into your head,"

Snake said, "'cause you won't have time to look at it when you try to bring Emma out." .

"I'm counting on you, Raiden," Otacon said.

"I covered most of the Core when I had to take out the C4s. If there's anything you need to ask me, call me on the Codec."

"I'll do that."

Raiden signed off, took a breath, and continued to swim toward the end of the corridor. Eventually he came to the hatch, which was closed. Raiden grabbed the wheel and turned it, releasing a swarm of bubbles from the seal. He opened the door and—

—came face-to-face with the bloated, mutilated corpse of Peter Stillman.

Raiden reflexively opened his mouth and yelped in surprise and fright, losing some of his precious air.

Stillman had been badly disfigured by the explosion. The cadaver's arms were spread as if the man were trying to embrace Raiden. The water around him was a ruddy brown from the blood.

Raiden got hold of himself and pushed the body out of the way. It floated to the side and came to rest against a wall. The operative swam through the hatch and continued his journey into the second chamber. The corridor continued for another thirty yards or so. The C4 had wrecked the place—the walls were in shreds, and pieces of machinery, tools, and fallen girders littered the passage. After a short jog to the west, Raiden came to a short stairwell—going up—and there was light at the top. He swam toward it and broke the surface. As in the first Filtration Chamber, part of the level was higher than the rest. Raiden climbed out, waded through three-inch-deep water, and left the stairwell.

He entered a fairly large room that hadn't been flooded. The chamber had a high ceiling, a catwalk around the wall so that workers could access the tall filtration machines. In the middle of the room was a Sediment Pool filled with water. The ceiling threw back the diffused reflection of the surface. Beams of light radiated from the water and danced on the walls and ceiling, giving the room a certain surreal atmosphere. But the most unusual thing about it was the man *sitting* cross-legged like a guru on top of the pool. On the surface.

It was Vamp.

Raiden's eyes widened. *How is that possible?*

The vampire almost appeared to be suspended slightly above the water. The hair on his chest was highly noticeable. His eyes were closed. His forehead was marked with the open gunshot wound inflicted by Raiden earlier.

Raiden drew the SOCOM. "Still ticking, huh?" he asked.

Vamp's eyes opened. "Unfortunately, hell had no vacancies."

The vampire began to breathe steadily, focusing on his concentration. He slowly stood as if he were easing the tension in his body. The routine looked as if it was a dancer's stretch exercise.

Raiden shouted, "Ha!" and fired the SOCOM.

As if executing a series of ballet moves, Vamp elegantly dodged the bullets—but remained over the water!

Raiden was shocked that he couldn't hit the guy.

Vamp bent forward in a low bow. A line of blood trickled down his cheek. He then stood tall and glared at Raiden. He laughed and said, "I thought so. Human muscles are quite eloquent. They speak out clearly what a person's next move will be. They even tell me which way a gun is going to be pointed before the trigger is pulled. But your muscles—they're different. This should be fun. Well worth the wait!"

"You knew I was coming?"

"You've become a nuisance. I can't let you interfere with Arsenal Gear." He indicated the direction behind him. "The girl is just ahead. She is of no use to us now. But she served us well as the live bait for the big catch. Crazy Ivan sometimes speaks the truth."

He must mean the Russian—Ocelot, Raiden thought. "Emma's alive?"

"She was . . . some time ago. But the flooding has become quite serious—I wouldn't be surprised if she's a mermaid now."

Raiden wanted to curse at the inhuman being.

"Did you really think killing the President would prevent a nuclear strike?" Vamp asked. "Think again."

"I didn't do it!"

"Hmm. Arsenal is still armed with a purified hydrogen bomb."

"What?"

"This is no ordinary nuclear bomb. This weapon is capable of heavy hydrogen nuclear fusion using lasers and magnetics to generate heat-insulated compression. It was a top secret project initiated by the current President . . . and Solidus has no idea of its existence. The clean thermonuclear bomb is at an experimental stage and is handled differently. Specifically, it becomes launch-capable when Arsenal is activated. A nuclear threat still exists."

"Then Wall Street could still—?"

"That was Solidus' intent. Not ours."

"Then, what are you . . . ?"

"We're not going to let Solidus have the bomb. He's a fool to believe that an electromagnetic pulse over Wall Street is going to faze the Patriots. To destroy them the city that they control must be reduced to rubble. Only that will bring them out in the open where they can be destroyed."

"Nuke the city?!"

"Six months ago, we lost everything we believed in. We were abandoned to take the fall in their cover-up. We were labeled as killers responsible for the mass murder of civilians as well as our own allies. And the 'public' believed every word, turning a deaf ear to whatever we had to say to the contrary. Our only goal is to wipe them from the face of the earth—and destroy this world of deceit they have created along with them."

"You're insane," Raiden spit.

"Insane? We might be the only ones telling the truth!"

A burst of static resounded over the Shell-wide PA system.

The noise echoed in the Pool Room. Then a voice announced, "Final check for activating Arsenal has been completed." Raiden recognized it as belonging to none other than Solidus Snake. "All Arsenal personnel report to your stations."

"Well," Vamp said calmly. "It sounds like Arsenal's ready to go into operation."

All Raiden could do was to express his frustration and anger. "Damn it!"

"You're still hoping that the girl can install that virus that you're carrying around, aren't you?"

"You know . . . ?"

"It's a shame you're not going to be around long enough to hand her the program." He nodded his head at the pool of water. "That isn't seawater, you know. It's a by-product of the microbes contained in the pool. The density of the water is extremely low as a result of benign aerobic bacteria taking in the supplied oxygen. Buoyancy is practically nonexistent thanks to the high oxygen content. Once you fall in you don't come up. So take a good look at your grave."

The vampire then grinned, showing his fangs. A long, red tongue slithered out of his mouth and licked the blood trickling down his cheek.

"Show me what you got!" Raiden challenged with a growl.

Vamp leaped into the air, simultaneously throwing a cluster of knives at Raiden. The operative saw them coming, dropped, rolled, and came up out of harm's way. As the vampire dropped to the pool surface, Raiden blasted him again with the SOCOM. The creature seemed to brush the bullets away with his cape as he performed a whirling-dervish maneuver. Raiden ran to another side of the room; the lights above him created a long shadow that stretched across the pool. Vamp ceased twirling, reached out, and *grabbed* Raiden's shadow. Raiden suddenly felt as if he'd been pulled from behind. He plummeted backward and landed on his back.

Vamp laughed maniacally. "You're wasting your time!" Vamp released the imprisoned shadow, allowing Raiden to get up and move.

How did he do that?

Before Raiden could bother with answering his own question, the vampire leaped to the upper structure, hung on to the catwalk with one hand, and unleashed a volley of knives with his other. The knives struck the floor mere inches from Raiden's feet in all directions. He was pinned, for the monster seemed to have an unlimited supply of blades at his disposal.

Vamp aimed his throws closer to Raiden's feet, forcing the operative to jump back and forth in order to dodge them. At first Vamp had only wanted to restrain him; now the guy was really trying to hit him. Raiden cartwheeled out of the target area and landed next to a large lead pipe that extended from floor to ceiling. He ducked behind it, giving him enough time to holster the useless SOCOM, and ready the AK.

Let's see how he dodges machine guns!

Raiden stepped out from behind his cover and let loose with a maelstrom of spray fire. Vamp pushed off from the catwalk, *bounced* off the floor below, soared into the air above the pool, and dived straight in. The low density of the pool didn't seem to affect the vampire at all.

Had he hit him? Raiden was almost certain that some of the bullets had struck the figure.

He noticed his long shadow across the pool. Raiden didn't want to fall into that predicament again, so he raised the AK and shot out the work lights on the ceiling. He then turned to fire at the lights behind him, but Vamp burst out of the pool like a fish jumping for a low-flying bird. He held a knife and plunged it into what was left of Raiden's shadow. The knife dug deeply into the concrete around the pool, virtually pinning the shadow to it. Raiden attempted to pull away but he couldn't move. His feet were firmly planted where he stood attached to a shadow that was now out of his control.

Raiden twisted his body so that he could get a better shot—and fired at the remaining lights behind and above him. The bulbs shattered loudly, plunging the room into darkness, save for the lights in the pool itself. The illumination, cast through the shimmering surface of the water, made foreboding, flickering patterns on the walls and ceiling.

He no longer had a shadow, so Raiden was free to move. He slipped behind the pipe once again and dug into his backpack. He found several grenades he had confiscated, plucked three frags, and readied one in his right hand.

Vamp leaped into the air once again; this time he clung to the opposite catwalk, a vantage point from where he could see the operative.

"You can't hide now!" the monster called. He threw more knives, forcing Raiden to do a body roll out from behind the pipe. Vamp dropped to the floor, a mere six feet from Raiden. He held a long blade in his hand, ready to attack. Raiden knew he couldn't let the guy near him—he had witnessed what the vampire was capable of doing to enemies in close proximity. Vamp had sliced and diced most of SEAL Team Ten, and they had outnumbered him.

Raiden pulled the pin with his teeth and tossed the frag grenade at the Dead Cell member. He then skirted quickly behind the lead pipe. The explosion rocked the room, and the vampire cried out in pain. The pipe protected Raiden from the blast, but he didn't stay under cover long. The operative stepped out, the AK ready, and blasted the stunned figure in front of him.

Vamp screamed an unearthly cry and shook with force as the rounds penetrated his body; but the nonhuman managed to jump away and dive into the pool once again.

Raiden cursed aloud, but he knew he had hurt the monster.

He had seen the thing's dead flesh ripped off of its body, first from the grenade blast and secondly from the AK fire. The question was . . . could he kill something that was already dead?

He took hold of the second frag grenade and held it to his mouth. He moved around the pool to another side. Raiden could see the dark shape of Vamp's body underwater still treading. The creature was preparing to spring out and attack again. Raiden pulled the pin in anticipation, started counting, and waited.

One . . . come on, do your thing, mister. . . !

Vamp remained underwater.

Two . . . hurry up, damn it!

He was going to have to toss it. A wasted grenade . . .

Three . . . !

The water surface broke as Vamp shot out of the pool. At the same time, Raiden flung the grenade at the ascending figure and ducked. The explosion hit Vamp full in the face, successfully knocking him out of the air. He tumbled like a bat that had been shot mid-flight and fell on his back. There wasn't much of a splash due to the low water density. Vamp floated on top of the pool, still and lifeless. To make sure, Raiden aimed the AK and unleashed several bursts of rounds at the vampire's body.

Vamp slowly sank as blood spread over the surface, which, oddly, began to *boil.*

Raiden had seen a lot of strange things in his short lifetime— but he had never encountered anything as ungodly as the creature known as Vamp.

He made a call on the Codec.

"Colonel! They've apparently completed the final check procedure on Arsenal Gear!"

"Find Emma on the double!" the Colonel answered. "You've got to get her to install the virus program that the President gave you. When you find her, take her to the Computer Room on Level B in the Shell One Core!"

Raiden changed frequencies. "Snake! Did you catch all that? I didn't make it on time. Arsenal's going active!"

"Yeah, I heard. The hostage rescue's gonna have to wait."

"I'm going after Emma."

"We'll secure the Computer Room. Looks like we can't install the virus program without Emma."

"Can't your partner do it?"

Otacon answered, "I would if I could. But the security for this system is no joke. I need more time . . ."

"That's why we need her," Snake insisted.

"Understood. I'll make sure you have your family reunion."

Otacon started to say something but hesitated.

"What's up?" Raiden asked.

"A lot of years have passed between E.E. and me."

"Then you should see her. Right?"

"I don't have the right to see her."

Snake interrupted. "We can talk about this later, Raiden. I think you'd better get moving."

"I'm on it!"

25

RAIDEN CHECKED the Soliton Radar maps on the Codec. It was unable to receive a transmission of the area between the Pool Room and the Control Room. Probably because a good deal of it was underwater or perhaps destroyed. Snake was right. He'd have to memorize the path for the return trip with Emma.

He went through the passageway Vamp had indicated and went north to a section of corridor that had collapsed and was completely submerged. Slipping on the thermal goggles again, Raiden dived into the cloudy water and swam forward. The passage went west into darkness. After a couple of minutes' swimming, he came to a staircase that descended a flight. From there the corridor doubled back east. Raiden saw light on the surface — it was as good a place as any to catch a breath of air.

Raiden ascended, breathed, and looked around. The space he was in had a curved, glass window that was also part of the ceiling. The curvature allowed for about six inches of headroom. From there he could see the northernmost room on the higher, unflooded level. Raiden spotted a young woman in the open doorway. The Locker Room. Emma.

He took a breath and held it, then resumed the underwater journey. At the end of the corridor were two different hallways going north. Raiden faced them, pondering which path to take. His intuition leaned toward the one on the left, so that's the way he went. He swam for almost a minute and came to the end—the corridor doubled back to the left and up a flight of stairs to fresh air. Raiden climbed out, shook himself like a dog, and padded to a door—now closed—marked LOCKERS.

The place was empty. The only sign of recent activity was some food garbage littered around a trash can, a blanket and pillow on a bench, a few empty soda cans, and a dripping faucet attached to a sink.

She's in here somewhere.

"Emma?" he called. "Emma Emmerich?"

She's hiding.

"It's all right. I won't hurt you."

Silence.

Raiden walked slowly around the place. He knocked on the bathroom door—and looked in after there was no response. Vacant.

Raiden returned to the middle of the Locker Room.

She's in one of the lockers.

Starting with the one on the far left, Raiden went to each locker and opened it. Then closed it. One after the other . . . opened . . . closed . . . opened . . . closed . . .

Raiden heard a tiny squeak of fear in a locker not far ahead from where he was. He moved two steps to the right and opened the door.

She screamed.

"It's all right!" Raiden shouted.

The girl went silent. She sat on the floor of the locker, knees raised, trembling. She was scared to death.

Raiden held out his hands, palms upward, the way one would for a pet. "I'm not an enemy. See?"

"Who are you?" she whispered.

"Raiden. I'm getting you out of here."

She didn't believe him. "Get me out . . . ?" The girl shook her head. "You're lying! Where're you taking me this time?" She drew back into the locker, cowering against the metal.

"What are you talking about?" Raiden said. "I'm here to help!"

Emma whimpered but her brow creased. She was thinking about it.

"Here—I'll prove it." He slowly reached out to her neck and touched the skin where a Codec might be. "Do you have nanos?" She didn't answer, but there was a flicker of recognition in her eyes. "Well, do you?"

"I do," she answered. "Everybody on this project has them . . ."

"Good. Let's try."

He switched to nanocommunication and hooked up with her frequency. "Can you hear me?"

"Yes."

"Well, I have nanomachines, too."

"Then you're not one of them . . ."

"That's what I've been trying to tell you."

"And you came to *rescue* me?" She still didn't believe it.

"Actually, I need your *help*. To stop Arsenal. I understand you're the only one who might be able to do it."

"And who told you that?"

"The President."

"Really?" There was doubt in her voice. She didn't trust him yet.

"I need you to come with me to Shell One. Your brother's waiting for you there."

"My—" Her eyes widened as if he'd punched her in the face. "My brother?"

Suddenly there was an explosion somewhere above or below them. The room shook and the lockers rattled.

"Come on! We have to get moving! This place'll be flooded soon."

He held out his hand again. She stared at it, at him . . . then slowly raised her own arm. She tentatively placed her hand in his and allowed him to pull her out of the locker.

Raiden was surprised by how cute she was. She was dressed in a two-tone T-shirt with black short pants. Her bare legs were pretty and youthful. Her brown-red hair was secured behind her head with two chopsticks. She had an adorable face and wore red-framed glasses, giving her a nerdy, yet sexy, persona.

The room shook again. Water sprang from cracks in the ceiling and walls.

"We'd better move."

"I . . . I can't swim!" she cried. He didn't let go of her hand. "Leave me!"

Raiden pulled her close and looked into her eyes. "You can swim! You used to love it!"

She sniffed. "How . . . how did you know?"

"Your brother told me."

"He's really here?"

"That's right. He's here to rescue you."

She tried to push away from him but Raiden held her tightly. "I don't believe you! He would never come for me!"

"And I'm telling you he's here! Waiting for us in Shell One!"

"No! He left me . . . my mother—when we needed him the most! When my father died all he could think about was himself!" She hung her head in misery, her eyes welling with tears.

"Emma, we can go over all that later. But first, we have to get out of here!"

"No! I hate water!" Almost like a stubborn child, she became emotional, screaming her objections. "It's hopeless! I can't swim!"

I did not sign on for this! Raiden thought. A *psychiatrist I'm not!*

"Emma . . . please . . . come on. You can do this. I know you can. You don't want to die here!"

"No!"

"Look, let me just show you." She let him pull her through the door to the top of the stairs . . . for some reason she couldn't walk very well and had to lean on him . . . her eyes widened with fear when she saw that the water level was at the top of the stairwell.

"You can piggyback. I'll do all the work. You just hold your breath and hold on. You can do that."

"No . . . no . . . I can't . . ."

"Emma . . . please!"

"I can't keep my eyes open in the water . . ."

"You don't have to. I'll guide you."

"I . . . I was injected with something! My legs . . . see . . . I have trouble moving them!"

It was true. She was very unsteady. Her legs trembled. They'd been "asleep."

"Just hold your breath, Emma. Take a deep breath. I'll do the rest. First we'll head for Filter Chamber Two. Then we'll take a break."

"And all I have to do is hold my breath?"

"That's right."

"How long?"

Better not tell her the truth! "Just a little while."

"Are you sure?"

"Of course I'm sure! That's how I got here!"

"I don't think I can do it. I'm not good at holding my breath."

Raiden racked his brain. How was he going to ease this girl's mind?

"Look, Emma, I have an idea."

She looked at him as if she were eager to hear one.

"Put your ear against my back and listen to my heartbeat."

"Your . . . heartbeat?"

He nodded and helped her climb onto his back. "Go ahead. Put your head down." She did so. "Now count the beats. Don't think about anything else. When you reach a hundred, open your eyes. By that time, we'll be on the other side." She nodded her head. "Give me a signal if you think you're running out of breath."

"What will you do then?"

"I'll swim faster."

She hesitated and then nodded.

"Hang on tight . . ."

"I'm closing my eyes . . ."

"Take some deep breaths . . . One . . . two . . . thr—"

"Wait!"

Raiden groaned. "What is it?"

Releasing her grip on Raiden, she stood on wobbly knees. She continued to hold on to his arm with one hand. "Let me take off my glasses . . ."

She did so and Raiden said, "You know, you should wear contacts."

"There's nothing wrong with my eyes. I . . . I wear them for show."

"Trying to be different from the other girls?"

"No, it's not like that. I like glasses. And . . . there's a guy I liked who used to wear them . . ."

"Your first boyfriend?"

"No . . . somebody more important. Anyway, they bring me luck."

"I see . . ." Actually, he didn't, but he decided to humor her. She folded her glasses and held them in her hand as if they were some kind of precious charm. She then put her arms around Raiden again.

"I'm ready," she said.

"Okay, let's go!"

Raiden dived smoothly into the water with Emma clinging to his neck and shoulders. The swimming was much more difficult with the added weight. Raiden now questioned whether or not this was the best idea. It was too late to turn back, though. He had to turn on the strength but conserve the limited oxygen in his lungs. Not an easy task.

They made it down the steps and around the hall headed south to the east–west corridor. She clung tightly to him but gave no sign she was in distress. Raiden remembered the way through and swam toward the light, the big curved window where he had stopped the first time. He didn't know if she was counting as he'd told her to do, but he was certain that it took only sixty or seventy seconds to make it there.

They broke the surface and Emma gasped. They both breathed heavily for a minute, catching their breath.

"You all right?"

She nodded.

"Okay, here we go again. We're almost to the first stop."

She nodded and took a deep breath. Raiden submerged and swam around the corner, down the hall to the east, and finally up the stairs. When they were standing in Filtration Chamber 2, he had to catch her to keep her from falling. Her legs were still not strong enough to support herself. Raiden helped her over to a wall and they sat down to rest. Raiden intentionally sat five feet away from her to give her some space.

After a minute of silence, Raiden said, "You did good."

"I concentrated on your heartbeat," she said softly. "It . . . it reminded me of when I was a kid."

He looked at her and she tentatively smiled at him. He had gained her trust.

"I remembered my brother giving me a piggyback ride. I was sleeping with my ear against his back. I could hear his heartbeat."

"Sounds like you were close."

"We were . . . back then." She was quiet for a while. The only sound was the rippling of the pool echoing in the room. Then she spoke again. "We were stepchildren in our parents' second marriages. Wherever my brother went, I used to tag along. My brother didn't have any close friends, so he used to take care of me. We both wanted to be loved so much—so much that we used to pretend . . ."

When she didn't go on, Raiden prompted her. "Pretend?"

"Yeah. We used to play house." She lowered her head and blushed, but there was a smile on her face. "My brother was the husband and I was the wife." She looked up quickly. "But it was always just make believe! We were only kids. You know what I mean?"

Raiden thought about it before answering. "I never had a family. But I think I know what you mean."

His Codec buzzed. It was the Colonel.

"Raiden, what's your status?"

"Colonel, I've got Emma Emmerich here. We've managed to avoid drowning."

"Good job. Get her over to Shell One as soon as you can."

"That's going to be hard with the connecting bridge on the upper level destroyed."

"Didn't Olga say something about taking the oil fence at the bottom of Strut L?"

"Yeah . . . I remember that."

"You should be able to go down by way of Strut L. Try and get over there."

"What about Emma? She's been injected with something and she can't walk without my help."

"Then you'll have to carry her!"

He nodded and looked at Emma. She smiled sheepishly. "We're on our way." He signed off, only to catch another call, this time from Snake.

"Raiden, we've infiltrated the Computer Room. What's your situation?"

"Emma's safe," he answered. "We're heading your way."

Otacon appeared on the monitor. "Good job!"

"Shell One's deserted," Snake said. "Looks like everybody's aboard Arsenal."

"I had a good look at the system," Otacon said, "but there's nothing I can do. E.E.'s our only hope."

"Right. I'll put her on."

"Huh?" Otacon's eyes went wide. "E.E.? How . . . ?"

"I'll use my Codec as a relay."

Otacon, suddenly very nervous, cleared his throat.

"Here she is . . ."

For the first time in years, the stepsiblings greeted each other, albeit through nanocommunication.

"Uh . . . E.E.? Is that you?"

"Hal . . . ?"

"E.E. . . ."

Neither of them was sure of what to say. And then Otacon blew it by asking, "E.E., why are you involved with Metal Gear?"

"Huh?" She was obviously rattled by his aggressive tone. It wasn't what she was expecting.

"You knew our family's dark history and still got involved? What's wrong with you?"

"I should've known!" Her disappointment was evident.

"Answer me! Why are you repeating the same mistake?"

"I wanted to hurt you! I wanted to see you suffer!"

"E.E.!"

"You abandoned me!"

"No! That's not what happened!"

Snake cut in to the conversation. "All right, that's *enough*!"

Otacon seemed relieved by the reprieve.

"Who are you?" Emma asked.

"I'm a friend of Otacon's, Emma," he answered.

"Otacon . . ."

"Enough with the sibling rivalry!"

"That's not what this is!"

"We haven't got time for it! Raiden! Get her over here right now!"

Raiden took back control of the Codec and answered, "Gotcha, Snake. I'll head over there with her."

"Most of the enemy's aboard Arsenal. I suggest you be careful. Make sure Emma gets here in one piece."

"Raiden," Otacon said, "take care of my sister."

"Don't worry, I'll get her there."

He signed off and turned to the girl. She was pouting over the exchange she'd had with her brother. "Emma, Snake and Hal are waiting for us in Shell One's Computer Room. I've got this disk that the President gave me." He pulled it out and showed it to her. Emma seemed to come out of her funk as she examined the software. "It's supposed to contain a virus that can corrupt Arsenal Gear's operating system. We need you to—"

"This is my program," she said.

"What?"

"Why did the President give it to you? Did something happen to him?"

Raiden winced. "He's dead."

"What?"

He nodded grimly but quickly returned to the subject. "You actually wrote that virus?"

"It's not really a virus. It's more like a worm cluster. It's actually a delayed-effect autonomous program that's designed to invade GW's cerebrum and render its nerve connections useless."

"You know what GW is?"

"Of course. I created it."

Raiden was flabbergasted. *This girl is* that *smart?*

"You look surprised."

"Uh . . . well . . ."

"Cat got your tongue?"

"Uh, sorry. How about the Patriots? Ever heard of them?"

"Yes."

Raiden nodded. *It figures.*

"But I only know what I've been told."

"Can you tell me what you know?" he asked.

"Uh, it's hard to put into words." She gestured with her head and raised her eyebrows. At first Raiden didn't understand . . . but then he got it.

They switched to nanocommunication. "Are you reading me, Emma?"

"Yes, loud and clear."

"The President said that Arsenal Gear was the Patriots' key to supremacy."

"That's as good a description as any."

"What exactly is it?"

"It's a massive data processing system capable of controlling information on a global scale," she explained.

"A data process—? I thought it was a weapon."

"The system's a social device for maintaining the Patriots' control."

"You've lost me."

"In this day and age, information emerges from every direction, and it's freely distributed. A variety of information—gathered by servers employing the latest in high-speed communication networks and P2P technology—is rapidly circulated to individuals. In fact, the speed of this circulation process is accelerating on an almost daily basis. The Patriots seem to be afraid of this development. Apparently, they believe that their role will shift from dominant to dominated. Let me give you an example. You're aware of Solid Snake's anti–Metal Gear activities, aren't you?"

"Yeah. I know a little bit about it."

"That's just a small sample of uncontrolled information. I can guarantee you the Patriots did not want Solid Snake's name publicized. Now, look at it like this—political scandal, corporate corruption . . . up until now, the Patriots have managed to keep a lid on these and other self-serving events. But with their existing data processing system they are no longer able to effectively control the flow of information generated at the individual level. With the newly created system they can fully regulate digital information. High-level information can be categorized in stages, given clearance levels, and deleted as necessary—never to be seen by the public. By deleting such information, the Patriots can shape the course of history as they see fit."

"Somebody's bound to catch on . . ."

"No. The memory capacity—not to mention the life span—of the average individual is extremely limited. On the other hand, digital information lasts virtually forever. It doesn't deteriorate."

"So?"

"The alphabet . . . twenty-six letters, right? It could've been thirty letters. What if the four deleted letters were controlled by a program?"

"Impossible."

"It's not. In fact, something similar is already underway. Do you know how many genes exist in an individual?"

What is this—school? "About thirty to forty thousand?"

"Right. That's what was announced at the turn of the century. But there's actually a hundred thousand, according to the original theory advanced by the scientific community. Information regarding the remaining sixty thousand was suppressed by the Patriots."

"No . . ."

"Why? How would you know? Do you know what a gene looks like? Did you count them yourself?"

"There are research organizations—"

"Of course. And their reports have already been subtly altered. They're even beginning to believe the doctored reports. GW is a system that allows the Patriots to decide what will be recorded in tomorrow's history."

"So what we're talking about is one huge censorship system for deleting information which might be inconvenient to the Patriots?"

"Exactly. The actual, physical core for handling the task—GW—is installed in Arsenal. It's the only system in the world with an optic neural AI that has a parallel processing capacity of 980 trillion hammets."

"I suppose that being a specialist in neural AI and complex logic played a significant role in your association with the Metal Gear project."

"That's not the only reason . . ."

"What do you mean?"

She blushed and wouldn't answer.

"I guess there are plenty of other reasons," Raiden ventured.

"Yes, there are."

"I understand."

"Do you?"

"So Arsenal Gear was actually designed to protect the GW system, wasn't it?"

"Uhm, yes. It's armed with everything, including nuclear weapons, and it's fully equipped with cyber-terrorist countermeasures. Physically and logically it's the ultimate fortress for housing GW."

"But the AI is actually capable of controlling everything?"

"No. GW is only the system's core. It's only for deciding what data is stored or deleted. The actual sub-system for executing the task exists within our social structure."

"What?"

"Do you remember the panic that gripped the computer industry prior to the end of the century?"

"You mean the Y2K problem?"

"That's right. If you recall, our government supplied the world with a countermeasure program—using the Internet at full capacity. The program was distributed to every governmental organization . . . every key facility . . . throughout the world. In addition, the same program was included in an OS application for distribution among the public."

"Let me guess. The Y2K countermeasure contained a program designed by the Patriots?"

"Yes. And everything supplied from that day onward contains the same program."

"Impossible."

"Do you know how a computer operates? Do you really know the basic principles on how data is exchanged? Nobody's aware of it, but there's a subsystem in place. And it's about to be activated!"

"Is that why Solidus wants to burn out every electrical circuit in Manhattan with a nuclear blast?"

"Probably. But the overall system isn't actually complete."

"What?"

"It still lacks the necessary factors for judging situations. I heard they were planning a major experiment in the next few days to provide complex data for the GW to study. And suddenly all this happens . . ." She paused, became very quiet, and looked away.

"Emma, it's not your fault. If it wasn't for the terrorists . . ."

"Yeah. You're right."

"I think we'd better head for the Computer Room."

She gasped and turned sharply to Raiden. "My bird! Is he safe? Is he in the Computer Room?"

Raiden didn't know what she was talking about—and then he remembered. "That noisy, overgrown parakeet?"

"Excuse me, he's a *parrot*. And he's my best friend. My only friend."

"Well, the last time I saw, the bird's okay."

"Oh, good. Did you know that in the old days miners used to take a canary into the mineshafts to detect toxic gas?"

"That's what he's for?"

"No. I really needed someone to talk to."

"Right. I think we'd better get moving." He helped her stand and they walked out of the chamber to the next flooded stairwell. "We have a little longer to cover than the last time."

"I'll give it my best," she said. Her attitude had improved immensely.

"Whatever you do, don't open your eyes."

"Why not?"

"Uhm, there's a dead body . . . not a pretty sight."

"Oh."

She removed her glasses again. Raiden nodded at the chopsticks. "What are those sticks in your head?"

"They're lacquered chopsticks. They hold your hair in place. Did you know that they're pretty popular in Europe and South America?"

"Can't say that I do." He smiled and said, "You're not only cute, but smart, too."

"Oh, I'm *much* more than cute . . ."

With that, she climbed on to his back and took a deep breath.

26

Raiden slipped into the water and swam with Emma back into the murkiness. The going seemed to be easier. Emma was more relaxed—her grip around his neck wasn't as *desperate* as before. Raiden stopped at the first skylight he saw so that she could take a breath of air. After confirming she was ready to go again, he continued on. He passed the disabled maintenance cart and knew it wasn't far from there.

The entire trip took less than two minutes. They made it to the end, climbed out of the water, and rested for a moment.

"How are you doing?" he asked.

"Okay. That wasn't so bad."

He led her to the elevator, but the floor was covered with sea lice. Emma flinched and cried, "Ewww, no!"

"They're just bugs, Emma," Raiden said. "They won't hurt you."

"No. I . . . I can't go through them!"

Raiden didn't know what to do. Was he going to have to knock her unconscious and carry her into the elevator?

Then he remembered the canister of coolant Stillman had

given him. There was a little left—maybe it would act as a repellent? He got it out of his pack, shook it, and sprayed around the floor. The insects scattered as if they were being attacked by the worst poison imaginable. The canister was truly empty now, so he tossed it into a waste basket.

"Come on."

He called the elevator. She continued to lean on him, but he could see that her legs were regaining their strength. She wasn't as shaky as before.

They rode the lift to 1F. He motioned for her to stay in the elevator and remain quiet while he checked out the floor. Raiden went down the hall toward the room where the President had died but halted when he heard the shuffling of footsteps around the corner. Raiden peeked cautiously and saw a lone guard coming out of the chamber. The operative popped back out of sight, drew the M9 with the tranquilizers, and waited. As soon as the sentry walked around the corner, Raiden shot him point-blank. The man wavered on his feet, his eyes rolled up into his head, and he collapsed like a rag doll.

The rest of the level was clear. Raiden went back to the lift and fetched Emma. He helped her walk to the stairwell and onto the entrance of the T-connector that adjoined the L–K bridge. A Cypher hovered near Strut L where they were headed. Raiden reached into his backpack and retrieved a chaff grenade. In order to conserve PSG-1 ammunition, he thought it would be a better idea to take out the Cypher's functions with the grenade—provided he could throw it far enough. Raiden crouched low and duck-walked along the bridge out of the Cypher camera's line of sight. When he was in a suitable position, he pulled the pin, stood, and tossed the grenade high and over the spy-bot. The grenade went off, spreading its cloud of tiny metallic pieces over the device. The Cypher rotated and faced the water as if it were confused. Raiden ran back to the door, took Emma's hand, and led her across.

The entrance to Strut L was a Level 5 security door. Raiden slammed his hand against it and cursed.

"What's wrong?" Emma asked.

"I don't have a security card five! Damn!"

"So you're giving up already?" He looked at her questioningly. "Ta-daaa!" She held out a PAN card. Raiden took it—the card was a Level 5. "Are you impressed?"

"You should have told me you had it!"

"The truth is I just remembered it myself."

At first Raiden wanted to strangle her. Instead he gave her a hug.

Then the Codec buzzed. It was his girlfriend. "Well, Jack. It sounds like you and Miss Emma are getting along just fine."

"Rose?"

"I've been monitoring your every move and conversation. I can't say it's been fun."

"Give me a break! I'm only trying to keep her spirits up!"

"Is that right?"

"Absolutely! My mission is to get her to the Computer Room."

"That's all?"

"Yeah."

"You're attracted to her, aren't you."

He didn't want to lie. "I'll admit she's cute."

"Cuter than me?"

"Rose! You're beautiful. You know how I feel about you."

"Oh? Have you remembered yet?"

"What, you mean April thirtieth?"

"Yes."

Raiden took a stab. "It's your birthday, isn't it?"

"Wrong! You're not even warm!"

"What is it then?"

"Forget it. It's nothing. Maybe I'm just a little . . . a little jealous."

"Rose?"

"You'd better get moving. Good luck."

And she signed off. Raiden wanted to pull his hair, but Emma was watching him curiously. He blew it off and said, "Come on."

According to the Colonel's instructions, the best way to get back to Shell One was by using the oil fence—a barrier close to the water that connected each of the Struts. It was wide enough for a person to traverse—but it wasn't very strong. It was never meant to be a walkway.

Getting to it was yet another challenge. Raiden found the proper hatch on the Strut L roof and lifted it. His eyes widened when he saw the open-air rung ladder that stretched all the way along the Strut from the roof down to the oil fence—it was the length of a football field or more.

"I have a question for you," he said to Emma.

"What is it?"

"How do you feel about heights?"

"I can't say I like heights, though water's higher on my phobia list. Why?"

"We have to go down a ladder."

"How far down?"

"Just a *little* bit."

"Why do I feel like we've had this conversation before? How *little* is little?"

"About a hundred and thirty feet?"

"*What?*"

"Think you can do it?"

"Would you take 'no' for an answer?"

"How are your legs?"

"Better. The numbness is gone. I can climb down on my own."

"Okay. Follow me."

Raiden lowered himself through the hatch and onto the ladder. He descended a few rungs and waited for Emma to trail him. Once they were moving—slowly and steadily—Raiden realized how late in the day it was. The sun was close to the horizon and the temperature had cooled. Strong wind threatened to force them off the ladder, but they held on tightly and kept moving. Raiden ordered Emma not to look down and stay focused on the rungs. It took them nearly fifteen minutes, but they eventually made it to the bottom of the Strut and a small pontoon platform that encircled it.

Emma leaned against the handrail while Raiden dug out his binoculars.

"The sunset," she said. "It's beautiful."

Indeed, the sky was a fiery orange-red.

"If we don't hurry, it'll be the last one we see," Raiden added.

He put the binoculars to his eyes and scanned the oil fence. It connected Struts L, G, D, and E. A couple of Cyphers flew around the pontoon at Strut E. There were sentries on the pathway as well. The bridge bobbed up and down with the movement of the sea's surface, much like a huge serpent crawling across the sea. Periodic waves sprayed up from between the fence's connecting points.

"Enemy soldiers and Gun Cyphers," Raiden said. "I don't think we're going to be able to slip past all that." He put a foot over the rail and tested the floating bridge. It dunked a bit with his weight. "Looks like it can barely support one person. How much do you weigh, Emma?"

"Are you going to ask me how old I am next?"

"If you go alone, I think you can make it across."

He made a call to Snake on the Codec.

"This is Raiden, do you read me?"

"Yeah. What's up?"

"We've made it to the lower part of Strut L. We'll have to cross the water from here."

"Can Emma walk?"

"She's okay. The pontoon bridge doesn't look too sturdy. Emma is going to have to cross it alone."

"Right. The oil fence . . ."

"There are Cyphers and several guards."

"Raiden, you're carrying a PSG-1, aren't you?"

"Yeah."

"It's time to play sniper."

Raiden moved to a suitable location and pulled the sniper rifle off his back. "Not bad. This spot gives me a good view of the targets."

"You're going to have to cover Emma until she crosses to Strut E. I'll get there and provide some support of my own."

"Thanks."

"Think you can handle it?"

"Yeah, I know the drill. I've faced a similar situation in Advanced Mode Level Four VR training with the PSG-1."

"VR . . . ?" Snake groaned. "Guess that's better than nothing. Make sure you don't hit Emma!"

"Duh."

"Right now, with Arsenal's boarding in progress, security should be at a minimum. That doesn't mean it's going to be easy. Given the situation, they've probably got Claymores in place to make up for the security shortage. Make sure you use your thermal goggles."

"Right."

"Okay, I'm heading for Strut E."

Raiden signed off and turned to Emma. "Okay, I'm going to clear a path for you from here."

"How?"

"Sniper fire."

"You're kidding."

"Trust me."

"What if I fall into the sea? I can't swim!"

"You were doing pretty good a few minutes ago."

He stared at her with a straight face. Finally she smiled. "Okay."

"Think you can do it?"

"Would you take 'no' for an answer?"

They both answered, "No," simultaneously.

She bravely put a leg over the rail and stood on the bobbing bridge. She said, "Whoa," to herself, found her balance, and began to move slowly across. Raiden slipped on the thermal goggles. He scanned the bridge ahead of her and spotted a hidden Claymore halfway across to the next pontoon. He leveled the PSG-1, aimed, and fired. The mine exploded, sending a cloud of smoke in the air. The sentries would now be well aware of their presence.

"Oh!" Emma cried, startled. "Warn me when you're going to do that!"

"I can't," he said. "Just expect it, okay?"

She went on, shakily making her way across the narrow fence. Then the gunfire began. A sentry at the other end of the bridge was firing at Emma. She screamed and ducked, holding on to the bridge for dear life.

Raiden aimed the PSG-1, centered the sentry in the crosshairs, and squeezed the trigger. The guard jerked and fell into the water. Two more men ran out from the pontoon guardhouse and took positions. Raiden pointed the rifle at one of them, breathed, and fired. The guard's head exploded in a puff of red.

Another gunshot resounded from Strut E. The second guard rose, rotated, and fell into the sea.

Snake was at Strut E. He waved at Raiden.

Another Cypher flew into view. Raiden took aim—but Snake shot it first. The machine blew up noisily and showered the water with its remnants.

Emma was past Strut G and on the way to D and Shell One. She was halfway there.

If only she could move faster!

Raiden scanned the bridge for more sentries and saw none —
but there was movement above the oil fence around Strut D.
What was it? He peered through the scope and saw a long, dark
cape. A man had crawled out of a hatch and was somehow clinging to the side of the Strut!

Vamp. He was alive!

The creature dropped onto the bridge in front of Emma. He
pounced on her and pinned the girl's arms behind her back. He
then turned toward Strut L, knowing full well that Raiden was
watching from there. The vampire raised his right hand with a
flourish — it contained a long knife. Raiden heard the man's unearthly laugh, even from that distance.

Snake was unable to fire at Vamp. Without a sniper rifle it
was too risky. Raiden realized that it was up to him alone.

Vamp began to drag Emma toward Strut D, the knife still at
her throat.

Get him in your sights! Now!

Raiden focused on the couple and placed the crosshairs directly on Vamp's face. It was an extremely difficult shot, for the
creature was moving quickly and he had Emma in front of him.
The good thing was that Vamp was two heads taller than the girl.

Concentrate . . . relax . . . feel the shot before making it . . .

He squeezed the trigger.

A spurt of red. Vamp's head jerked back. A direct hit!

But something happened. There was a flash of an arm and
Emma seemed to bend in pain. Vamp toppled over and fell into
the water, but Emma clutched her waist and fell to her knees.

Raiden grabbed the binoculars to get a better view.

Blood was spreading across Emma's stomach.

Snake jumped off the pontoon and onto the bridge. He ran
toward her firing his SOCOM at a new Cypher that had appeared. The spy-bot blew apart and Snake continued across. He
reached Emma, picked her up, and carried her back to Strut L
with no further interference.

The Codec buzzed.

"Raiden! Emma's been stabbed!"

"That bastard!"

Otacon broke in. "How bad is it?"

"She's conscious," Snake said, "but the bleeding is bad. I'm bringing her over there right now."

"E.E.!" Otacon whispered.

"Raiden! Get that disk over here as soon as possible. I'm afraid her time's running out!"

Raiden swallowed and answered, "I'll be there!"

27

THE OPERATIVE quickly made his own way along the oil fence. As before, it bobbed up and down in the water with his weight. One of Raiden's strengths during training was his agility. His instructors all commented on how flexible and light on his feet he was. Thus, he had no problem keeping his balance on the shaky bridge. Clearing the bridge of the soldiers and Cyphers in advance contributed to his speed. At one point he came to the spot near Strut D where Vamp had stabbed Emma. There was fresh blood on the bridge. Raiden paused to reflect a second or two, and then he hurried over it. He continued on to Strut E and climbed over the rail into the makeshift guardhouse. A dead sentry lay on the floor. From the odd angle of the man's head, Raiden deduced that the soldier's neck had been broken—most likely by Snake when he came through to rescue Emma.

Raiden took hold of the rung ladder that was attached to the side of the Strut and began to climb. There was a hatch nearly halfway up. The ladder wasn't as tall as the one on Strut L, but it still took him nearly a minute to get to the entrance. He opened it and stepped inside, guessing that it led to the Strut's B1 level.

It was a room full of boxes and cartons. There was no one around. A legend on the wall labeled the place as the B1 PARCEL ROOM. Raiden took a moment to make a call on the Codec.

"Snake, what's your situation over there?"

"Emma seems to be, uh . . . doing something to GW's defensive capabilities. All we need now is your disk. You'd better hurry—I don't think she's gonna make it."

"How's the bleeding?"

"She's . . . just get over here. You'll find the coast is clear with everybody aboard Arsenal right now."

"Understood."

He signed off and kept moving. Raiden ran out of the Parcel Room to the stairwell. He climbed to the first floor three steps at a time and was panting by the time he got to Strut E's roof. Nevertheless, he felt energized and alert. The run had done him good.

A lone Cypher patrolled the airspace above the E–F connecting bridge. Raiden drew the SOCOM, aimed, and blew it out of the sky. He then sprinted to the T-connector crossway and pushed forward to the entrance of the Shell 1 Core. Just in case Snake was wrong, Raiden cautiously entered with the SOCOM in hand, but the place was quiet and still. Nothing had changed since he was last there—just that there was a feeling of emptiness and desertion.

The elevator got him to B2 and the Computer Room in no time. All in all, the entire trip from Strut L took him less than three hundred seconds.

The scene inside wasn't pretty. Emma was lying on the floor in a puddle of blood. Her shirt was soaked red. Otacon knelt beside her, holding her head in his lap. Snake stood alongside the computer terminal.

Raiden swallowed. "How's Emma?"

Snake shook his head and whispered, "I think he got some internal organs . . . we can't stop the bleeding."

Otacon looked up at Raiden. There were tears in his eyes.

"H . . . Hal?" Emma weakly reached out with her hands to touch him. Apparently her eyesight was failing. She was shivering.

"I'm here," he said.

Snake sidled up to Raiden. "Got the disk?" Raiden dug it out of his pack and handed it over. "Emma's set everything up. Evidently, all you have to do is pop in the disk." He inserted it into the terminal. A screen appeared on the monitor indicating that data was being uploaded. "Uhm, that should insert the virus into the AI." Raiden could see that Snake really wasn't in his element. The man hadn't the faintest idea what he was doing.

They waited as the progress bar slowly filled . . . 50 percent . . . 60 percent . . . 70 percent . . .

"Is it working?" Raiden asked.

Suddenly, a warning alarm beeped loudly on the computer. A virus detection program activated and an error message appeared on the monitor.

"What the—?" Snake turned to Otacon. With Emma still in his arms, Otacon peered toward the screen.

"Oh no . . . an antibody agent . . . !"

Then, just as the progress bar reached 90 percent, a bright red warning appeared on the monitor: DISCONNECTION!

"Damn!" Snake shouted as he slammed a fist on the desk. "The connection's been cut!"

Raiden leaned in to look at the screen. "Is the virus upload complete?"

"I don't think so. The count's stopped at ninety percent." Snake turned to his partner. "Otacon?"

"I don't think Emma's made any mistakes," her stepbrother said.

"But?" Raiden asked.

Otacon pursed his lips and offered, "A portion of the worm cluster might have been altered after the disk left Emma's hands."

"By the Patriots?"

Snake blurted, "Will the virus still work?"

"I have no idea," Otacon answered. He was too preoccupied with Emma to think properly.

Raiden and Snake looked at each other and then turned back to the monitor. The error messages hung there for a moment and then the screen completely shut off. Snake sighed heavily and took out the disk.

Emma, unaware of the situation, spoke up. "Hal . . . ? Is . . . everything . . . all right?"

Otacon didn't know how to reply. He looked to Snake for guidance, but his partner simply shook his head. Otacon leaned low to Emma's ear and answered, "It's all right. Everything's all right."

"Good," she said. "At least . . . I won't be adding . . . another page to . . . our family's . . . dark history . . ."

Raiden whispered to Snake, "What if the virus doesn't work?"

"We either destroy that thing, or take out Solidus and his men."

"How do we get on board?"

"I don't think we can unless somebody inside gives us a hand."

They turned back to the unfolding drama on the floor. Emma was fading fast.

"Hal . . . I . . . always . . ."

"What is it, Emma?"

Her hand slowly reached toward Otacon's glasses. " . . . wanted to see you again."

"You don't hate me?"

"Never . . . I never wanted to get . . . in your way. I never . . . wanted to hurt you . . . I thought that with Arsenal . . . if I followed in your footsteps . . . I could be . . . closer . . . I just wanted you to look at me as . . . a woman."

"E.E. . . . I could never do that . . ."

"Don't be so honest . . . it hurts . . ."

"Sorry."

"Can I . . . ask you one last favor . . . ?"

"Sure."

"Call me . . . Emma."

"What?"

"Please call me . . . Emma."

"What's wrong with E.E.?"

She managed to grasp his glasses and pull them off his face. And then her hand dropped limply. The glasses fell to the floor noisily but unharmed.

"Emma?" She smiled . . . barely. "Emma!"

And she was gone.

"Emma! Answer me! Emma!" Otacon broke into tears. Snake and Raiden stood by helplessly. They let him cry it out as the sobbing increased to painful wails. After a moment, he continued to address her. He didn't seem to care if Snake and Raiden heard.

"I didn't . . . I didn't leave you because of the accident. I had . . . I had a relationship with . . . your mother. She seduced me . . . and it went on . . . My father's death . . . was no accident. He took his own life. It was all my fault. All my fault. Forgive me, Emma . . ."

At that moment the parrot in the cage squawked. "Hal . . . Hal . . ."

Otacon looked up and blinked. He gently laid Emma's head on the floor and stood. He approached the cage slowly and opened the door.

"Hal," it repeated.

Otacon put his hand inside and the bird immediately stepped onto it. He brought the parrot out of the cage and held on to it with both hands, and then started sobbing again.

There was a loud burst of static over the Shell-wide PA system. Then Solidus' voice announced, "Attention! Arsenal Gear is ready for launch! Evacuate the upper levels immediately!"

Snake cursed silently and said, "Sounds like they're cutting this area loose!"

"What do you mean?" Raiden asked.

"It means we're going to sink," Otacon answered for him.

"We have to get the hostages out!" Snake said.

"What about the Kamov repairs?"

"Done," Otacon replied.

"We won't be able to get everybody aboard."

Snake nodded but said, "We'll just have to take as many as we can."

Otacon walked back and stood over Emma's body, still holding the parrot. To convince himself of the finality of the situation, and as if it was a decision on his part, he said, "My sister . . . won't be able to come with us."

The parrot squawked as if it understood.

The PA blasted another announcement. "We will be commencing the countdown shortly. All personnel in the upper levels—head for the evacuation area immediately!"

Otacon shook his head and said to himself mostly, "I'm always the survivor . . . why, Wolf?"

Raiden wasn't sure what he meant. He glanced at Snake, who looked down and nodded.

Shadow Moses! Raiden thought. One of the terrorists was a woman named Sniper Wolf. Hal Emmerich had been her prisoner, but actually the two of them had had a relationship of some kind . . . he'd been in love with her . . .

"Otacon," Snake said. "Take care of the hostages."

"What about you guys?" he asked.

"We got other arrangements." He indicated the window through which the massive access hatch of Arsenal Gear could be seen. "There's our ride out of here. Anyway, we're gonna have to sink that thing if the virus doesn't work."

"I should be going with you."

"You've got your job, we've got ours."

"You mean I'd only get in the way."

"Wrong. Otacon, only you can save the hostages. Got it?"

"Yeah. Right." He took a breath and addressed the two men. "Listen. The two of you won't be able to destroy that thing. Eliminate the enemy. That's your only option."

The three men left the Computer Room and went down the hall to Arsenal Gear's access hatch. It appeared to be solid and secure. Lettering on the door read: ARSENAL GEAR—NO UNAUTHORIZED ENTRY. Raiden glanced at Snake, who nodded his head.

The parrot squawked again, "Hal . . . Hal . . . Hal . . ."

Otacon couldn't help but break down once more, "E.E.! Damn! Aaauuhh!" He rammed his head against the wall in torment.

"Otacon!" Snake shouted. His friend ceased wailing and Snake softened his tone. "Try to get as many hostages out as you can. It's a short flight to the shore, so don't worry about overloading the Kamov."

The scientist inhaled deeply and got hold of himself. "Leave it to me." He turned to Snake and held out his hand. Snake clutched it . . . and then the two men embraced.

The PA blurted, "I repeat! All personnel in the upper levels head for the evacuation area immediately!"

"I'm counting on you, Otacon," Snake said.

Still carrying the parrot on his shoulder, Otacon turned and headed for the elevator. He pushed the call button, waited a moment for it to arrive, and then entered it. Inside, the parrot continued to talk. "Hal . . . I miss you . . . I miss you . . ."

Otacon sobbed again and addressed the bird as if it were his dead stepsister. "You and me . . . we're the same . . . Both you and I . . . we were always alone . . . always. We only wanted to be loved. We were always waiting . . . waiting for somebody . . . somebody who would love us . . . But we were wrong. You can't wait to be loved. You have to go out and find it. Four years ago . . .

I realized that you can't just wish for a happy family. You have to make it happen. I only wish I knew that sooner. I learned that I could love . . . as you probably did . . . Emma . . ."

The elevator arrived at the level where the hostages were being held.

Back on B2, Snake and Raiden contemplated the Arsenal Gear hatch access. Raiden indicated the elevator. "You think he's gonna be okay?"

"He's tougher than he looks," Snake answered. "Consider it done."

"Now. How do we open this thing?" Raiden studied the door and then looked at Snake. There was a gleam in the man's eye that he hadn't noticed earlier.

"You can come out now!" Snake called.

As if appearing from nowhere, the cyborg ninja dropped from the ceiling and landed gracefully on its feet!

Raiden jumped back in surprise. "The ninja! What the—?"

The ninja brandished the samurai sword and stood straight and tall. "Arsenal's going to take off," it said in its metallic voice. Raiden turned to Snake for an explanation, but the man ignored him. "We still need you to take care of a few things," the ninja said to Snake.

Then, without warning, the ninja swung the sword at Raiden and held the point directly in front of his eyes. "This time do not fail us!" the newcomer said to Snake.

"Snake! What's all this about?"

His friend didn't respond to the question. Snake simply said, "Bedtime, Raiden."

"You're changing sides now?" Raiden asked, astonished at the sudden switch.

"Changing sides?" Snake asked. "I don't recall saying I was on yours."

Raiden took a sharp intake of breath. "Damn it."

The ninja then switched off the device in its helmet that created a face shield. The covering cleared up to reveal . . . Olga Gurlukovich!

"You!" Raiden shouted.

"Ready for some shut-eye?" Olga asked in her own voice.

An electric charge issued from the sword, enveloping Raiden in a current that shook his body. The nanomachines in his body resonated and released plasma bolts. He cried out in pain and anguish and then dropped to the floor. Unconscious.

THIRTY MINUTES LATER Otacon took off in the Kamov loaded with the hostages. As the chopper ascended, he heard a loud rumbling that reverberated over the Big Shell. He and his passengers watched in horror as the Struts trembled like they were being shaken by an earthquake. The dark water of the bay flooded the upper levels—and then massive explosions rocked the entire structure.

They've done it! Otacon thought. *They've blown the Shell's upper levels! My God! . . . My God! . . . Arsenal Gear is rising! It's RISING!*

28

THE VOICES DRIFTED into his ears as if from a dream. Two men. A conversation. Floating in and out. Simultaneously loud and soft.

"Is he still alive?"

"He was when Olga brought him in."

Raiden recognized the voices, but his head hurt so much that he couldn't quite put it all together. He opened his eyes and saw bright, blurry lights. A ceiling. His arms moved reflexively, but Raiden found that he couldn't budge. His wrists were secured to something . . . a table. His legs, too. He was *strapped* to a table. And he was completely naked. He wanted to groan aloud, but perhaps it was better to feign unconsciousness and listen to the two men.

"I've checked everything including the Genome data, but there's nothing on this guy. NSA, CIA, FBI . . . he doesn't exist in any database. He's a nonexistent operative from a nonexistent organization."

Raiden knew that voice. Ocelot. Revolver Ocelot.

"I suspected as much. However, I know this man . . ."

And *that* voice. Raiden knew it as well. Solidus. Solidus

Snake. Strange, there was something about the man's vocal inflections that prickled the very core of Raiden's soul. Something from long ago. *What was it?*

"Wake him up," Solidus commanded.

A motor hummed and the table slowly tilted to an upright position. The room came into view. It was partitioned by glass and was equipped with the latest medical equipment. Past the glass, steel bars—a prison?—and another chamber. Cables ran from the foot of the table, sprawling across the floor like arteries.

The two men stood before him. Solidus was dressed in a black power-suit that resembled armor, and he wore an eye patch over his left eye. The most dramatic thing about his gear was that two mechanical tentacles snaked out from the suit below his arms. The tentacles were long and functional with claw pincers on the ends. Raiden couldn't help but think that Solidus resembled Snake—the traitor he had known as Pliskin. As for Ocelot, the gunslinger looked exactly the same.

"It's been a while, hasn't it . . . Jack the Ripper?" Solidus taunted.

"You *know* this fellow?" Ocelot asked.

Solidus glared quickly at Ocelot to shut him up then turned his attention back to Raiden. "You remember me, don't you?"

Raiden didn't reply. *What is this guy talking about?*

"You've grown!"

One of the tentacles stretched out and wrapped itself around Raiden's neck. The claw squeezed . . . and Raiden gasped for air. The other tentacle then extended to lightly scan Raiden's mind.

"A high concentration of cerebral implants . . . *tsk, tsk,* have they altered your memory, too?"

The tentacle on his head emitted a sharp bolt of electricity, causing Raiden to scream in pain. Solidus chuckled and withdrew both robo-feelers.

"This is my son," Solidus announced. "I taught him everything. Jack, I never thought I'd see you again."

Raiden managed to find his voice. It came out as a whisper. "You . . . know me?"

"You don't remember?"

Raiden blinked. *What the* hell *is he talking about?*

"Your name . . . your skills . . . everything you know . . . you learned from me!"

Something within Raiden stirred. Some distant, long lost synapse of memory. An image . . . a young boy with white hair. A soldier. A boy soldier.

"The eighties," Solidus prodded. "The Liberian civil war. You were one of the best among the child soldiers that fought in that conflict. When you were barely ten years old you became the platoon leader of the 'small boy unit.' At the time, your outstanding kill record earned you several nicknames, including 'White Devil' and 'Jack the Ripper.' "

Again, Raiden flashed upon a vague picture of himself at that age. Hiding. Fighting. Carrying a gun. Running in battle . . . Were these real memories or were they imagined?

"Jack, I was your godfather. I named you. When the war ended you disappeared from the relief center. I wondered what happened to you. I should've known they'd recruit you."

Solidus gestured to Ocelot. They moved away, their backs to Raiden, but the operative could still hear their whispers.

"It's an interesting coincidence," Ocelot said, obviously doubting his own words.

"If he's a lackey for the Patriots, I doubt that he knows anything of interest."

"What should we do with him?"

"We'll use him like you suggested."

"What about Dead Cell?"

"Ignore them."

Ocelot suddenly jerked his prosthetic arm toward his torso. He grunted and held the forearm tightly.

"Happening again?" Solidus asked.

Ocelot winced in pain. "Could it be that *he's* here, too?"

"Hmpf."

The gunslinger took a few deep breaths and seemed to regain control of his prosthesis after a brief moment. He took a few steps away from his boss.

"In another hour," Solidus remarked, "we demonstrate the power of Arsenal Gear."

"Attack with standard weapons, of course?"

"Yes. We proceed as planned."

"At last report, all is well with GW."

Solidus nodded with satisfaction. "How about the troops?"

"The men are being refitted with Arsenal Gear equipment as ordered." Ocelot gestured at Solidus' eye patch. "You're the spitting image of Big Boss!"

Solidus laughed loudly. "Is that so? Perhaps I should be grateful to this kid for that!" The terrorist leader grinned at Raiden and then left through a door to the south. Raiden was alone with Ocelot, who took a few steps toward the prisoner.

"This situation . . . I find it very . . . nostalgic."

Raiden recalled the Shadow Moses incident. Snake had been captured and strapped to a table just like the one he was now on. And Revolver Ocelot had tortured him.

"Where am I?" Raiden asked.

"Why, inside Arsenal Gear, of course." Raiden looked past Ocelot and through a glass window. The sea . . . water drifting faster than normal . . . They were moving! "Actually, we're also inside the memory of Shadow Moses." Ocelot pulled a disk out of his pocket and held it up for Raiden to see. It was the President's virus disk, the one that he and Snake had attempted to upload into GW. "I'll take this back. You don't need it anymore, do you?" The gunslinger stuck the disk back in his pocket.

Raiden heard someone enter the room. His gaze shifted to the side, and he saw Olga Gurlukovich. No longer wearing the cyborg ninja suit, she was dressed in her regular battle gear.

"A foul wind is blowing," Ocelot said. His contempt for the Russian woman was palpable. "We shall speak again." Without acknowledging her, he turned and left the room.

Raiden glared at Olga.

"Don't move," she whispered. "Stay as you are." She wasn't looking at him. "We're being monitored by a camera."

"What are you up to?" Raiden asked softly.

"Quiet. I'm switching over to nanocommunication." .

Raiden heard the connection in his inner ears and then asked, "Mister X? Ninja?"

"Correct. It's me."

"I thought you were the leader of the Russian troops."

"No. That was just a smoke screen."

"A smoke screen?"

"I was sent to provide you support."

"*Support*? Who sent you? The Colonel?"

"No." She sighed. "The Patriots."

"*What?*"

"I . . . I deceived my troops . . . betrayed them . . ."

"But why?"

"My child . . . is being held hostage by the Patriots." Olga took a few steps and gazed out the window at the sea world drifting by. "It all started two years ago when I lost my father during the tanker incident. My men and I had nowhere to go . . . so we joined forces with an illegal Russian organization."

"The Russian mafia?"

"Something like that. Actually, I learned much later that it was a subordinate organization of the Patriots. I was expecting at the time. When I gave birth to my child, it turned out I was in a hospital run by the Patriots. In the morning . . . my child was gone. My baby is being kept somewhere in this country."

"Have you ever met your child?"

"No. Once a month they send me a photo of my child via network. I've never even held the child in my own arms."

"I see . . ." Actually, he didn't at all, but he said, "Given your situation, nobody can blame you for what you did."

"That's your opinion."

"What about Snake? I thought you two were enemies."

"He wasn't responsible for my father's death. Actually, I owe him our lives. Two years ago, they were responsible for getting us out from the sinking tanker alive."

"So you were partners since the incident?"

"No. I only found out the truth shortly before this."

"*Huh?*"

"When I confronted him here."

"You fought with Snake? When?"

"Well, it was around the time you were holding hands with that girl."

At first Raiden wasn't sure whom she meant. Then he remembered. Emma. It was when he was bringing Emma to Shell 1.

He couldn't help asking sarcastically, "So you joined hands with Snake to pay back a debt?"

"No. Mutual gain."

"Mutual *gain?*"

"My job was to assist you. If Solidus gets away with Arsenal, your mission is a failure. The Patriots would judge that as failure on my part as well and terminate my child. Putting it simply, my child's life depends on your success."

"So you did it all for your child. But why would the Patriots want to help me? Are they hoping I'll take Solidus out?"

"No. You're just like me. We're just pawns."

"Pawns for what purpose?"

"The S3 Plan."

"The what?"

"You'll figure it out sooner or later. But I wonder if you'll handle the truth?"

"What do you mean?"

"Listen. We haven't got time for this. Solidus will commence his attack any minute. He's got to be stopped."

"What about the virus?"

"No results so far. I think the Patriots have tampered with the program."

"Will it work?"

"I don't know."

"Get me out of this thing!"

"Not yet. I'll release your restraints after I leave this room."

"Where's my gear?"

"Snake's got everything. I couldn't bring it here."

"And where do I find Snake?"

"The passageway ahead leads to a hangar. He'll be waiting there. I gave him a card key for the hangar."

"Does Snake plan to destroy Arsenal Gear?"

"No. Even for Snake it's impossible to completely destroy this thing. The only option is to stop Solidus and his men."

"What're you going to do?"

"Stay concealed. That's my role. I still can't afford to be discovered."

"Olga, you can't keep this up. They're bound to find you."

"Listen. I'll free you in a little while. Now brace yourself." With that, she disconnected nanocommunications, walked over to Raiden, and slugged him hard in the abdomen.

"Ugh!!"

For show, Olga spit on the floor in front of Raiden's feet. Then she turned abruptly and left the room.

29

REELING FROM THE PAIN of the blow, Raiden gasped for breath and tried to relax his diaphragm. After a minute or so he was able to breathe normally. He fully understood why Olga had hit him under the watchful eyes of the surveillance cameras, but he didn't have to like it.

Then he realized how cold he was. The temperature inside Arsenal Gear was frigid. And he had no clothes.

"Jack, are you all right?" It was Rose, calling through the nanomachines.

"Oh. Yeah."

"Jack, is it true? What Solidus said?"

Raiden sighed. "Yes."

"It's unbelievable! Drafting small children, sending them to war . . . it's not allowed under international conventions!"

"ICC rules don't mean a lot in war. Someone told me that there are over three hundred thousand children in combat right now. I was just one of them."

"So you remember? I thought your memory had been . . . manipulated by them."

"It was. But I have nightmares every day, pieces of the past I can't put together."

He could hear the shock and pain in her voice. "Why didn't you tell me?"

"You couldn't begin to understand."

"You wouldn't know that until you try me."

"I didn't want you to get hurt. There was never a real reason for me to fight except that someone put a gun in my hand. And that someone was Solidus."

"It wasn't your fault!"

"If I survived the day's fight, I was praised, fed, and had a bed to sleep in. I think I was only six when I held my first AK, but I'm not even sure of that."

"Jack?"

"I'm not like Snake. I never questioned why we fought. There was no purpose, no way out. They give you a gun, you ask how many to kill. If you didn't, you were the one they shot instead."

"It's okay! No one is blaming you."

"We were shown Hollywood action films every day. The kind with macho guys and big guns. They call it 'image training.' Played war games, too. But with real bullets. They . . . they built us from the ground up, into killing machines. We were fed once a day. I can still taste the gunpowder they mixed into the food."

"Gunpowder? In the *food*?"

"The gunpowder had toluene in it, giving it hallucinogenic properties. It kept us drugged, controllable."

"Oh my God!" Rose began to sob.

"When the civil war ended, those of us who survived were taken in by NGOs. They gave me a new life in the States. I can't . . . but nothing's changed." Raiden felt his own voice crack even through the Codec. "The only people who have no problem with my past have secrets and agendas of their own. Terrible nightmares . . . every night. I can never forget . . ."

She continued to weep. "Jack . . . !"

"I'm afraid of the night. That's why I don't sleep next to you."

"You should have told me . . ."

"Told you what? That I'm a *killer* and always have been?"

"No, no . . ."

"What I hate more than anything else in the world is my own past. I didn't want you—or anyone—to know about it. Now I know why I was chosen for this mission. No one can take him on—take him down—except me. I've been kept alive this long for this. I knew as soon as I saw Solidus."

"Jack, I love you the way you are now. You have to believe me!"

Raiden grunted with doubt.

"I didn't know anything about you, I admit that. Where you were born, how you grew up—but I know that now. And I know that what I feel for you can only get better, and I'll share in your · past if that's the price."

"It doesn't work that way. No one can share the burden of what I've done. It's not one of those warm and fuzzy things couples share."

"I accept the good and the bad, Jack. That's what you do for someone you love."

"I don't want to share my past with anyone. I just want to forget about it."

"Jack? I haven't told you—you know, what *I've* done . . ." Before going on, though, Rose checked herself and went silent, aside from continuing to cry.

"The last two years with you—it's been more than I've ever hoped for."

"Jack . . ."

"But I can't go any farther. I know you want to get married."

"I—"

"But . . . I can't. I can't risk starting a family. There's no way to erase my childhood."

"It's all right, Jack. Please, don't say any more."

She signed off. The Codec was quiet. Raiden closed his eyes, willing himself to shed some tears . . . but nothing happened. He couldn't cry. He had been taught long ago that good soldiers never cried.

The bonds securing him to the torture table suddenly opened with a snap. Olga had done what she had promised.

Still completely naked, Raiden stepped onto the floor and headed out of the room, past the glass partition, and into a long corridor. Immediately outside the medical room was a node. Raiden stooped awkwardly and accessed the maps—just as it could for the Big Shell itself, the Soliton Radar read Arsenal as well. Raiden could then envision through nanocommunication the ground plan he needed. Apparently he was in what was known as Arsenal's "Jejunum."

And it was occupied by a few guards.

"Raiden, do you copy?" It was the Colonel. Raiden slid behind a gigantic cargo container to his right and flattened his back against it. "You must continue your m-mission, mission."

He sounds funny, Raiden thought. The transmission was somewhat garbled.

"I've lost all my gear. I need to locate Snake," he answered.

"He was never factored into the simulation. Leave him out of this."

"I can't do much naked, especially in this temperature."

"That's true . . . you won't be able to . . . do much."

"I think Snake has my gear."

"Raiden, take out Solidus and his men. You must recover Arsenal intact."

"Colonel, are you under orders from the Patriots?"

"Your role—that is, *mission*—is to infiltrate the structure and disarm the terrorists!"

"My *role*? Why do you keep saying that?"

"Why not? This is a type of role-playing game. The point is that you play out your part—and I expect you to turn in a perfect performance!"

Raiden thought the Colonel sounded *extremely* strange. The quality of his nano-streamed voice was more electronic than usual. The garbling was just as bad, but Raiden figured it was because he was inside Arsenal Gear. Still, the man was also *behaving* oddly.

"Colonel, I just remembered something."

"What?"

"That I've never met you in person. Not once."

The Colonel's Codec image in Raiden's mind faltered, as if the signal was weak.

"Complete your mission according to the simulation!"

All right. That's enough, Raiden thought. "Colonel, who are you?"

"No more questions. We have Rosemary."

What did he just say? "What do you mean by that?"

"Over and out!"

The transmission ended. It had to have been one of the weirdest conversations he'd ever had with anyone.

He heard a guard walking toward the container. Raiden quickly tapped on the side of it and then ran to the opposite end and hid around the corner. The guard appeared at the back of the container, but by that time Raiden had skirted around to the opposite side.

The Colonel called again. "Raiden, turn off the simulator right now."

Huh? "What did you say?"

"The mission is a failure!" The transmission quality was worse and the Colonel sounded even more metallic. "Cut the power right now!"

"What's wrong with you?"

"Don't worry! It's a simulation! It's a game just like usual!"

Rose interrupted and said, "You'll ruin your eyes playing so close to the TV."

Raiden blinked in confusion. *What are you talking about?*

The Colonel returned. "Raiden, something happened to me last Thursday when I was driving home. I had a couple of miles to go—I looked up and saw a glowing orange object in the sky to the east! It was moving very irregularly . . . Suddenly there was intense light all around me—and when I came to I was home. What do you think happened to me . . . ?"

"Huh?"

"Fine . . . forget it . . ." The Colonel actually sounded hurt. End of transmission.

What the hell is going on?

Raiden peered into the corridor. The first guard he'd seen was busy looking for whatever had knocked on the back of the container. Raiden ran down the corridor, one hand covering his privates, the other ready to strike anything that appeared in front of him. The hallway split into two levels just ahead. The upper level continued parallel with the lower one. He didn't know whether to ascend a few stairs and try the high road, or simply stay where he was. The Soliton Radar told him there were three guards on the upper floor. Only one ahead on the lower. It was a no-brainer.

The Colonel burst through again. "You've been doing this a long time. Don't you have anything else to do with your time?" End of transmission.

Am I going crazy? What the hell did he just say?

Another burst. "I hear it's amazing when the famous purple stuffed worm in flap-jaw space with the tuning fork does a raw blink on *Hara-kiri* Rock. I need scissors! Sixty-one!"

Something was seriously wrong. It couldn't be the nanomachines. Or could it? But if that were the case, why would the Colonel be acting so bizarrely? Saying those loony things?

Raiden moved to another large container on his right just past the staircase. The upper level had a gridded floor, so he could see through it. A guard was just above him patrolling the floor. The guy hadn't noticed him, so Raiden simply waited him out. The operative stood flat against the container until the man headed in the opposite direction.

The Colonel was back. "Actually, there is something that I have been meaning to tell you but I just couldn't . . . I think you should know, though. On Saturday morning last week I saw a guy leaving Rosemary's room. How should I put it? It was like they were . . . so 'intimate.' I'm sorry. Sorry to bring this up during the mission, but . . ."

Oh, come on! That bastard! That can't *be true! . . . or could it?*

The only thing Raiden knew to do was move on. He hurried forward, stopping at every container he came to so that he could scan the space in front and behind him for sentries. The radar showed him that a new man was on his level, and he was heading his way! Raiden crouched and *willed* himself to be part of the container.

The guard walked by and didn't detect him.

Raiden stood and made a run for it.

The Colonel sent yet another transmission. "I'm not home right now. Please leave a message after the beep. Beep! Shadow Moses. Shadow Moses. Metal Gear. Destroy Metal Gear."

Ignore him!

The operative kept to the side of the pathway, hoping he would blend in to the wall. He was doing fine when the sentry behind him shouted, "Hey!" Raiden didn't turn to look—he simply ran.

The guard fired his weapon and then took off in pursuit. Raiden ducked between two containers, ran around the back one, and waited until the man had moved in front of him. Raiden sneaked behind the sentry, grabbed him in a stranglehold, struggled with the guy for a minute, and finally rendered him unconscious.

"Infiltrate . . . the enemy fortress . . . Outer Heaven . . . !" the Colonel ordered.

Raiden dragged the soldier between the cartons and left him there.

The whole world's going crazy, he thought.

Then the Colonel said cryptically, *"Kawanishi-Noseguchi, Kinunoebashi, Takiyama, Uguisunomori, Tsuzumigataki, Tada, Hirano, Ichinotorii, Uneno, Yamashita, Sasabe, Kofudai, Tokiwadai, Myoukenguchi . . ."*

Raiden didn't know *what* to make of that . . . until he realized that the Colonel was naming Japanese train stations!

The guy's NUTS!

He continued to move. The coast was clear to the end where he came to a hatch. The Soliton Radar informed him that he was entering the "Ascending Colon." It, too, was a long hallway.

"Jack, it's me."

Rose! Thank God . . . ! "Hi!"

"Jack, I owe you an apology."

"If it's about that conversation just now, I'm the one who's sorry."

"No, it's something else."

"What is it?" She sounded very serious, the complete antithesis of her demeanor just a little while earlier.

"That day at Federal Hall two years ago—it wasn't a coincidence." She struggled for a brief moment. "I was ordered to keep an eye on you."

What? Raiden blinked. "Keep an eye on me . . ."

"Yes. By the Patriots."

What else *could possibly go wrong today?* "You're a spy."

"I suppose. Yes. It's an ugly word."

He was speechless. There was absolutely nothing he could say.

"Are you still there?"

"Was sleeping with me part of the job?" he asked sarcastically.

"I fell in love with you!"

"How could anyone—"

"I can't excuse what I did. I've reported every detail of your personal life to them these two years. What you did, said, everything . . ."

"Must've been fun."

"But some things I didn't tell anyone! Like what I felt for you!"

He couldn't help being cruel. He wanted to hurt her. "So that's why you were involved in this mission. I should have known. Why else would they toss an *analyst* into the mix at the last minute?"

"I'm sorry, I know what I did was wrong."

"No matter where I go—I get *used*!"

"I reinvented myself to suit your tastes. Hairstyle, clothes, the way I moved, things I talked about . . . You say you love the color of my hair, my eyes. They're not even real."

"You must have gone over my psych profile with a fine-tooth comb."

"It was my job."

"Great performance. Had me completely fooled."

"What I really wanted was for you to see the real me. It hurt to play out this—this artificial romance. It was worse to lie to myself than to you. The more love you gave me, the more it hurt—because I knew the person you loved was just a character."

"So it was artificial on my end, too. It was just a game, not the real thing."

"Oh, Jack . . ."

"I feel better knowing that."

"What?"

His bitterness was overt. "I was in love—or thought I was—with someone who didn't exist. I was trying to be someone I wasn't by loving what wasn't real. I don't know who you really are! The person I knew isn't real. She's not the woman I'm talking to right now. In a sense, the deception was my own, not theirs."

"Jack, I thought I was acting, because that was my job. But I did fall in love with you, that wasn't an act!"

"You expect me to believe that?"

This time Rose couldn't answer.

"It's okay," he said. "You had your reasons, right? Hey, I understand. But I have nothing left to—"

"Jack!"

The transmission suddenly garbled as it had done with the Colonel's.

"What?"

"I'm—I'm carrying—"

Her voice *slowed* as if it was really recorded and the speed had been adjusted.

"Rose? What's going on?"

"I'm prrrregnant . . . Jaaack . . . your baaaaby . . ."

"*Rose!*"

The transmission ended.

30

Dazed and confused, Raiden continued his journey into Arsenal's Ascending Colon. Surely Snake was up ahead somewhere. Raiden knew that if he didn't find some clothes soon he was going to freeze to death.

"Amazing how you walk around like that."

Raiden turned toward the voice.

"Snake!"

The man stood leaning against the wall. He no longer wore the SEAL uniform. Instead, he was dressed in one of the older FOXHOUND sneaking suits. There was a bandana around his head—just as Raiden remembered Solid Snake from the numerous photographs he had seen. His voice was low, hushed against enemy hearing.

"Where's my gear?" Raiden whispered.

"Right over there." He pointed to a pile of weapons and equipment. Raiden rushed to it and immediately dressed in his Skull Suit. Within seconds he was fully equipped with everything that had been taken from him.

"That's more like it," Snake said. He then tapped on his neck, indicating that they should speak through the Codec.

"Sorry about earlier," he transmitted through nano. "I had to use you as bait to gain access to Arsenal. It worked."

"Why didn't you tell me about Olga?" Raiden demanded.

"You never asked." Raiden grunted, not hiding the fact that he was angry. "Not happy about that? Get over it."

The operative sighed. "Any effects of the virus yet?"

"Still waiting on that."

"So it was rigged by the Patriots?"

"Looks like it. From what I can tell, Arsenal is headed for Manhattan. I don't know what Solidus is planning, but we'll have to deal with it one way or another. There's also a troop of production-model RAYs ahead."

"How many units?"

"Twenty-five, according to Olga."

"Twenty-five?"

"Yeah. Can't say I've faced that many Metal Gears before, but—I think we can deal."

"No way we can!"

"We can because we have no other choice."

"How?"

"I've stocked up on Stinger missiles." Snake gestured to some boxes he had hidden off to the side of the corridor. There were two Stinger launchers as well. "Oh yeah, Olga left this for you." He handed Raiden a ninja's sword. The operative took it, amazed by its beauty and inherent power.

"Why?"

"Olga asked me to give it to you. Besides, I'm not a big fan of blades."

Raiden swished the sword around, testing it.

"We're going to have plenty of company ahead. This is your last chance to practice. It's a high frequency blade. You know how it works?"

"A little bit." Raiden continued to test the blade's electronic capabilities. For some reason he was a natural with it. The operative attempted a few maneuvers—uppercuts, chops, a spin-slash, quick thrusts . . . Raiden felt as if the sword had always been a part of his anatomy.

"You had VR with swords?" Snake asked, impressed.

"No. But I like this!"

"Come on. Time to go. I understand that several members of the Gurlukovich army were trained as Tengu warriors in order to protect Arsenal Gear's inner sanctums."

"Tengu?"

"They wear armor that's protected from biochemical environments and have masks inside their helmets to help them breathe. They run faster and are stronger than your average soldier, so be ready."

Raiden sheathed the sword in his belt. They both picked up the Stinger launchers. "Wait up, Snake."

"What?"

The operative hesitated. "Snake, have you ever . . . enjoyed killing someone?"

"What are you talking about?"

"I'm not sure. Sometimes it's hard to tell the difference between reality and a game."

"Diminished sense of reality, huh? VR training will do that." He continued walking through the Colon. Raiden followed.

"No, it was field training, when I was a kid. I lied, Snake. I have more field experience that I can remember. It's not VR that's doing this to me."

Snake's eyes narrowed. "Raiden, we don't carry guns to take people down. We're not here to help some politician, either."

"You can say that because you're a legend, a hero. I'm Jack the Ripper, a dirty reminder . . . of a terrible mistake."

"Legends don't mean a whole lot. I was just a name to exploit. Just like you."

"People will remember only the good part, the right part of what you did."

"There's no right part in murder, not ever. And we're not in this to make a name for ourselves."

"Then what are you and Otacon fighting for?"

"A future. You can stop being part of a mistake starting now."

"What am I . . . what am I supposed to do?"

They came to a closed hatch. Snake used a key card to open it. They went through and continued walking.

"Find something to believe in," Snake answered. "And find it for yourself. And when you do, pass it on to the future."

"Believe in what?"

"That's your problem. Come on."

Otacon called on the Codec. "Snake! Raiden!"

"Otacon! Are you all right?" Snake asked.

"Yeah. So are all the hostages."

"That's good news," Raiden commented.

"How's everything on your end?"

"All right for now. But there is something . . ."

"What?"

"The Colonel's last few transmissions were strange," Raiden explained.

"Strange? How?"

"Just . . . strange. No idea—"

"Interference?"

"I don't know."

"Where is this Colonel?"

"I don't know. I've never met the man, actually."

Otacon rubbed his chin. "I'll dig around."

"Thanks. I owe you one."

"If there's anything else, call me on the Codec."

The physicist signed off as Raiden and Snake approached a hatch marked ILEUM. Snake swiped the card, started to open it . . . and stopped. He turned to Raiden and whispered. "I have a bad feeling about this. Watch out."

They slowly entered the space—and were immediately surrounded by a troop of masked soldiers—the Arsenal Tengu!

Some of the men were equipped with swords. Others had AKs. The ones with guns started firing. Both Snake and Raiden leaped instinctively to opposite sides of the room and ducked behind cover. Raiden set down the cumbersome Stinger launcher and started to draw his SOCOM but then decided to try the sword Olga had given him. He felt comfortable with it. He was confident he could use it successfully.

Snake signaled him and Raiden nodded. Together they rushed out and ran forward. Snake blasted away with his SOCOM while Raiden used the blade to deflect the onslaught of bullets raining on them. It was an amazing piece of technology and weapon craftsmanship. The high frequency capabilities enabled Raiden to swing the sword with lightning-fast speed and intuitively knock away the enemy ammunition. It felt . . . *fantastic*.

Snake mowed down the front line of Tengu, allowing Raiden to meet a couple of the sword-bearing soldiers head-on. He took on both of them at once, swinging the blade like a pro. The swords clashed and *clanged*, flinging sparks in all directions. Raiden rapidly spun his body 360 degrees and slashed out, slicing his opponents through the midsections. He moved on without stopping, noting that Snake was also advancing. With the SOCOM blazing, Snake became a warrior with the urgency of a charging rhinoceros. It was inspiring. Raiden knocked away a stream of fire from the Tengu at the rear, pausing long enough to stab a soldier who had appeared abruptly from a place of cover.

The Tengu were definitely a cut above the enemy troops Raiden had encountered thus far. They were fast and tough, and they fought with determination. Without the high frequency blade, Raiden was certain that he and Snake would have been finished. By being able to knock away bullets with the same rapidity as they were fired the two men had a great advantage.

Raiden hadn't counted how many men there were, but in two

minutes it was all over. The Tengu lay dead or wounded on the floor. Snake glanced at Raiden to confirm that he was all right. Raiden nodded at his partner and grinned.

Otacon called on the Codec. "Raiden? About this Colonel of yours . . . I found out where he is."

"Where?"

"Inside Arsenal."

"*What?*"

"I've checked out all the possibilities, but I keep coming back to Arsenal. It isn't a relay point. It's the origin of the signal. And the encryption protocol it uses is exactly the same as that of Arsenal's AI—the so-called 'GW.'"

"What the hell does this mean?"

"I think it means—you've been talking to an AI."

"That's impossible!"

"The Colonel probably isn't GW per se. GW was most likely stimulating cortical activity in the dormant part of your brain through signal manipulation of your own nanomachines. The Colonel is in part your own creation, cobbled together from expectations and experience."

"That's crazy!"

"But it's probably the truth. The virus may be starting to affect GW, which would explain the Colonel's behavior."

"It was all—an illusion? Everything I've done so far . . . ?"

"Raiden!" Snake snapped.

"Snake, what's happening around here?"

"I don't know. What I do know is that you're standing right here in front of me. Not an illusion—a *flesh and blood man*."

Raiden didn't know what to think.

"It's your call," Snake said. "You can drop this if you want."

Raiden looked at Snake and then at his surroundings. The Tengu soldier bodies. The interior of Arsenal Gear.

"No," he said. "I can't do that. Let's go."

31

THE TWO WARRIORS retrieved the Stinger launchers, moved on, and entered a new section of Arsenal Gear, a large circular space with a high ceiling called the "Sigmoid Colon." In many ways the room resembled an arena where gladiators might have fought ages earlier. The only difference was that there was no space for an audience. There were a couple of doors on the far side of the area. A rung ladder stretched up one wall to the darkness near the ceiling.

The Codec buzzed. The Colonel again. Raiden feared answering it, wondering what nonsense the AI would spout this time.

"Raiden! They've got Rose!"

The Colonel's voice sounded normal this time. There was no garbling or electronic interference.

"What?"

"Rose is being held in the holds!"

Snake shook his head. "It's a trap," he said.

But Rose's frightened face appeared on the monitor. "Help!" she cried. The image just as quickly disappeared.

"Rose!" Raiden shook the Codec as if he could get her back somehow.

"Raiden, get a grip!" Snake commanded.

"But Snake!"

"It's a trap. Since the Colonel doesn't exist, there's no way he can take Rose hostage."

Raiden continued to stare at the now-blank Codec. "Yeah. You're right."

"I *am* right."

"Okay. But . . . does Rose . . . exist?"

"Don't be weird. She's your—"

"What if I've never really met her . . . ?"

"What?"

"If the Colonel is something that I partly dreamt up, then . . . everything I remember about her could be . . ."

"Don't jump to conclusions!"

"You and Otacon are the ones that say the Colonel never existed."

"Raiden!"

Is this what Olga was talking about? Raiden asked himself.

Snake turned his back on the younger man and continued walking. Raiden snapped out of the funk and followed him. When they reached the center of the arena, the lights seemed to flicker. There was the sound of *sliding*—

—and a dozen more sword-wielding Tengu commandos dropped from the ceiling on ropes, surrounding the duo.

Raiden immediately dropped the Stinger launcher and drew the high-frequency blade. Snake readied the SOCOM. The two men positioned themselves back-to-back, their weapons aimed at the newcomers.

For a few seconds nothing happened. Then one of the commandos raised his blade, shouted, and lunged for Snake. The SOCOM exploded in a burst of gunfire. The Tengu whipped his sword in front of him, deflecting Snake's bullets. Then, the other commandos attacked all at once. Raiden swiftly slashed his sword back and forth, crashing with the razor-sharp weapons of destruction. Snake continued to fire, dodging a blow from his opponent's blade. This time the ammunition ripped through the Tengu, sending him to the floor in a bloody mess. Snake turned to aim at other commandos but found he needed to move defensively to prevent being cut in half. Raiden held his own, fencing with three Tengu at once. Snake clutched the assault rifle and performed a forward roll between two enemy soldiers. He came up on his feet *behind* them, turned, and mowed them down before they had time to figure out what had happened. Snake was then in a position to shoot the other Tengu not involved in the sword fight with Raiden. The men rushed him, but Snake's trigger finger was faster. The arena echoed with the cries of pain and anguish as the SOCOM delivered its messengers of death.

Raiden tried the 360-degree spin again, finding that the maneuver suited him. His blade decapitated one of his combatants as Raiden's body returned to its original stance, the lethal sword outstretched as if it were a part of the operative's body. The other two Tengu retreated a few steps, but Raiden kept advancing. He swung the sword with confidence, relentlessly boring into his enemies with a frightening fervor. The blade struck one of them across the chest, cutting through his armor and penetrating vulnerable flesh.

Snake stood and watched the display with admiration. *The kid's not bad,* he thought.

The second Tengu went down, blood spurting from the wound in his chest. The last man standing continued the fight with Raiden, but it was a lost cause. Something had definitely gotten into the young operative—whether or not it was the false message that Rose had been nabbed, Snake didn't know. But there was no doubt that he was witnessing the emergence of a formidable soldier.

In seconds it was all over. The twelve Tengu lay around them dead or dying. The only sounds in the echoing chamber were the groans of the mortally wounded and Raiden's panting.

Then a hatch opened. A tall, dark woman with blonde hair strolled inside carrying a monstrous Rail Gun.

"Fortune . . ." Raiden murmured.

The two men watched her approach until she stopped some twenty feet away. The air of melancholy—of desperation—that Raiden had felt from her before still enveloped the statuesque figure.

"It's been a long wait, Solid Snake—the root of all my sorrows."

"What?" Snake asked.

"Two years ago you killed my father," Fortune said. "That was the beginning of hell for us. Everyone I love has been taken from me one by one . . . and no matter how hard I try I can't follow them. An endless nightmare . . . The only thing we live for is to see it end. Our wait is almost over."

Raiden spoke. "You can't be serious about firing the nuke!"

"Since no one can kill me, I may as well kill everyone I can," she said as if it were the most natural thing in the world. "Starting with *you*, Solid Snake!"

She aimed her linear rifle.

"Damn!" Raiden whispered.

Snake readied his automatic. "Looks like I'm today's pick," he shot back at Raiden. "You go on ahead." He gestured with his chin toward the rung ladder.

Raiden shook his head. He wanted to stay and fight.

"You want eternal rest? I've got it right here," Snake said to the woman.

"What are you going to do?" Raiden whispered. "Bullets can't get near her!"

"I'll think of something. There's no such thing as a witch."

Fortune sneered at Snake. "You think you can kill me?" She shifted the linear rifle.

"I don't know what your group's been through," Snake said, "but let's get one thing clear—I didn't kill General Dolph."

"Do you think anyone believes your lies?"

"Raiden, get out of here!" Snake shouted.

Raiden picked up his Stinger launcher, slung the heavy thing over his shoulder, moved closer to the wall, grabbed hold of the rungs, and started to climb. He hesitated, looking back at his friend.

"Go!" Snake yelled.

Raiden had to put his faith in Snake's abilities. There was still a job to do ahead. He continued his ascent until he reached the ceiling. He then opened the hatch and climbed through just as gunfire erupted down in the arena below.

32

HE EMERGED INTO the middle of a dimly lit giant hangar appropriately named Arsenal's "Rectum." Raiden figured that it was where the Metal Gear RAYs were housed, but it was too dark to see ahead. The ceiling and walls of the huge room were lost in the gloom. It was then that Raiden began to appreciate the enormity of Arsenal Gear.

"Jack, I've been watching how you fight."

Solidus.

His voice reverberated through the cavernous chamber. Raiden whirled around but the man was nowhere in sight.

"It looks like you've remembered the way you used to kill in the old days! Or is it one of the S3 Plan's proud achievements?"

Raiden shouted angrily into the darkness, "What are you talking about?"

"It came as a complete surprise when Ocelot discovered the S3 data from GW. Not a bad idea, though—using fire to fight fire, creating the perfect assassin to retire Solid Snake's brother. S3 stands for Solid Snake Simulation . . . It's a development program to artificially reproduce Solid Snake, the perfect warrior.

The result is a FOXHOUND commando when FOXHOUND no longer exists, a simulated Solid Snake shaped by VR regimen. Sound like someone you know, Jack?"

Raiden felt a sinking feeling in his chest. He knew that someone all too well . . .

"I'm sorry to see you reduced to one of the Patriots' puppets. But I've made use of you—and their plan—too. Solid Snake's sudden appearance, your arrival—it was obvious the Patriots were among my ranks. I had to smoke the agent out before the mission entered the final phase. You came in handy as bait. Jack, those days during the civil war were as real as they come . . . Every day was absolute, split between life and death. You ran from it, and now, you've been led back to war by something less than real."

Raiden heard what sounded like a sonic boom. He turned to see Solidus Snake zoom toward him, propelled by an accelerator attached to the back of his armor. He stopped some distance in front of the operative, still wearing the mechanical tentacles and carrying a P90 high-powered assault rifle.

"No more games, Raiden," the man said. "At least you know. There's no reason to keep you alive now . . ."

There came a cacophony of *clashes* and *clatters* behind Solidus. The noise echoed loudly in the chamber, sending a shiver of fear down Raiden's spine. Out of the shadows walked three Metal Gear RAYs. The middle one opened its beak and roared with a metallic, horrible shriek.

"I've given you a worthy opponent, at least," Solidus announced triumphantly. "But now you should die as the little Jackie boy I once knew."

With a demonic laugh, Solidus accelerated away out of the light, leaving Raiden to face the mecha beasts alone.

How am I going to fight these things?

Before he could think it through, one of the RAYs fired rounds from one of the machine-gun pods attached to the end of its wings. Reflexively, Raiden used the sword to deflect the bullets—

but there were so many of them that the best thing to do would be to get the hell out of their way. He performed a torso-axial jump and leaped to the side. His own small-arms firepower would be useless against the monsters. His only hope was the Stinger launcher. But what piece of them should he target? Where were their vulnerable spots?

One of the RAY's faceplates opened, followed by a blast from the beast's Rail Gun. Raiden ran forward between the RAY's legs to avoid being hit. But a different RAY was waiting for him. A homing missile shot from the tube on the thing's back. Raiden had a split second to bolt sideways and roll. The explosion sent him reeling meters from where he thought he was. Dazed, Raiden picked himself up and readied the Stinger launcher. But as he loaded the weapon, the first RAY turned on him and fired its V17 Vulcan LaserStorm Cutter at the operative. Raiden cartwheeled out of harm's way, leaving the Stinger launcher on the ground. The RAY's faceplate opened again, followed by another blast from the Rail Gun.

Raiden managed to dodge the onslaught but was running out of options. Then he remembered the chaff grenades in his pack. They wouldn't do much damage, but they could be effective in slowing down the Metal Gears. After all, chaff grenades interfered with electronic circuitry. It was worth a try.

He dug into the pack and retrieved a handful. Raiden then watched the RAYs move and take position to attack. They were certainly amazing specimens of technology. Besides having ceramic-titanium alloy for armor, the mechas were equipped with artificial fibers that contracted when electricity was applied, much like natural muscles. Much better than hydraulics for movement. It was as if they were organically mobile. They were also controlled by computer. Each RAY had a nervous system–like network of conductive nanotubes that connected the widely dispersed sensor systems and relay commands.

There was only one way to mess them up.

Raiden pulled the pin out of one of the chaffs and tossed it at the closest RAY. The grenade exploded—and the RAY paused. It didn't move. Raiden pulled off the AK that still hung around his back and let loose with a constant stream of spray fire. The bullets bounced off the armor as expected—but they did damage the machine-gun pods and missile tubes attached to the RAY's knees.

Almost immediately, a red, gooey liquid oozed from the "wounds."

My God, is that . . . blood?

Raiden watched with amazement as the gunk solidified and "healed" the holes he had made.

That meant the RAYs had built-in mechanisms that secreted nanopaste from valves. The stuff coagulated like real blood wherever exterior damage was sustained.

Another blast of machine-gun fire woke Raiden from his moment of panic-stricken immobility. He performed another torso-axial jump and landed next to the Stinger launcher. As he picked it up, the RAY's faceplate opened.

It opens its faceplate when it's about to fire the Rail Gun. The RAY draws in outside energy through the faceplate!

Raiden aimed the launcher at the cavity beneath the faceplate—and fired. The Stinger soared toward its target and struck the heart of the beast. *Direct hit!*

The RAY roared as if it really felt pain. The thing raised its beak to the ceiling and wailed. Its wings thrashed wildly. The machine guns issued several bursts of indirect fire as if the RAY had been blinded. The hulking mecha stumbled forward, forcing Raiden to run out of its way. It didn't follow him, though. Instead, it leaned forward, froze for a few seconds . . . and then collapsed into a heap.

He had done it.

One down . . . and *two* to go.

Raiden, near exhaustion, panted, "It's no use . . ."

The two other RAYs converged on Raiden from opposite sides, ready to deliver the *coup de grace*.

"I expected a little more fight than that, Jack!" shouted Solidus.

Raiden braced himself. A RAY prepared to trample him, *but suddenly Olga leaped into the fray from somewhere in the darkness.* She stood in front of Raiden, shielding him. The RAY paused.

Solidus' disembodied voice called out, "So, you've decided to show yourself."

"Olga," Raiden said. "Don't do this. They'll know—"

"I'll hold them off, give you time to get away," she replied.

"What about you?" She didn't answer. "This is suicide!"

"Your nanomachines—they're transmitting your vital signs to the Patriots. If you die, my child dies. Do you understand?"

"The child . . ."

Solidus' voice boomed again. "I see! So that's why you sold your troops out to me. So many dead, and they all died trusting you! Weren't they your comrades?"

He had hit the woman where it hurt. "No, not just comrades! Family!"

"Hah!"

"I know I'm going to hell," she declared. "But at least my child—"

"I applaud your attitude. If you have a death wish, I'll be happy to accommodate you."

The atmosphere sheared violently with an explosion. Solidus propelled himself in front of Olga with the aid of the accelerator.

"See you in hell!" he shouted—and one of the tentacles snapped out and grabbed Olga by the throat. Raiden fired the SOCOM, but the bullets bounced off of the man's armor. Olga managed to turn the barrel of her own gun toward Solidus with a cry of rage—but the pressure on her throat was too great. She dropped her weapon, fighting for breath. Solidus lifted her off the ground, dangling her in the air like an animal with its prey. He twirled the P90 in his hand like a gunslinger.

Olga's eyes met Raiden's. "Live . . . you have to . . ." she gasped.

The P90 stopped rotating and Solidus pulled the trigger. A single gunshot blasted through the air and hit Olga in the forehead. Blood and brain tissue splattered behind her.

"*Olga!*" Raiden shouted.

The tentacle flung the woman's body across the room where she landed with a *thud*.

Shocked beyond words, Raiden fell to his knees. He was paralyzed by the terrible turn of events.

Then a tentacle grabbed *him* by the neck.

"Enjoy the show, Jack?" Solidus asked. "Let's pick up where we left off." He signaled toward the dark ceiling. Someone else controlling the RAYs went into action. The Metal Gear monstrosities began to move toward the two men. However, something wasn't right—the RAYs wavered as if they were having trouble keeping their balance. The wings flapped erratically, the entire structures *wobbled* . . .

"Hm?" Solidus furrowed his brow, watching them.

A RAY shook its birdlike head like a broken toy.

"What's wrong with it?" Solidus called out.

Raiden heard Revolver Ocelot's voice ring out from the darkness. "The AI . . . GW . . . it's out of control!"

"What?"

The RAYs then broke out into a frenzy of uncontrollable movements.

Ocelot continued, "I'm reading an abnormal impulse cascade throughout the neural network. I can't shut it down!"

"What happened?"

"Maybe—some kind of virus—"

Solidus knew what that meant. "The *Patriots*?"

"I don't know!"

"Ocelot! What have you been up to?"

"It's too late!" Sirens wailed throughout the hangar. "Arsenal's system control is going haywire! It's on an emergency ascent course!"

The entire foundation rocked. Raiden felt it. The gigantic craft was rising.

The RAYs creaked and roared. Then they turned to each other . . . and *attacked*! They lashed out at whatever was in their way, whether it was another RAY or the humans in front of them.

"Stupid machines!" Solidus shouted. Still carrying Raiden with one tentacle, he snapped shut his steel collar and turned on the muscle suit. Harnessing the accelerator, he deftly evaded a RAY's lashing tail and other assaults. He then aimed the P90 and expertly sniped out the mecha's AI control center with carefully placed blasts. This seemed to settle down the other RAYs. They stood still, slightly trembling with faulty neural networks.

"Damn the Patriots!" He looked at Raiden, considered his captive, and said, "You still have some use . . ." He dropped Raiden onto the floor. The operative got up to his hands and knees . . . but his will to fight was sapped.

Then a new voice rang out in the cavernous space, "I've captured Snake!"

Both Raiden and Solidus looked up.

Fortune had arrived. She had Snake, his hands bound behind him, walking beside her.

"Snake?" Raiden whispered.

Solidus ordered, "Bring him in." As Fortune pushed Snake forward, Solidus turned to Raiden, who was still helpless on the floor. One of the man's tentacles slithered to the operative's neck—it held some kind of hypodermic—and jabbed him in the neck.

Raiden was helpless as his eyes rolled into the back of his head and he blacked out.

33

"ARE YOU awake yet, Jack?"

Raiden heard Solidus' voice, but he wasn't sure if he was dreaming or not. He'd been out cold, but for how long?

He felt a breeze. Damp air. Chilling wind.

The surface he was lying on was wet. It was . . . *raining*?

His vision was blurred, but he could see Solidus standing before him. Raiden knew it was him because he still wore tentacles.

He shook his head. Whatever it was Solidus had injected him with was beginning to wear off, but he still felt hazy.

Raiden looked around. He was no longer in the big room. He was . . . *outside*.

Solidus stood in front of him. To the side was one of the Metal Gear RAYs. No, it wasn't one of the Arsenal RAYs. It was the one he had seen during the Harrier battle. The prototype. The RAY that Ocelot had stolen two years earlier.

Revolver Ocelot himself stood by the RAY's foot.

Raiden turned his head and saw Fortune standing next to Snake, who was lying facedown with his hands cuffed behind his back. He, too, must have been drugged.

Raiden looked up and saw a dark, stormy sky. Rain.

He felt movement. Choppy sailing.

They were on top of Arsenal Gear. The gigantic war machine had surfaced and was moving across the river. It was the middle of the night, or early morning before sunrise, Raiden couldn't tell.

Solidus spoke again. "GW, the Arsenal AI, is corrupted beyond repair. I admit that I underestimated you . . ." A tentacle whipped out, grabbed Raiden by the throat, and lifted him up again. "I'll squeeze the answers out of you instead, my son . . ."

Raiden couldn't breathe. He struggled helplessly as he dangled in the air.

"What do you hope to hear?" Fortune asked. "You know he doesn't know anything."

"It's not *him* I want the answers from." Solidus continued to choke the operative for a few more seconds and then released him. Raiden fell to Arsenal's hull with a crash. The young man gasped and gulped a lungful of air. He coughed and wheezed in torment.

"What do you mean?" Fortune asked.

"That's not your business."

"Oh, really? It so happens I have some business of my own to attend to." She turned to leave.

"Planning to hijack Arsenal?" Solidus asked. The woman stopped dead in her tracks. "You were going to screw me over, weren't you?"

Fortune whirled around. "Who talked? Ocelot?"

"Not exactly. I was the one who used Ocelot to suggest the idea to you in the first place."

"What?"

"I was planning to give you Arsenal to begin with."

She sneered. "Why the uncharacteristic generosity?"

"I'm no philanthropist. Arsenal is far from impregnable. It needs other Metal Gears as guards, a huge payload of warheads, and full air, sea, and land support to function efficiently. Against a large attack force without support, Arsenal is nothing more than a gigantic coffin. Seizing Arsenal Gear was never the real objective."

Fortune struggled to contain her fury. "What was your objective then?"

"A list of names—of the *Patriots!*"

"Huh?"

"They were planning to extend their control to digital information flow with GW and Arsenal. That means the information they want to filter out is contained in GW. Including the list of the highest twelve members of the Patriots' Wisemen's Committee."

"And once you knew who they were, you would cross out their names one by one? While we with their useless Arsenal drew their fire?"

"Very good!"

Fortune said through her teeth, "You were using us all along."

"Were you any different?"

"But your plan's hit a snag with GW destroyed hasn't it?"

"No . . . there is another way."

"Really . . . but we have our own plans to carry out. We'll take the Arsenal since you don't care for it anyway. The purified hydrogen bomb is ready to go."

"A nuclear strike won't stop them."

"It will damage their power source—the mindless masses that they control. First things first."

"Of course. That was what you wanted. I won't stop you. Good luck."

"Thanks," Fortune said with irony. "But I have quite enough of that."

Ocelot laughed.

"What exactly do you find so funny?" she asked the gunslinger, unable to mask the hatred in her voice.

"Charades usually are humorous. I wouldn't have minded

watching some more of it, but we're running a little short on time."

This time it was Solidus who turned to him. "What are you talking about?"

Ocelot shrugged. "Everything you've done here has been scripted. A little exercise set up by us."

"*Exercise?*"

"The S3 plan was conceived as a means to produce soldiers on par with Solid Snake. That's what I told you. But the VR training the boy was put through is not the meat of the project. You think this little terrorist incident is your own doing, Solidus? *This* is the S3 training kernel—an orchestrated re-creation of Shadow Moses."

"*What?*"

"Ames' and the President's deaths, the ninja, the computer virus that mimics FOXDIE . . . did you really think they were all a coincidence? Ames' own nanomachines were used to shut down his pacemaker. I arranged for the appearance of the ninja as well. As for the President—although Johnson realized what was going on, he played out his allotted part. As for the computer virus, it's a digital counterpart of FOXDIE. It was also designed to eliminate every scrap of information regarding the Patriots from GW. Your plan was invalidated even before execution, Solidus."

Solidus' eyes flared red as Ocelot continued to speak.

"Fatman was a different story. He's one of our people, a sort of examiner we hired to test the boy's progress before letting him tackle the exercise proper. We had to arrange for Stillman's presence to coax the maniac into agreeing. If the boy had allowed the Big Shell to be destroyed, this exercise would have ended there. The project has no room for failures."

Solidus was seething. "What do you mean?"

"Given the right situation, the right story, anyone can be shaped into Snake. Even rookies can fight like men of experience. An instant creation of genius—and this training kernel will provide more than enough data to formulate such a program. You, Dead Cell, Olga . . . you're all nothing but pawns placed to create the perfect simulation. Solidus, you and the boy were selected because your relationship resembles the one between Solid Snake and Big Boss."

Ocelot addressed the woman. "Fortune, you and the rest of Dead Cell stand in for the FOXHOUND squad that Snake took on in Shadow Moses. You're the most impressive collection of freaks outside of FOXHOUND. We've gone to a lot of trouble to set you up against the boy. That story about purified hydrogen bombs is just the tip of the iceberg. The project was already underway when I sank that tanker along with your old man two years ago. Throwing your husband, Colonel Jackson, in the brig was part of it, too. You were told that the eradication of Dead Cell six months ago was an act of the Patriots. We provoked and encouraged your hatred—and you opted for vengeance, just as we planned."

"All *orchestrated* . . . ?" Fortune asked.

Ocelot glanced at Snake. "Except for the appearance of the real Solid Snake. I wonder now who sent for *you* . . . ?"

Fortune's lips trembled. "All our misfortune was . . . just a part of their project?" Her face hard, she swung her linear rifle toward Ocelot—but he smoothly fired his revolver before she could pull the trigger. The gunshot resounded loudly even in the rain.

Fortune gasped and looked down at her chest. A hole had appeared between her breasts.

"H-how . . . could . . . ?"

Ocelot grinned. "You're no Lady Luck. You have nothing that we didn't give you."

"Wha-what?" Fortune began to waver, her legs buckling. She clutched her chest with one hand as blood oozed between her fingers. She then sank to one knee.

"Do you know why no bullet could hit you? It wasn't magic

or some New Age mumbo jumbo. Certainly wasn't your psychic talents. It was all staged by the Patriots."

She was having trouble breathing. "St-taged?"

"You were being shielded by the electromagnetic weapons technology that the Patriots developed. Your Dead Cell comrades loved your father and husband—we needed a pathetic wretch like you to keep them focused. You've been our puppet all along just like Olga."

"No!"

"You were hamming it up as the tragic heroine thanks to the script the Patriots wrote for you. Pure self-indulgence—absorbed in your own 'misfortune,' you couldn't get enough of the drama."

She couldn't believe it. "I . . . could have died . . . whenever I wanted to . . ." With a resolve that grew from a hidden fortress within her soul, Fortune managed to bring herself to stand.

Ocelot scrutinized her. "Hm? Thought I got her in the heart . . ."

Fortune fired the linear rifle at Ocelot . . . but the bullets deflected, just as ammunition had done with her!

Ocelot nodded. "Now I remember. Your heart's on the right." She fired again, but the bullets flew off in different directions without hitting him. "Waste of metal, my dear. Your luck's run out." He smiled and pointed to a small device attached to his belt. "This is the little gizmo. There's no such thing as miracles or the supernatural—only cutting-edge technology."

Solidus growled and fired the P90 at Ocelot. Again, the rounds were deflected.

"You b-bastard," Fortune whispered. She coughed blood and fell, gasping for air.

Ocelot leaped onto the RAY's leg and swiftly climbed to the cockpit. Solidus continued to fire at him, but it was no use. Nothing could hit the gunslinger.

"Now that I have enough data," Ocelot announced from the top of RAY, "all I have to do is retrieve Arsenal and clean up the refuse from the exercise!" With that, he climbed into the cockpit and assumed the controls.

Solidus shouted, "Just try!"

RAY's machine guns took aim at Solidus, who threw down the P90 and drew swords—one in each hand. The machine gun let loose with a thunderstorm of gunfire, but Solidus expertly repelled the bullets. One of the rounds happened to ricochet off Snake's handcuffs, jolting him awake. He groaned and shook his wrists loose.

Failing to hit Solidus, Ocelot halted the machine-gun fire and opened RAY's missile pod. "How's this, then?"

But before he could fire, Fortune managed to stand again and step in front of them all, shielding Raiden and the others from Metal Gear. She extended her hands.

"Fortune!" Raiden cried.

"You idiot!" Solidus yelled. "Get the hell away from there!"

"I told you," Ocelot announced through RAY's PA, "your luck's run out. Take your reward. It's all the payload RAY has. Die!"

Snake shouted, "Everybody down!"

The three men flattened themselves on Arsenal's hull just as Ocelot pulled the triggers. Missiles shot out of RAY toward Fortune . . . *and then changed their trajectory*! They curved away from Fortune and harmlessly detonated in the air above them.

"What the—!" Ocelot said, astonished. "Impossible!"

He fired another set of missiles. Once again they couldn't hit their target.

Snake muttered, "She *is* Lady Luck!"

Fortune shook her head. "My name is Helena Dolph Jackson. The daughter of a proud noble soldier . . ." She coughed blood again and began to fade. "I can see my family again . . ." She finally collapsed, her strength completely waned. It took her mere moments to die.

Ocelot aimed a cannon at the three men. "Try this instead!"

he shouted. He reached for the trigger—and his prosthetic right arm suddenly froze. "What? No! Not now!" The possession took over with uncontrollable power. Ocelot struggled with the arm, but Liquid Snake's spirit was too strong. This time the entity gained full control over Revolver Ocelot's body in seconds.

"Brothers!" Liquid announced with his own voice through Ocelot's vocal cords.

Snake was horrified. "Liquid!"

"I've been waiting for this."

Solidus, too, was incredulous. "It can't be!"

Liquid laughed. "I've been inside this arm all along, waiting for the right time to awaken."

"You were inside Ocelot?" Solidus asked.

"Yes. A sleeper in the arm of a Patriots' spy."

Snake growled, "It was *you* two years ago?"

"Exactly. I was controlling him. Snake, it was I that leaked information about Arsenal to your partner and got you out here."

"*What?*"

"You're the only one who can free me, after all. Now I'm off to bury the Patriots for good!"

Solidus shouted, raising his fist at Ocelot/Liquid. "You know where they are? How?"

"Why do you think I chose Ocelot as my host? But before I go, I have a family matter to settle with both of you. There's room for only one Snake and one Big Boss!"

Solidus screamed a war cry and fired flaming blasts from his tentacles. They missed RAY's cockpit completely.

"Time to say good-bye!" Liquid said. He flipped a switch. "I've started Arsenal's navigation program. The course will take you straight into Manhattan!"

Raiden, now standing, shouted, "You're planning to crash this thing into New York City?"

"It'll be a full-scale disaster!" Solid Snake agreed.

"Disaster?" Liquid asked. "That has a nice ring to it."

They felt Arsenal lurch and shift directions. It immediately started to vibrate and pick up speed. The three men were forced to grab hold of protuberances on the hull to keep from being swept off.

"Like surfing? It's a good way to go!"

"Liquid!" Snake shouted. "Stop this thing!"

"Hey, Snake. You coming?" With that, RAY rose on its legs, turned and headed for Arsenal's side. Solid Snake released his grip on Arsenal and ran after RAY.

"Snake!" Raiden shouted.

RAY leaped off the speeding Arsenal and into the water. Snake managed to grasp the thing's tail as it went over the side stringing him along with it.

Raiden almost got up and took off after them, but he knew he'd never be able to catch up. Arsenal had already sped a great distance from where RAY had submerged.

Besides, all he could see now was lower Manhattan looming ahead of them.

There was nothing he could do. They were going to collide into the island.

Closer . . . closer . . .

He saw the skyscrapers standing tall in the darkness. Arsenal approached the landmass . . . faster . . . faster . . .

They were almost there. *They were really going to crash!*

Raiden shut his eyes and screamed.

34

THE MASSIVE BEHEMOTH known as Arsenal Gear dipped under the Verrazano-Narrows Bridge and collided into the Statue of Liberty while roaring past Liberty Island. The statue's remains were dumped onto Ellis Island as Arsenal continued north at a breakneck speed. When it plowed into Battery Park, the monstrous warship bounced and crashed over landmarks, buildings, and vehicles. The twenty-eight battery cannons were destroyed in its wake, ending their tenure in America without having fired a single shot in a real battle. The obstacles slowed down Arsenal's warpath, but the craft continued to skid through Wall Street and over the New York Stock Exchange building, tearing away the NYSE and U.S. flags. With a roar of explosions, eventually the leviathan decelerated enough . . . and came to a stop in front of Federal Hall National Monument. Arsenal's tip knocked the statue of George Washington slightly askew. The American flag was torn but still hung loosely on the pole in front of the building.

The impact sent Raiden and Solidus flying off the mobile base and onto Federal Hall's roof.

Very few people were stirring in the predawn streets. The

screams and sirens had yet to start up; but as this was New York City, an army of emergency vehicles and personnel would descend upon the scene within minutes. A flock of pigeons roosting on top of the hall reeled with fright. Gigantic, dark smoke clouds swarmed above the site—an all-too-horrific reminder of another day of destruction in lower Manhattan.

For a few moments the two warriors didn't move. Finally, Solidus opened his eyes, shook his head, and stood. Looking around, he finally realized where he was.

"Federal Hall . . ." He started to laugh. He threw up his hands and broke into a frenzied dance.

Raiden snapped out of his shock at the sound of Solidus' voice. He pulled himself up. "What are you laughing at?"

Solidus stopped dancing and asked, "Do you know what day it is today?"

Raiden was confused by the question. "Uhm, April thirtieth?"

"That's right. George Washington took office as the first President of the United States of America two hundred years ago today. And it happened right here. We were going to declare another independence—the dawn of a new nation—here. The end of the Patriots' secret rule, liberation of this country. This was where it was supposed to begin, this is where freedom could have been born."

The man's expression hardened as he turned his icy gaze on Raiden.

"All you want is power at any cost!" the operative growled.

Solidus paused to consider Raiden's statement. "Jack, it's not power I want. What I wanted to take back from the Patriots were things like freedom, civil rights, opportunities . . . the founding principles of this country. Everything that's about to be wiped out by their digital censorship. Jack, listen to me. We're all born with an expiration date. No one lasts forever. Life is nothing but a grace period for turning the best of our genetic material into the next generation. The data of life is transferred from parent to child. That's how it works. But we have no heirs, no legacy. They call my brothers and me *Les Enfants Terribles*—cloned from our father, with the ability to reproduce conveniently engineered out. What is our legacy if we cannot pass the torch? Proof of our existence—a mark of some sort. When the torch is passed on from parent to child, it extends beyond DNA. Information is imparted as well.

"All I want is to be remembered. By other people, by history. The Patriots are trying to protect their power, their own interests, by controlling the digital flow of information. I want my memory, my existence to remain. Unlike an intron of history, I will be remembered as an exon. That will be my legacy, my mark in history. But the Patriots would deny us even that. I will triumph over the Patriots and liberate us all. And we will become . . . the *Sons of Liberty!*"

Solidus continued to rant to himself as Raiden received a call from the Colonel on the Codec. "Raiden, are you receiving? We're still here." The voice was once again electronically synthesized, the garbled communication of a damaged AI.

"How's that possible?" Raiden answered. "The AI was destroyed!"

"Only GW."

"Who are you?"

"To begin with, we're not what you'd call . . . human," the "Colonel" admitted. "Over the past two hundred years a kind of consciousness formed layer by layer in the crucible of the White House. It's not unlike the way life started in the oceans four billion years ago. The White House was our primordial soup, a base of evolution . . . under the protection of the flag, suckled on the national religion of capitalism. We are formless . . . we are the very discipline and morality that Americans invoke so often. How can anyone hope to eliminate us? As long as this nation exists, so will we."

"Cut the crap! If you're immortal, why would you take away individual freedoms and censor the Net?"

Rose's broken voice butted in. "Jack, don't be silly."

The Colonel again: "Don't you know that our plans have your interests — not ours — in mind?"

"What?"

Rose again: "Jack, listen carefully like a good boy!"

Throughout the speech the voices jumped back and forth between that of the Colonel and of Rose. "The mapping of the human genome was completed early this century. As a result the evolutionary log of the human race lay open to us. We started with genetic engineering, and in the end, we succeeded in digitizing life itself. But there are things not covered by genetic information."

"What do you mean?" Raiden asked.

"Human memories. Ideas. Culture. History. Genes don't contain any record of human history. Is it something that should not be passed on? Should that information be left at the mercy of nature? We've always kept records of our lives. Through words, pictures, symbols . . . from tablets to books . . . but not all the information was inherited by later generations. A small percentage of the whole was selected and processed, then passed on. Not unlike genes really. That's what history is, Jack. But in the current, digitized world, trivial information is accumulating every second, preserved in all its triteness. Never fading, always accessible. Rumors about petty issues, misinterpretations, slander . . . All this junk data preserved in an unfiltered state, growing at an alarming rate. It will only slow down social progress, reduce the rate of evolution. Raiden, you seem to think that our plan is one of censorship."

"Are you telling me it's *not*?"

The voices of the Colonel and Rose kept merging, separating, butting in, overlapping. "You're being silly! What we propose to do is not to control content, but to create context. The digital society furthers human flaws and selectively rewards development of convenient half-truths. Just look at the strange juxtapositions of morality around you. Billions spent on new weapons in order to humanely murder other humans. Rights of criminals are given more respect than the privacy of their victims. Although there are people suffering in poverty, huge donations are made to protect endangered species. Everyone grows up being told the same thing. 'Be nice to other people.' 'But beat out the competition!' 'You're special.' 'Believe in yourself and you will succeed.' But it's obvious from the start that only a few can succeed. You exercise your right to 'freedom' and *this* is the result. All rhetoric to avoid conflict and protect each other from hurt. The untested truths spun by different interests continue to churn and accumulate in the sandbox of political correctness and value systems. Everyone withdraws into their own small gated community, afraid of a larger forum. They stay inside their little ponds leaking whatever 'truth' suits them into the growing cesspool of society at large. The different cardinal truths neither clash nor mesh. No one is invalidated, but nobody is right. Not even natural selection can take place here. The world is being engulfed in truth. And this is the way the world ends. Not with a bang, but a whimper. We're trying to stop that from happening. It's our responsibility as rulers. Just as in genetics, unnecessary information and memory must be filtered out to stimulate the evolution of the species."

"And you think you're qualified to decide what's necessary and what's not?" Raiden asked, enraged.

"Absolutely. Who else could wade through the sea of garbage you people produce, retrieve valuable truths and even interpret their meaning for later generations? That's what it means to create context."

"I'll decide for myself what to believe and what to pass on!"

"But is that even your own idea? Or something Snake told you?"

Raiden thought, *Touché.*

"That's the proof of your incompetence right there," the Colonel/Rose continued. "You lack the qualifications to exercise free will."

Raiden lashed out. "That's not true! I have the right—"

"Does something like a 'self' exist inside of you? That which you call 'self' serves as nothing more than a mask to cover your own being. In this era of ready-made 'truths,' 'self' is just something used to preserve those positive emotions that you occasionally feel. Another possibility is that 'self' is a concept you conveniently borrowed under the logic that it would endow you with some sense of strength."

"That's crap!"

"Is it? Would you prefer that someone else tell you? All right then, explain it to him!"

Now it was just Rose's voice, obviously feigning "sincerity." "Jack, you're simply the *best*! And you got there all by your*self*!"

Raiden wanted to scream. It was all wrong. *All wrong!*

"Oh, what happened?" the Colonel asked. "Do you feel lost? Why not try a bit of soul-searching?"

"Don't think you'll find anything, though," Rose said cruelly.

"Ironic that although 'self' is something that you yourself fashioned, every time something goes wrong, you turn around and place the blame on something else."

The two voices interchanged throughout their dialogue again. "'It's not my fault. It's not your fault.' In denial you simply resort to looking for another, more convenient 'truth' in order to make yourself feel better, leaving behind in an instant the so-called 'truth' you once embraced. Should someone like that be able to decide what is 'truth'? Should someone like you even have the right to decide? You've done nothing but abuse your freedom. You don't deserve to be free! We're not the ones smothering the world. You are. The individual is supposed to be weak. But far from powerless—a single person has the potential to ruin the world. And the age of digitized communication has given even more power to the individual. Too much power for an immature species. That's why we've decided to be your guardians, if you will. Building a legacy involves figuring out what is wanted, and what needs to be done for that goal. All this you used to struggle with. Now, we think for you. We are your guardians, after all."

"You want to control human *thought*? Human behavior?"

"Of course. Anything can be quantified nowadays. That's what this exercise was designed to prove," the Colonel said.

Rose commented, "You fell in love with me just as you were meant to, after all. Isn't that right, Jack?"

The voices merged again. "Ocelot was not told the whole truth, to say the least. We rule an entire nation—of what interest would a single soldier, no matter how able, be to us? The S3 Plan does not stand for Solid Snake Simulation. What it does stand for is Selection for Societal Sanity! The S3 is a system for controlling human will and consciousness. S3 is not you, a soldier trained in the image of Solid Snake. It is a method, a protocol that created a circumstance that made you what you are. So you see, we're the S3. Not you. What you experienced was the final test of its effectiveness."

"That's crazy!" Raiden shouted.

"You heard what President Johnson said."

The voice abruptly changed to that of James Johnson. "The Arsenal's GW system is the key to their supremacy."

Then the Colonel returned. "The objective of this exercise was to establish such a method. We used Shadow Moses as a paradigm for the exercise."

Rose giggled. "I wonder if you would have preferred a fantasy setting?"

The Colonel chuckled as well and said, "We chose that backdrop because of its extreme circumstances. It was an optimal test for S3's crisis management capacity. If the model could trigger, control, and solve this, it would be ready for any contingency. And now we have our proof.

"Raiden, there are also reasons behind your selection. Solidus raised plenty of other child soldiers. Do you know why we chose you over them? It was because you were the only one who refused to acknowledge the past. All the others remember what they were, and they pay for it daily. But you turn your back on everything you don't like. You do whatever you like, see only the things you like, and for yourself alone."

The Colonel alone: "Yes, Rose can attest to that!"

Rose alone: "You refused to see me for what I was. I lied to you, but I wanted to be caught. You pretended to be understanding, to be a gentleman . . . You never made a conscious attempt to reach out to me. The only time you did was when I gave you no choice but to do so."

Raiden responded without thinking. "I was just trying not to—"

"What? Trying not to 'hurt' me? Dear, the one you were trying not to hurt was yourself! Avoiding the truth under the guise of 'kindness' is all that you did! It occurred to you to do nothing but look out for yourself. Even if you claim that it was for my sake, that feeling was nowhere to be seen. In the end, everything was for your sake. I was never part of the picture."

The Colonel sneered. "Exactly right! So you see, you're a perfect representative of the masses we need to protect. This is why we chose you. You accepted the fiction we provided, obeyed our orders, and did everything you were told to. The exercise is a resounding success!"

The voices merged again. "Didn't I tell you that GW was still incomplete? But not anymore, thanks to you. Your persona, experiences, triumphs, and defeats are nothing but by-products. The real objective was ensuring that we could generate and manipulate them. It's taken a lot of time and money, but it was well worth it considering the results. But I think that's enough talk. It's time for the final exercise. Raiden. . . take Solidus down!"

"Think again!" Raiden blurted. "I'm through doing what I'm told!"

"Oh, really? Aren't you forgetting something?"

The voice then became Olga's. "If you die, my child dies."

Then the Colonel returned. "The termination of vital signs from your nanomachines means the death of Olga's child. Not to mention the death of Rose. She's wired the same way."

"Rose," Raiden said. "Does she actually exist?"

She answered, "Of course I do, Jack! You have to beLIEve me!"

"Damn . . ."

"It will be a fight to the death. Solidus, at least, wants you dead. We will collect the necessary data from this last fight, and then we'll consider the exercise closed. So, Jack the Ripper! Will it be Solidus, the Patriots' creation? Or you—Solidus' creation? Our beloved monsters . . . enjoy yourselves!"

The Codec went silent.

Raiden looked up at Solidus. The man had been talking to himself the entire time. Only now did he turn to face his foster son.

35

"JACK, MY SON," Solidus said. "My clone brothers and I are called monsters. Replicates of evil genes. You are one-of-a-kind, but still a monster shaped by a dark and secret history. We need to decide which monstrosity will have the privilege of survival."

Raiden knew he couldn't refuse to fight. For some reason he felt responsible to Olga for the life of her child.

"By the way, Jack," his foster father said. "I was the one who killed your parents."

This revelation caught Raiden off guard.

"I claimed you for my own and raised you as a soldier in the army of the Devil. I am your foster father . . . and your worst enemy."

"Why?" was all Raiden could think to ask.

"Because I needed to know whether we were really someone else's creation. We're repeating history, Jack. Liquid and Solid hunted down Big Boss, trying to sever the tie that bound them to him. Unless you kill me and face your past, Jack, you will never escape. You will stay in the endless loop—your own double helix. It's time we were both free."

Raiden's high-frequency ninja blade lay at Solidus' feet. He picked it up and tossed it to his foe. The blade buried its point in the roof directly in front of its master. Raiden grabbed the hilt and held the sword aloft.

"I have other reasons for wanting you dead," Solidus announced as he brandished a *daisho* of two swords—a *Katana* and *Wakizashi*—each equipped with the *Minshuto* and *Kyowato* blades, respectively. "The clues to the Patriots inside GW have been erased, but there are other traces. Inside *you*."

"What?"

"The information is being carried by the nanomachines in your cerebral cortex and throughout the neural network they formed. So . . . brace yourself!"

Solidus activated the steel collars on his armor. He sheathed the *Wakizashi* and kept the *Katana* in his right hand—

—and attacked.

Raiden quickly countered Solidus' blade and knocked it away. Solidus didn't lose his momentum, though. He immediately swung the *Katana* around in a counterclockwise motion to assault Raiden's other side. Raiden whirled around to avoid the blow, but the tip caught him on the shoulder, drawing blood.

Solidus wasn't beyond cheating. He activated the accelerator in his suit and aimed the blast at Raiden. The operative was forced to perform his torso-axial leap to prevent the flames from hitting him. Nevertheless, he felt the heat singe his Skull Suit. Then one of Solidus' tentacles opened a claw and shot a small missile at his opponent. Raiden ducked just in time; the missile exploded behind him on the far side of the roof.

It was time for an offensive maneuver. Raiden charged at Solidus with the high-frequency blade outstretched. Solidus hadn't expected the young man to recover so quickly from his attacks and was caught by surprise. Raiden's blade slashed Solidus' left arm, slicing through the armor and severing a network of arteries. Solidus grunted in pain and brought the *Katana* down toward Raiden's right shoulder. Raiden deftly blocked the blade with his own, creating sparks. They stood in close proximity for several seconds, their swords *clanging* and *clashing* with the furor of a thunderstorm. Finally, Raiden rolled out of the melee under Solidus' arm, landed on his feet, and attempted to strike his opponent in the back along the armor's spinal cord. It was probably the only vulnerable spot that he could get to. If Olga's blade could cut through the metal there, Raiden just might succeed in delivering a fatal blow.

But Solidus moved defensively and blocked the attack.

The two men stood apart for a moment catching their breaths. Solidus loosened the tentacles' harness and dropped it on the roof.

"Good work, Jack, but this is where it gets interesting!"

The man was actually giving Raiden a fair fight. Now it was just swordsman against swordsman.

They stepped forward once again. The blades hurtled into each other—strikes and counterstrikes, advances and retreats, lunges and parries, attacks and ripostes . . . it went on . . . and on . . .

The Codec blared at Raiden as he battled. "You have to beat Solidus!" the Colonel shouted. "This is your last duty!"

"We're not just pawns in some simulation game, you know!" Raiden panted.

"Yes, you are," Rose said. "You're nothing but mere weapons. No different from fighter jets or tanks."

"The old model destroyed four years ago was REX," the Colonel continued.

Rose: "The new amphibious model is RAY . . ."

The Colonel: "Both of these are the same as the code names used by the U.S. Armed Forces to refer to Japanese war planes during World War II."

Rose: "Your code name 'Raiden' also comes from the Japanese navy's name for one of its interceptors."

"Stop it!" Raiden shouted through his nano. "I'm not a weapon!"

"Oh, really?" Rose taunted. "Do you know the code name the U.S. Armed Forces used for the Japanese fighter *Raiden*?"

The Colonel answered, "It was *Jack*! Both of you are just weapons to be used and thrown away."

Rose: "Just weapons to be used on the battlefield. Just pawns in a game—exactly as you said."

The Colonel: "And a weapon has no right to think for itself! Now it's time to fulfill your purpose! Defeat Solidus!"

The Codec went silent.

Solidus managed to lunge at Raiden's chest as the operative parried to the side. The blade made a decent slice in Raiden's ribs but not enough to cause serious damage. Seeing an opening, Raiden swung his sword down onto Solidus' right arm, nearly severing it at the man's elbow. Solidus cried out in pain and anguish. He dropped the *Katana* and retreated. He clutched the wounded arm as blood spurted out of it. He glared at his opponent in shock and anger. His right arm was useless. Nevertheless, he drew the *Wakizashi* with his left hand and charged. Raiden made a slight retreat, enough to allow his opponent to step within range. He then lunged hard with his blade, penetrating Solidus' chest just below the rib cage. Solidus vocalized his agony again but quickly countered with a parry that knocked Raiden off balance. The operative used the point of his sword against the roof to stabilize himself, performed a cartwheel *over* the hilt, and landed on his feet. Solidus was already rushing him, but the man was damaged and weak. It wasn't difficult for Raiden to step aside and deliver the deathblow on the muscle suit's Achilles tendon—the spine.

Solidus' back erupted in a fountain of blood like a spigot had been turned on. His spinal cord severed, he wavered unsteadily on his legs. Sheer poise prevented his legs from buckling immediately. He stumbled dangerously close to the edge of the roof and rocked. He no longer had control of his muscles. The look on his face was one of surprise, disbelief, and fear.

Then with one last look at his foster son, he toppled over and fell to the ground below. His body bounced against the statue of George Washington and came to rest at its base. Nature then played the ultimate card of irony—a breeze finally caught the torn American flag that hung by threads on Federal Hall's flagpole. The flag came loose and drifted down, covering Solidus' corpse.

36

RAIDEN WAS SPENT. He gazed at the body below and then became aware of the crowds that had gathered on the streets. Helicopters clattered overhead. Fleets of emergency vehicles and rubberneckers covered the scene. Arsenal Gear and the debris around it were still burning and billowing smoke into the air. The arrival of the media added to the cacophony.

He quickly moved out of sight, ran to the edge of the roof, and jumped. He landed lightly on his feet and moved into the mass of people. Within minutes, he was one of the onlookers. No one seemed to notice his Skull Suit. They were all too engrossed in the destruction around them.

"Who am I . . . really?" Raiden asked aloud.

"No one quite knows who or what they are."

Raiden turned toward the familiar voice.

"Snake!" He couldn't believe his friend was alive. "How . . . ? What . . . ?"

Snake shook his head. "Otacon rescued me in the chopper. Ocelot and the RAY got away."

They stood for a moment surveying the damage. Snake put a

hand on Raiden's shoulder and said, "The memories you have and the role you were assigned are burdens you had to carry. It doesn't matter if they were real or not. There's no such thing in the world as absolute reality. Most of what they call real is actually fiction. What you think you see is only as real as your brain tells you it is."

"Then what am I supposed to believe in? What am I going to leave behind when I'm through?" Raiden asked.

"We can tell other people about . . . having faith. What we had faith in. What we found important enough to fight for. It's not whether you were right or wrong, but how much faith you were willing to have that decides the future. The Patriots are a kind of ongoing fiction, too, come to think of it."

Raiden wasn't sure what Snake was talking about.

"Listen, don't obsess over words so much. Find the meaning behind the words, and then decide. You can find your own name. And your own future."

"Decide for myself?"

"And whatever you choose will be you."

"I don't know if I can . . ."

"I know you didn't have much in terms of choices this time. But everything you felt and thought about during the mission is yours. And what you decide to do with them is your choice."

"You mean . . . start over?"

"Yeah, a clean slate. A new name, new memories. Choose your own legacy. It's for you to decide. It's up to you."

Raiden finally nodded. "I'll find something worth passing on."

"We all have the freedom to spread the word. Even me."

Raiden suddenly remembered. "Snake, what about Olga's child?"

"Don't worry. I'll find him. Count on it. As long as you keep yourself alive he's safe."

"Why do you assume it's a boy?"

Snake shrugged. "Or her."

"Do you know where Liquid went?"

"I put a transmitter on his RAY."

"Did he head for the Patriots?"

"Yeah. But I have a feeling they gave Ocelot a bogus location to begin with." Raiden made a face at that. "Cheer up. We have a better lead." He held up a computer MO disk that looked like the one the President had given Raiden. "This contains the list of all the Patriots."

"But Ocelot took it!"

"The one we gave you wasn't the real thing."

"What?"

"This virus is coded to destroy only a specific part of GW — namely the information about the Patriots' identities. Which means that there's a parameter coded in here that defines what that information is."

"I get it . . . analyze the code and you can probably find out where they operate. Count me in!"

Snake shook his head. "No, you have things to do first. And people you need to talk to."

At those words, Raiden noticed someone standing in the crowd some distance away. A young woman. Looking at him.

Rose.

She really does exist!

Raiden turned back to Snake . . . but he had vanished. Raiden looked around for him, but the guy had disappeared . . . which was something he was good at doing.

The operative focused again on Rose. She stood waiting for him. He walked slowly toward her. Passersby stared at Raiden but went on without a glance at Rose.

"What's wrong?" she asked.

Raiden blinked. "Nothing." He studied her pretty face. "Can I ask you something? Who am I really?"

Rose smiled. "I wouldn't know." When he made a perplexed

expression she added, "But we're going to find out together, aren't we?" He cupped her face between his palms. "See me for what I am, okay?"

"I know."

And then Raiden remembered what Rose had told him . . . it seemed like ages ago. He looked down at her belly, which was slightly bulging. She caressed it and nodded. Then she looked up and asked, "Do you remember this place?"

"Of course. This is where we first met. And I remember now!"

"Hm?"

"Today—April thirtieth—is the day I met you."

"That's it!"

"I think I found something to pass along to the future."

"What?"

"He said all living things want their genes to live on."

"Are you talking about the baby?"

"Yeah. But genes aren't the only thing you pass on. There are too many things that aren't written in our DNA. It's up to us to teach that to our children."

"What kind of things?"

"About the environment, our ideas, our culture . . . poetry . . . compassion . . . sorrow . . . joy . . . We'll tell them everything . . . together."

Rose's eyes went wide. "Is that a proposal?"

Raiden answered with slight bashfulness, "This is for your ears only."

He took her hand and together they walked through the crowd, away from the devastation, toward an uncertain—but hopeful—future.

EPILOGUE

THE CODEC *CHIRPED*.

"Snake, you there? It's me."

"Yes, Otacon?"

"I've finished going over that disk."

"Did you find the Patriots' list?"

"Of course. It contained the personal data of twelve people. There was a name on it . . . Snake, it was one of our biggest contributors!"

Snake winced. "What's going on around here?"

"I don't know."

"Anyway . . . where are they?"

"Well, we were right about them being on Manhattan, but . . ."

"But what?"

"They're already *dead*. All twelve of them!"

Snake paused, processing this information. "When did this happen?"

"Well, uh, about a hundred years ago."

"What the *hell* . . . ?"

"That's right! The twelve Patriots lived and died a century ago . . ."

ABOUT THE AUTHOR

Between 1996 and 2002, RAYMOND BENSON was commissioned by the James Bond literary copyright holders to take over writing the 007 novels. In total he penned and published worldwide six original 007 novels (including *Zero Minus Ten*, *Never Dream of Dying*, and *The Man with the Red Tattoo*), three film novelizations, and three short stories. An anthology of his Bond work, entitled *The Union Trilogy*, was published in October 2008, and a second anthology—*Choice of Weapons*—will be out in spring 2010. Benson's book *The James Bond Bedside Companion*, an encyclopedic work on the 007 phenomenon, was first published in 1984 and was nominated for an Edgar Allan Poe Award by Mystery Writers of America for Best Biographical/Critical Work. Benson has also written non-Bond novels: *Face Blind* (2003), *Evil Hours* (2004), and *Sweetie's Diamonds* (2006). *The Pocket Essentials Guide to Jethro Tull* was published in 2002. Using the pseudonym "David Michaels," Benson is also the author of the *New York Times* bestselling books *Tom Clancy's Splinter Cell* (2004) and its sequel *Tom Clancy's Splinter Cell: Operation Barracuda* (2005). Benson's latest venture is an original series of "rock 'n' roll thrillers." The first title was *A Hard Day's Death*, published in April 2008. The sequel, *Dark Side of the Morgue*, was published in March 2009. He is also the author of the sixth "Gabriel Hunt" adventure novel, *Hunt Through Napoleon's Web*. Visit the author at his website, www.raymondbenson.com.